THE ROSE GROWER

THE ROSE GROWER

MICHELLE de KRETSER

Chatto & Windus
LONDON

Published by Chatto & Windus 1999
2 4 6 8 10 9 7 5 3 1

First published in Great Britain in 1999 by
Chatto & Windus
Random House, 20 Vauxhall Bridge Road,
London SW1V 2SA

Random House Australia (Pty) Limited
20 Alfred Street, Milsons Point, Sydney,
New South Wales 2061, Australia

Random House New Zealand Limited
18 Poland Road, Glenfield,
Auckland 10, New Zealand

Random House (Pty) Limited
Endulini, 5A Jubilee Road, Parktown 2193, South Africa

The Random House Group Limited Reg. No. 954009
www.randomhouse.co.uk

A CIP catalogue record for this book
is available from the British Library

ISBN 0 7011 6917 6

Papers used by Random House are natural,
recyclable products made from wood grown in sustainable forests;
the manufacturing processes conform to the environmental
regulations of the country of origin

Printed and bound in Great Britain by
Biddles Ltd, Guildford

For my mother
& in memory of my father

Small change, small change.

Napoleon Bonaparte, surveying the dead
on a battlefield

1789

On a cloudless summer afternoon in 1789, labourers working in the fields around Montsignac, a village in Gascony, saw a man fall out of the sky.

The balloon had drifted over a wooded ridge and into their valley. The farm-workers, straightening up one by one, shaded their eyes against the dazzle of sun on crimson and blue silk. The thing hung in the sky – sumptuous, menacing – like a sign from God or the devil.

Then there was thunder and fire, and a man plummeting earthwards.

It was the 14th of July. The world was about to change.

*S*tephen opened his eyes and fell in love.

It was right and natural that it should happen that way: he believed, like so many of his generation, in the *coup de foudre* – the lightning flash which reveals the lie of the land between a man and a woman. 'An angel,' he sighed, not caring who might hear.

At once her face moved away, out of his field of vision. There was the sound of vigorous scratching.

He was propped up against cushions on a crimson sofa carved with scallop shells. There was slanting light, mote-speckled, and the scent of roses. He took in the old-fashioned beams, on which blue and red flowers had once been painted, and the unpapered walls. But as usual it was the pictures he really noticed: the large one directly opposite him showed a maiden with a basket of fruit, and the rest were no better. He had imagined that kind of thing would be different in France.

An elderly servant, long and thin as a nail, served him from a decanter on a silver tray. He sipped – was it brandy? something that made him choke – and looked around for her.

She was seated by the window, her head bent over a small garment at which she was stitching. But a child of about eight, solemn-faced and weighed down with dark curls, planted herself in front of him.

'Are you fatally injured? If you live, will you take me ballooning?'

'Mathilde, someone who has suffered an accident is ill-equipped for your conversation.' Stephen turned his head and saw a stout man in a mustard-yellow waistcoat, standing in front of the fireplace. 'I envisage a speedier recovery for our visitor if you remove yourself from his vicinity. And take Brutus with you.'

Unperturbed, the child continued to gaze at Stephen with expectant curiosity. 'I adore children,' he said and smiled at her. 'They are so ... *innocent* and yet so perceptive in their apprehension of the world.'

'Oh no – another Rousseauist,' said the child with unconcealed disappointment. 'I'm not like that at all.'

As she spoke, something manifested itself on the far side of the room. Stephen saw a squat black form, a squashed-in muzzle, a formidable underbite that exposed a row of yellow fangs. Swiftly and noiselessly, the apparition padded up to him and thrust its cold nose between his legs.

His knuckles whitened around his glass.

A tall young woman, whom he had not previously noticed, said, 'Brutus!'

The creature withdrew its muzzle an inch or so and sneezed, scattering cold droplets. Its eyes were amber and unwavering, and made no secret of its low opinion of the intruder.

'It's quite all right,' the child said kindly. 'He doesn't bite many people these days. He used to be much worse.'

'I trust you find the intelligence reassuring.' The stout gentleman crossed the room, obliging the dog to give reluctant ground. Stephen found himself looking up at panoramic grey eyebrows, and sharp brown eyes that pinned an enormous beaky nose into place. 'Jean-Baptiste de Saint-Pierre' – holding out his hand – 'Welcome to Montsignac.'

'Stephen Fletcher.' He attempted to get to his feet but Saint-Pierre wouldn't allow it, waving him back onto the cushions. Brown eyes and yellow ones continued their unhurried scrutiny of his person.

Eventually: 'English?'

'American.'

'Really? Then no doubt you have an opinion about turkeys.'

Stephen had just decided that a turkey must be something entirely different in France, when his host added, 'But you speak our language very well.'

He identified it as a question. 'I'm afraid you exaggerate.

5

But my mother is a Frenchwoman, and since my father's death we've lived with her family.'

The explanation seemed to satisfy Saint-Pierre. 'Well, Mr Fletcher, you appear not to have suffered any serious harm as a result of your unexpected descent into our midst.'

He had been away from home long enough to recognise that he was being gently mocked. Old World conversations required athleticism, a series of leaps between words and what they might mean. That was another thing he had not been prepared for.

'No. That is, I mean . . .' He wriggled experimentally and regretted it: 'My ankle . . .' He drank more brandy and asked, 'What happened?'

'Reports vary. My own conclusion, based on the available evidence, is that you leapt from a balloon that had caught fire. Fortunately, you landed on one of my haystacks. Some villagers carried you here. A doctor has been sent for, but the town is a few miles away.'

One of the young women – not the angel but the tall one – said, 'Father, if the gentleman has hurt his ankle it'll swell up. He should take off his boot.'

At this, the servant creaked forward. 'No sense at all,' he remarked, to no one in particular, between bootlaces.

Saint-Pierre said, 'Allow me to present my daughters, Mr Fletcher. Mathilde you are already acquainted with. Then there is Sophie – ' she nodded shyly at him – 'and Claire, my eldest.'

The angel looked into his eyes and smiled. Not an angel after all, thought Stephen, but the Madonna herself, with that blue dress.

(Though not perhaps the way it clung to her body.)

'Madame la Marquise de Monferrant,' murmured Saint-Pierre, his head on one side, detached, observing.

Somehow the back of Stephen's hand struck the decanter, sending it crashing. The dog surged forward and fastened its jaws onto his shin.

When Saint-Pierre was twenty-four years old, Jean-Jacques Rousseau published *The Social Contract*. The philosopher was a controversial, even radical figure; Saint-Pierre found his book annoying, naively if passionately reasoned. His taste ran rather to the cynical wit of Voltaire, whose *Candide* he had bought in the original anonymous Swiss edition of 1760 and kept on his night-table ever since.

Yet when time had soothed the irritants of sentimentality and rhetorical excess, Saint-Pierre discovered Rousseau's arguments lodged pearl-like within him. The Genevan called for social justice, preached the essential goodness of nature, pleaded for substantial content over frivolous style. Saint-Pierre thrilled to it all. Which is not to be wondered at: we are innately lazy and selfish thinkers, and the philosophies we favour are inevitably those which correspond most closely to our own needs and inclinations. Saint-Pierre, despite the keenness of his mind, was no exception.

He was heir to one of the great southern families of the *noblesse de robe*, the judicial – as distinct from the military – nobility. But if he had been born within the cocoon of aristocratic privilege, life had instructed him in the essential flimsiness of that edifice. The Saint-Pierre family's troubles had begun with Jean-Baptiste's father, who at the age of twenty-two had forsaken his native Toulouse for the glitter of the capital. Well, of course: a young man, rich, ambitious, of noted brilliance. He had outgrown the provinces like a shabby suit of clothes.

He had social connections in the royal entourage and legal ones at the sovereign high courts. Thus he obtained a minor sinecure – Keeper of the Royal This or That – at Louis XV's Versailles as well as a place on the Parisian court of appeal. A year later he married the daughter of the president of the court. His future unrolled before him like cloth of gold.

Then he discovered two things about himself: he had a taste – and a talent, he believed – for gambling, and he was in love, hopelessly, unswervingly in love, with a woman who was not his wife. He would turn up of a night at the gaming tables with a bag of gold in each hand, and walk away whistling into the dawn with empty pockets. He found it necessary to spend more and more time at Versailles, to be near the chestnut-haired beauty who held his heart like a tremulous songbird in her plump little hand. On those occasions when luck went his way he bought her emeralds, which were what she loved best in the world.

His son associated Paris with sounds (his mother weeping and coughing, angry voices) and Versailles with smells (his father had a tiny set of airless rooms near the royal privies). Jean-Baptiste lived for the summers spent with his father's parents on their estate at Montsignac in Gascony: long, unreflecting, solitary days played out in forests and flower-filled lanes. There were dogs, meadows, vineyards, birdsong, the river's green expanse. He was his grandmother's darling, his grandfather's boast. There was no red-eyed mother spluttering behind a handkerchief, no red-faced father shouting that it had to be done, the land had to be sold and anyway it was only a temporary measure. No hard-faced boys jeered at him – their beaks jabbing peck peck peck – because his father was only a jumped-up magistrate from the provinces and not a proper courtier (unlike their fathers), nor a military commander (unlike their fathers), and horribly in debt (not unlike their fathers, but these things are different for courtiers and military commanders).

His mother coughed herself to an early grave. His father wept tears of self-reproach, hugging his son to his breast. Peering out from the embrace, the boy saw his father take a band of red and green stones from the dead woman's dressing-table and slip it into his pocket.

8

A whisper – it was no more – had begun to circulate about a judge whose judgment could be bought. Bribery in itself was more or less the order of the day; the scandal lay in being talked about. The president of the court found it expedient for his son-in-law to give up the judiciary in order to devote himself fully to his royal duties. Naturally, there was no appeal from the president's ruling.

The boy endured the decade that followed. Paris was the saddest, emptiest place. He worked hard at his books – he had the habit of scholarship easily acquired by lonely children – and his discipline was backed up by a razor-sharp mind: there at least his father hadn't failed him. As soon as he could, he made the journey in reverse, turning his back on the capital to enrol in law school in Toulouse.

The year Jean-Baptiste read Rousseau was the year his father died. The chestnut-haired woman, a widow for the past eighteen months, had accepted an offer of marriage from a distant, wealthy cousin, thus definitively spurning her former lover. They said old Saint-Pierre died of a broken heart, alone in his evil-smelling little room in the icy palace.

The son did what he could, with the help of his mother's money. The debts sucked up his inheritance and swelled, new creditors daily presenting their IOUs scrawled with his father's initials. He was glad to pay, glad to redeem the moral bankruptcy of his childhood. He saw himself as an *honnête homme*, an upright man. Early on in life, he had determined he would be the antithesis of the fawning courtier, the unfaithful husband, the judge who accepted bribes and robbed the dead. He gave up mortgaged estates with the lightest of hearts; Montsignac, which still belonged to his grandfather, was safe and that was the only parcel of his patrimony he cared about.

He chose to wear plain, slightly shabby clothes that would never have been tolerated at Versailles. He was rather proud of the fact that he was hopeless at dancing.

A position on the Toulouse *parlement* had followed naturally for the brilliant law student. Saint-Pierre told himself he had earned it by his own efforts, although he knew very well that his lineage weighed equally in his recruitment to the high

9

court, his grandfather having renounced his place on the bench in favour of his grandson. The essential thing, reasoned Jean-Baptiste, was that he took his work seriously and judged the cases that came before him with impartiality, careful to use his office in the interests of ordinary people, scrupulous in his dissection of privilege.

Thus are we defined by the influences we would most resist.

But perhaps you have the wrong impression of Saint-Pierre. It shouldn't be thought that he was a prig. He laughed readily, finding absurdity in most things, and was possessed of a slightly malicious turn of phrase. And like all true Gascons, he knew the pleasures of the table. Sober as a judge, so the saying goes, and Saint-Pierre took care to be, despite his partiality to armagnac and the wines of Bordeaux. But food was a source of harmless delight. He sucked the tiny bones of roast ortolans, smacked his lips over cassoulets made with good Toulouse sausage, devoured pâtés, soufflés, omelettes, lemon tarts, Marennes oysters, Corsican blackbirds, pigs' trotters stuffed with pistachios, *filet mignon* spiked with truffles, those small, round goat cheeses that have been rolled in wood-ash. He had a special weakness for *foie gras* made from the liver of the red-legged partridge. He allowed himself small gastronomic affectations, insisting that woodcock should never be drawn, but hung up by the feet until the feathers fell and the insides deliquesced and dripped out through the beak.

He had always been tall. Now he grew fat. He was proud of that, too: at Versailles, they watched their figures.

The girl he married came from a family which, although perfectly respectable, was neither wealthy nor well connected; his marriage could not be said to be spurred by greed, snobbery or desire for preferment. Not that anyone thought to look beyond the obvious motive for his choice: Marguerite, his eighteen-year-old bride, turned heads wherever she went. Along with the usual silver, linen and furniture, she brought with her a retinue of disappointed bachelors who hung mournfully around the household, importuning her with their eyes and assuring Saint-Pierre that he was 'a lucky dog'.

But the girl who could have had her pick of Toulouse was

in love with her husband, who made her laugh; and the young man who often woke from dreams of his mother crying and found his own face wet was utterly enamoured of his wife. Love matches, marriages welded together by affection rather than duty or material gain, were *à la mode*, and the Saint-Pierres, with their two sweet little girls, were the very model of domestic happiness.

There were sorrows of course – their son lived three days, Marguerite's sister was carried off by smallpox – and anxiety about money was never far away. The judiciary, for all its prestige, was not a lucrative career. Magistrates were expected to supplement their modest incomes, in theory from personal fortunes, in reality from a variety of venal practices. Saint-Pierre made a virtue of limited means; there were, nevertheless, certain appearances that had to be maintained. Like Rousseau, he could have said that although he lived economically, his purse insensibly exhausted itself: his daughters needed, his wife had to, his position required.

They spent every summer at Montsignac, where the big house stood empty since the death of his grandfather. Marguerite sat sketching on the terrace, worked in her garden, became acquainted with the village and its inhabitants. Dainty Claire, her father's favourite, clung to her mother's skirts, so it was Sophie who accompanied Saint-Pierre on his rambles through the countryside, scampering to keep up with his stride, memorising the casually recited names of birds and plants, filling her pockets with leaves, berries, a hedge-sparrow's nest, a curiously shaped pebble. Returning from these excursions, they would be met by Claire, who always ran to welcome her father home. He seized her wrists and whirled her off her feet while she shrieked with joy; he kissed her and scooped her up onto his shoulders. Sophie, standing a little way off, picked at the dusty hem of her dress.

One winter, when she had been married less than a dozen years, Marguerite began to cough. Saint-Pierre recognised that note instantly. Like his mother, his wife now turned her face away when he tried to kiss her.

So, finally, he had that too in common with his father.

11

He mortgaged Montsignac without hesitation and sent for doctors from Montpellier, Padua, Edinburgh, Vienna, even Paris. Depending on the remedies they confidently prescribed, he would stand over Marguerite until she swallowed the cup of ox blood or submitted trembling to the application of leeches. He piled layer upon layer of quilts over her small white body to sweat out the disease, stifling her protests. He insisted she spend the winter in Italy with her mother, although she wept and coughed and didn't want to go.

While Marguerite was away, Saint-Pierre's maternal grandmother died in Paris. Secretly he had anticipated this event, guiltily looking forward to the money he was sure he would inherit; although they saw each other very rarely, since he never went to Paris and she seldom left it, he was her only grandson. She had presented him with an extraordinarily ugly but undeniably valuable Sèvres dinner-set on the occasion of his marriage and she never forgot his name-day.

As it turned out, the old lady left him nothing but her husband's law books. Her Parisian son-in-law sent Saint-Pierre a curt letter informing him of the fact, and enquiring what arrangements he intended to make for taking possession of the volumes. Saint-Pierre wrote back asking for the books to be sold; he could imagine the sneer with which the implicit avowal of need would be received. Well, their good opinion meant nothing to him. That Montsignac would pass to his creditors was the only unthinkable thing. He sat in his library behind a desk where debts lay like leaf-fall and knew what he had to do.

By the time Marguerite returned from Italy everything had been decided and set in motion. The lease on the expensive townhouse was to be given up in the spring and its contents auctioned; the Saint-Pierres were moving to Montsignac where the clean country air would be far better for Marguerite's lungs than the stench and filth of the town.

Worn out from the long journey home, his wife lay on a sofa and tried to make sense of it. 'But how will we live? What will you do? Your work –'

'It's all settled,' he told her, not without a trace of pride at his resourcefulness. 'A vacancy on the appeal court in Castelnau comes up at the end of the sessions and I shall be filling it.'

From the *parlement* of Toulouse to the appeal court at Castelnau! 'You could have been president!' she whispered, appalled.

He went to sit beside her and took her hand. 'My dear,' he said gently, 'we have no choice. And we have always been happy at Montsignac, you know that.'

She thought, It is all very well for the summer.

*S*tephen's cousin had seen the Montgolfiers' first balloon rise up over Versailles in 1783. 'It was painted a brilliant blue and decorated with golden fleurs-de-lis. In the basket beneath it were a sheep, a rooster and a duck. They stayed aloft for eight minutes. Charles resolved to take up ballooning on the spot.'

'What happened to the sheep and the fowls?' asked Mathilde.

'I believe they were unharmed. Surprised, no doubt. It can't have been a pleasant experience. The fire that produced the hot air for their balloon was fed with straw, wool, old shoes and rotting meat. Charles says the smell was incredible. Think what it must have been like for the passengers.'

'I hope they weren't eaten, after all that.'

'The records draw a discreet veil over their eventual destinies.'

'It was inconsiderate of you to ruin your cousin's balloon. I might never have another opportunity to conquer the skies.'

Stephen contemplated the fragments lying in the courtyard. 'I'll commission a new one as soon as I return to Bordeaux. And I could show you how to build a model. All it requires is an ox bladder and fish glue.'

'Did you read that in an illustrated paper?'

'But what went wrong?' asked Sophie, who was wandering around the remains, poking now and then with the tip of her shoe at a charred wooden ring or a strand of metal from which a shred of wicker still dangled. She was conscious that his hair was pale gold. Not yellow – she had checked – but with a glint like metal in the sun. He was taller than she was, which seldom happened. His eyes were green shot with blue, as she imagined

14

the sea. Everyone knew Americans were inventive and unblemished; they loved freedom and thought nothing of travelling great distances. It was difficult not to stare.

Like everything in that house, the shirt Stephen had borrowed smelt of roses. It was also several sizes too large for him. Leaning on his stick, he flapped his arms to feel the breeze and waited for the sisters to smile. 'I was bringing the balloon down, I'd been drifting for hours and the meadows by the river seemed inviting. I remember pulling on the rope that opens the valve and allows the air to escape. Then there was the explosion. I must have thrown myself from the basket – and there I was lying on your sofa.'

'A foot either way,' said Mathilde, not without regret, 'and you would have been lying in a sea of gore.'

'Is landing always the most difficult part?'

He confessed that the disaster had occurred on his first solo flight, wondering why Sophie addressed her remarks to the ground or some distant point beyond his shoulder. 'But I followed Charles's instructions exactly. I've been up with him twice, and thought there was nothing to match that exhilaration – but to drift in solitude above the earth, to contemplate Nature undistracted by idle chatter ... That is sublime.' He shut his eyes and floated, for a moment, above a world made new for his delectation.

'But you said it was horribly smelly.'

He opened his eyes. 'No, no, this is – was – the very latest model, a balloon filled with flammable air. Wholly clean and scientific.'

'The villagers wanted to beat you to death,' confided Mathilde, slipping her hand into his. 'They took you for a creature of the devil.'

'It's a good thing your balloon didn't set fire to the barley,' said Sophie, 'or they probably would have killed you. The last few harvests have been bad. They're counting on this one.'

She had a habit, he noticed, of standing on one foot, the other wrapped around her ankle. He found her charming; deliciously strange, like all the French girls he had encountered.

Although nowhere near as pretty as her sisters.

'A few of the bolder men came up to the house this morning to see if you'd vanished or changed form – or dragged us all down to the hellfires that spawned you.' Mathilde hopped around him in one direction, then the other.

'I wish I'd been able to save my sketchbook.' Tilting his head back, he squinted at the sky. 'Boundless possibility. That was what I tried to draw.'

He had his back to the house, but recognising that light footfall on the gravel busied himself at once with his pipe. It was a recent acquisition that could not yet be reckoned among his accomplishments. Nevertheless, he felt it gave him stature; and something was necessary to mark his new life.

Mathilde said to the newcomer, 'He's not a balloonist really, he's an artist. So you can't blame Brutus for being suspicious of him.'

'I don't know how you can bear to be anywhere near that awful dog.' Claire stood close to him and smiled. 'It's very brave of you.'

'He didn't really hurt me,' he said bravely, drawing resolutely on his pipe, fluttering his enormous sleeves.

'He wasn't trying to hurt you. Just letting you know he had your measure.'

'Matty, have you done your lessons for today?' asked Sophie.

'Ballooning is scientific. Surely you wish my education to keep pace with the times?'

'Are you really an artist?' Claire was wearing a yellow cotton dress with a blue sash. There were blue stones at her ears, and around her throat.

'I'll have a studio in Paris in September,' he said, 'so then I will be.'

A nursemaid was seen coming up the drive. The baby she was carrying slept fitfully and cried often. She had walked down to the village with him, pointing out sights of rural interest – robins fluttering around a hedge, a field of pink-bellied oats, an astonishingly good-looking young man, with whom it had been necessary to exchange a few words – and on the way back the child had drifted off at last.

Claire called her over. 'You haven't seen my son Olivier, have you, Mr Fletcher? Isn't he a fine fat baby?'

'Please – you must call me Stephen.'

She stood there in her dress the colour of sunlight, cooing over the child. He thought of fields, roofs, vineyards, leaves, water and spires, of angles of vision that had once been impossible.

An orange butterfly wobbled past. Brutus's jaws closed over it.

The fine fat baby opened his eyes.

Opened his mouth.

Braced his body, and began to bellow.

Sophie and the nursemaid looked at each other.

*I*n 1789 Gascony is the vast unwieldy province of south-western France that reaches from the Atlantic to the Pyrenees, lunges north almost as far as Limoges, extends a grasping fist eastwards to Rodez. It is a multiplicity of tax districts, feudal territories, judicial systems, bishoprics, and obscure military subdivisions first imposed for the convenience of the Romans. Few of these boundaries can be defined with certainty; fewer still coincide; almost none can be accurately traced on a map. In 1789 Gascony, like France itself, is composite but not unified: it is ripe for rationalisation, centralisation, innovation; it waits to be seized by the future.

Deep within its untroubled green heart, two people are making their way along a hillside.

'What do you think of Fletcher?'

Sophie stoops to pick a sprig of the sweet wild mint they have been trampling underfoot. 'An enthusiast?'

Her father smiles. 'Enthusiasm appears to rule the day, if even half of what we hear from Paris is true.'

She remembers a time when she was ... five, perhaps, or six? The Saint-Pierres are having lunch and Sophie is carrying an apple tart from the sideboard to the table. The earthenware dish is heavy and still warm from the oven; she can barely manage the distance without dropping it. She knows she ought to place it on the pewter mat in front of her mother, but her mother is at the other end of the table. So she puts the dish down safely on the nearest corner and slides it over the polished wood.

'Careful!' exclaims Claire. 'You'll ruin the table. Look what Sophie's doing,' she says.

But, 'Well done, Sophie,' says their father. And to his wife, 'Did you see that? She thought about the problem and instead of trying to carry that dish all the way around to you and probably dropping it, she used her wits and found a more intelligent way.' He sits Sophie on his lap, feeds her apple tart and cream from his own plate, calls her his clever girl.

She is twenty-two years old now and still hungry for his approval. It might be withheld. Or dealt out spoon by sweet spoon.

She eats a mint leaf, noticing its slight furriness in her mouth.

Watered by seven rivers, this pocket of Gascony is intensely cultivated and entirely seductive. Small hedgy fields create a patchwork that pleases the eye and betrays the modesty of the average holding. Clumps of woodland – oak and chestnut, beech and hazel – are plentiful; they provide fuel, tools, grazing space. There are flickering poplars beside that stream, cypresses treading the length of this ridge. Vineyards yield any number of unexceptional wines, but local pride allows of no rival to the smooth dark brandy known as armagnac for which the region is famous. Everyone has a plum tree.

The Pyrenees are invisible in this fine summer weather; and anyway, they lie over sixty miles to the south. Here, the landscape never loses sight of human proportions. Its contours are varied enough to prevent monotony, gentle enough to avoid grandeur. Its unassuming hilltops afford wide views. It is prodigal with light.

Sophie and Saint-Pierre skirt a meadow that slopes up to meet an expanse of cloudless sky. Sophie likes to lie there, grass prickling against her skin, staring skywards until she has to hold onto the hillside with both hands to keep it from falling away beneath her. Although she doesn't know it, this habit of hers is remarked on in the village. It's one of her peculiarities, like being tall and husbandless.

Because it has been domesticated for so long, the countryside is veined over with footpaths. Most people have to walk wherever they need to go. Not that all the paths lead somewhere: a stranger might trustingly follow a green trail across fields and through spinneys only to find that it disappears on the edge of a marsh or vanishes into space on the sheer flank of a hill. Patterns of settlement and cultivation have shifted with the centuries, so that a telltale track ends at a cottage that is only a wild rose, fades away in a forgotten orchard long abandoned to the birds.

But Sophie and her father have turned onto a path that is well frequented, as it eventually joins up with the road to Castelnau. That road – and in fact this narrow, hedged track – were once walked by pilgrims on their way to Spain. The pilgrimage has long ceased to be fashionable, however; in the Age of Reason there are not many whose faith compels them over the mountains and to the holy city of Santiago. Many of the old leafy pilgrim trails are being forgotten, claimed by landlords greedy to extend their holdings, choked with brambles and saplings and falling into disuse.

Pink convolvulus, purple vetch and yellow ragwort flourish along the path, and fail to move Sophie, who is unsentimental about weeds. Scarlet poppies are rampant. There are blue campions and creamy foxgloves in the hedgerows, and honeysuckle coiling itself clockwise around bryony and dog roses. 'So called,' says Saint-Pierre, reaching up to knock down a cluster of papery brown petals with his stick, 'because it was believed that the root would cure the wounds inflicted by the bite of a mad dog.' Sophie first heard this piece of folklore as a child; her father repeats it unfailingly each summer.

They pass a small triangular pasture, intensely green, a secret place guarded by tall hedges of elder and hawthorn. A mud-coloured cow lowers her head and moos mournfully. Someone is late fetching her home for milking.

'I shall need some money,' says Sophie, 'a little more money for food, and the doctor.'

Her father makes a noise that might be assent or protest or both.

Later, he says, 'I liked that fellow who came instead of Ducroix – Morel, was that his name? Not a fussy old fool, anyway.'

'You only say that because Dr Ducroix advises you to eat less. And because he beats you at chess.'

'Of course,' he agrees serenely. 'What further evidence of the man's iniquity does the court require?'

They have reached the place near the crest of the ridge where their way forward is blocked by a thicket of blackthorn and they must turn left or right to continue. They always linger a little in this spot before taking the path that leads away from Castelnau and into the woods; it's an opportunity for Saint-Pierre to catch his breath without seeming to do so.

'Enthusiasm can be a fine thing,' he says now, leaning on his stick. 'But it's best to beware of enthusiasts. They mean well and that always tempts them into excess.'

Sophie glances at him sideways, trying to decide what he's referring to. But he's looking the other way, to where the late-afternoon shadows are climbing the hills; and anyway, she thinks, she would prefer not to know.

hen you couldn't find Sophie, you found her among her roses.

Stephen had not been at Montsignac ten days but he had learnt that. However, first there was Mathilde, lying reading in the grass. Brutus – he looked around at once – was nowhere in sight, at which he felt relief tinged with unease. Another thing he had learnt was that it was wise to have an idea of Brutus's whereabouts at all times.

He lingered awhile. Grass, flowers, leaves, sunlight: who could resist their conjuncture? 'Whenever I come through that door – it's like crossing the threshold into Eden.'

'You won't find your angel here. Nature has a ruinous effect on shoes.'

'What are you reading?' he asked fondly. He had his ideas about children. Like all notions that have been acquired without effort, they were not easily dislodged.

She handed him the book: *He had on no cloaths but a seaman's wastcoat, a pair of open kneed linnen drawers, and a blew linnen shirt; but nothing to direct me so much as to guess what nation he was of. He had nothing in his pocket but two pieces of eight, and a tobacco-pipe; that last was to me of ten times more value than the first.*

'I longed to be Robinson Crusoe when I was a boy.'

'It's quite a good story,' said Mathilde, 'but it would be better if he hadn't put in so much philosophy.'

'My brother and I used to play at castaways. He's older, so I was always Friday.'

'I'm going to be an explorer. Like Bougainville, but I'm not going to bother with the tropics. I shall sail north.' Mauve-tinted mountains of ice, lights dancing in the night sky, hoary sailors whose fingers had snapped off. Eyeless white monsters guarded fathomless caverns where waves crashed. She stood on the bridge of the ship, swaddled in furs.

Stephen went looking for Sophie.

It wasn't a large garden, but curving paths and cunningly disposed plantations gave the illusion of leafy rooms. That had been Marguerite de Saint-Pierre's doing, for gardens, like everything else, testified to the reaction against formality that had convulsed the age. Marguerite simply could not abide a parterre. Topiary made her feel ill. Fortunately Saint-Pierre's grandparents, old-fashioned people sequestered away in the countryside, had never succumbed to the worst excesses of symmetry and heraldic yews. Nevertheless, from the earliest years of her marriage, Marguerite had walked around Mont-signac and thought there was much to be done. She sent away for catalogues, made long lists of plants, filled page after page of her sketchbook with garden designs. She spoke, with shining eyes, of grottoes, cascades and something called a Serpentine Meander. She described glades radiating from the house on a *patte d'oie* plan. She hinted at a hermitage. Saint-Pierre asked for nothing more than to indulge her, but the imitation of nature looked set to ruin them. 'My dear,' he had to say at last, 'this isn't England.'

So the distressingly symmetrical lime trees survived in the park and schemes for a wilderness had to be abandoned. All was not lost, however. A good general seizes whatever opportunity comes to hand. Marguerite concentrated her efforts on the old garden near the house, where carnations, hollyhocks, tulips and cockscombs had been marshalled into rectangular beds bordered with boxwood, and the gravel was always neatly raked. Herbs and waving meadow plants soon transformed those formal flowerbeds; gravel gave way to grassy paths, which turned to mud in the winter but were undeniably more natural. Ingenious plantings softened straight lines into irregular arrangements of foliage. The carpets of dwarf evergreens vanished from one day to the next. A privet hedge was replaced by sweet-brier. Climbers and creepers climbed and crept everywhere. Luckily there was a Judas tree succumbing

23

to ivy's fatal embrace: it struck exactly the right note of melancholy.

Marguerite had ability, determination, a capacity for hard work. Her garden was a singularly pleasant place. Friends visiting from Toulouse declared themselves enchanted, solicited plants and advice. Walking in their wake, all she could think of was that she had fallen short of her aspirations. Worse still: she had only herself to blame.

The difficulty lay in her weakness for scented plants. Even lily-of-the-valley and wild white violets could not satisfy her craving, which demanded cultivated flowers. Hyacinths, wallflowers, stocks and freesias were allowed to intrude on the cow-parsley and mallow. She planted syringa. She had to have sweet peas. She wrote away for fragrant Virginia iris, reasoning that all American plants were authentically wild. She discovered, after a short, fierce struggle, that she was incapable of giving up roses: they rioted in sunny corners, scrambled up the courtyard wall, competed with jasmine and yellow-throated honeysuckle for possession of an arbour. 'But they're beautiful flowers,' said Saint-Pierre, bewildered by so much turmoil. 'They're not natural,' replied Marguerite sadly.

Sophie sat on the grass, listening to her parents and eating roses.

The summer she turned four her father told her the story of the Emperor Heliogabalus, at whose feasts guests were showered with such quantities of rose petals that most of them suffocated. 'What is suffocated?' she asked, and Saint-Pierre, already regretting his didactic impulse and wishing to avoid brutality, had answered evasively, telling her that for the Romans the rose was a symbol of eternal life because of its association with the gods. Shortly thereafter Sophie was discovered lying on her back in a sheltered angle by the wall, beneath a thick sprinkling of rose petals. 'I'm a Roman,' she informed her mother, 'I'm suffocating into a rose.'

Steadily, determinedly, in the years following Marguerite's death, roses had encroached on her garden. A stand of hazels was cut down because roses grow fat on sunlight. 'We'll sell the wood,' said Sophie, although no one had asked. 'Think of the money it'll bring this winter.' Screening shrubs – viburnum, goldenrod – were replaced with trellises so that more climbing roses could be accommodated. Delicate or demanding plants, abandoned to their own devices, drooped and died unremarked; the span of Sophie's attention was bounded by roses.

Those that grew in her garden, the hardy, long-lived roses of the eighteenth century, were far more tolerant of neglect than their modern descendants. But no gardener escapes hard work and pruning. In bleak December Sophie lopped back long side-shoots with the ruthlessness that is the hallmark of true desire. Twiggy dead wood was removed in spring. Careful trimming of flowering wood followed in summer, once the season was over. Garlic was planted around the bushes as it increased their resistance to disease. Leaf humus cooled their roots and kept weeds to a minimum when spread thickly on the beds. Watering involved Jacques, their ancient servant, and a cumbersome iron contraption called a water-barrow, and was arduous on both counts. Saint-Pierre's old mare was stalked for dollops of warm dung that Sophie stewed in an evil-smelling barrel until she judged the mixture sufficiently foul to satisfy her darlings. She went scavenging around towns and villages for new plants, knocked boldly on strangers' doors to beg cuttings when a spray overhanging a terrace snared her interest, had been known to steal if her request was refused. 'When it's roses,' said Mathilde admiringly, 'Sophie is shameless.'

Ruthless, bold, shameless: roses provided Sophie with an opportunity to be all these things.

Think of her: a girl with just enough education to awaken curiosity but not nearly enough to satisfy it, a woman with neither beauty nor wealth and therefore little prospect of marriage. Think of her days: the unimaginable, unavoidable drudgeries like making soap and sewing every article of clothing and linen, the tedium of winter evenings when a few expensive candles shed such poor light that the easiest (and warmest) thing to do was to go to bed. Think of her world: elsewhere, horizons were expanding – oxygen had been

25

isolated, the Pacific had been mapped, absolute monarchy was being dismantled – but science and history filtered down to Montsignac as anecdote and rumour, easily outweighed by a village scandal or the damage caused by an early frost.

You can see why Sophie needed roses.

Lying in bed with her eyes shut, she stroked her bare skin with a soft white flower.

In June, when no one was looking, she still ate rose petals.

But in late July the main flush of flowers was over, so that Stephen's eye was caught by a few clear pink stragglers on a bush with grey-green leaves. He picked one, and when he found Sophie on the far side of the brier hedge, he came up close to her and tucked the rose into her hair.

She turned the same colour as the flower.

He was charmed by the transparency – *the sincerity*, as he termed it to himself – of her response. That was what came of living in proximity to Nature. A basket at her feet contained lengths of string and a knife with a thin, curved blade; beside it, a basin of water held several green twigs. 'How fortunate you are,' he said, 'to toil in the open air, in the company of birds ... I've always wanted to be a gardener.'

'Well,' she said doubtfully, 'have you ever tried it?'

'I've often walked about in gardens.'

She had been standing to ease her back. Now she bent once more over a bed of young plants laid out in rows and he crouched beside her: 'Is that a rosebush?'

'Rootstock raised from brier cuttings I took from the hedgerows two winters ago. I'm grafting a rose onto it.' She had made a T-shaped cut in the brier stem at finger-height above the ground, wielding the lethal-looking knife with unconcerned precision. A different knife, one with a dull, rounded blade, was used to prise back the two folds of bark at the intersection of the cuts.

He saw her reaching for the basin, and passed her one of the twigs. With a nod of thanks she sliced out a short length, beginning just above and finishing just below a leaf bud. 'Look.' Her breath shook the green sliver balanced on the blade of her knife. She turned it over carefully and showed him the tiny patch of lighter-coloured wood on the other side. 'That must come out.' He looked on entranced as she removed the lighter wood while leaving the shield of bark that surrounded it intact. 'And now the bud goes into the space left by the two flaps of bark on the rootstock, like this' – he craned to see – 'and then it's tied on.'

'Let me help.'

Their hands touched. 'Firmly,' she said, 'but not too tightly.'

The tiny bud secured, he collapsed onto the grass: 'What backbreaking work.'

Sophie cut off the dangling end of string and straightened up to smile at him. 'It's easier with practice. And the surest method of propagation. I'll have two dozen new plants in the spring.'

'Is it very beautiful, this rose?' He was watching her face. When she smiled, the naturally serious cast of her features broke up and she looked ... almost pretty, he thought.

'Come and see,' she said.

She led him down paths and there it was: a small bush, smooth-stemmed, with dark, faintly glossy oval leaves and a profusion of red flowers. It was a charming sight – the cherry-red flowers, the deep-green leaves – and he said so. Yet from the way she looked at the ground, he could tell he'd disappointed her.

'Is it particularly rare?' he guessed, wanting to please.

'For someone who loves Nature, you don't know a lot about it, do you?' He swung around, startled. Mathilde, emerging from a thicket of leaves, smiled to herself. She had a game called Savages, which required moving about the garden without being seen. She was very good at it. 'Roses don't usually flower right through summer. This one comes from China, from the nurseries of Fa-tee near Canton. Sophie gave Rinaldi Mother's silver bracelet for it – only Father and Claire are not to know.'

'Matty!'

'But there are other roses in flower,' he objected, 'like the one Sophie has in her hair.'

'A Quatre-Saisons,' said Mathilde loftily, 'also known as an

Autumn Damask. An exception to the rule. It usually has a second flush of flowers late in the season but can't be counted on.' Adding with belated loyalty, 'Although Sophie's never fail. Rinaldi says she could plant a cabbage seed and it would come up a rose.'

'Rinaldi . . .?'

'The pedlar who sold me the red rose. Only when he was young, he used to be a sailor. On his last voyage, years and years ago now, he travelled to China where he saw roses like this, hundreds of them, growing in pots. In warm climates they flower all year round.' There was a dreamy note in Sophie's voice. 'Rinaldi recognised the value of a rose that flowers continuously, so he acquired as many as he could.'

'He brought them back planted in teacups,' put in Mathilde, 'that's how little they were.'

'Most of the plants didn't survive the voyage, and he sold those that did. But he kept two bushes for himself, on a plot of land he bought from the money he made. He intended to settle down, take a wife, raise children, keep a goat, live out his days cultivating his garden. But Rinaldi's a born wanderer.' Sophie shrugged. 'He grew bored, of course.'

Stephen had picked one of the red flowers and was sniffing it.

'The first thing anyone does with a rose is smell it,' said Mathilde. 'Have you noticed?'

'Children have such wonderfully enquiring minds,' he said, beaming at her.

'That wasn't children – that was *me*. I'm extremely advanced for my age.'

Stephen was still holding the flower to his face. 'We have music to train the ear and art to train the eye, we educate our palates with food and wine. Doesn't it strike you that our noses are shamefully neglected?'

'Perhaps that's why smells have such a powerful effect on us,' replied Sophie. 'We haven't been educated out of our instinctive response to them.'

'It's impossible to describe a scent,' he said. 'This one is delicate. And not what I expected. It doesn't smell like . . . like a rose.'

'I know.' Sophie stood on one foot and frowned.

He put his hand on her arm. She looked down at his long-jointed, large-knuckled fingers. There was a little scratch on the back of his wrist, among the fine, pale hair. 'I came looking for you because ... well, my ankle is quite healed, as you know, and I wouldn't wish to impose any longer on your kindness ...'

He's going away. Sophie had been bracing herself for this moment and here it was. She stood on the other foot.

'... but I wanted to ask if I might spend a few more weeks with you. I promise not to get in your way, I'll go for long walks, with a sketchbook ...'

'And an angel, perhaps,' said Mathilde. Very softly, to a bee.

That blackbird: had it been there all along on the courtyard wall, whistling like that?

*W*alking home along the leaf-shadowed lane that led from the village, Sophie was intercepted by Mathilde.

'He's arrived! I thought we were safe for another week?'

'Have you shut Brutus up?'

'*Vive la liberté.*'

Sophie quickened her steps.

In the courtyard, there were horses, a carriage, liveried servants. In the drawing-room, Claire and Stephen sat nowhere near each other. Sophie noticed that her sister was wearing one of her prettiest dresses, a rose-sprigged muslin; the sort of dress a wife might put on to welcome a husband she had not seen in over six weeks. If she had known she was going to see him.

Hubert paced around, talking and touching things. His hair was thinning but had kept its colour; he was proud of its dark lustre and rarely wore a wig. Sophie often told herself that a man with a high complexion and black hair cannot help looking angry; it was unfortunate for this theory that her brother-in-law usually was.

'What an unexpected pleasure. We thought next week –' Bending to kiss him, she flinched from the horror of his breath.

All this – the pacing, the touching, the flinching – was quite as usual.

'You've heard nothing, of course, stuck away in this back-water.' Confidence and accusation were endemic to Hubert's conversation. 'Those cretins in Paris have surpassed themselves. They sat up all night in the National Assembly and concluded it was their patriotic duty to suppress all feudal dues. Of course half those deputies have nothing of their own, which makes them all the keener to drag everyone down to their level.'

Stephen was looking from Claire to Sophie; explanation was plainly called for. Hubert had every intention of providing it: 'Privileges our families have exercised for centuries. Legitimate sources of income.' He began ticking them off on his fingers: 'River and road tolls, quit-rent, hearth taxes, taxes on the sale of merchandise at fairs, payment in kind, payment in money.' His ancestors had given their lives for France, eldest son after eldest son for untold generations. He chewed the inside of his cheek, overcome by the injustice of it all.

'Aren't you forgetting some of the more controversial privileges, my dear Monferrant?' asked Saint-Pierre from the doorway. Once, in the first year of Claire's marriage and in the interest of fairness, he had sat down to make a list of Hubert's good points. After *Keeps an excellent table*, he thought for a long while and came up with *Forthright*.

Hubert attacked a worn spot on the carpet with the toe of his boot. Men like his father-in-law were running the country into the ground. A wife who was beautiful and conscious of the difference in their rank was one thing; the problem was the relatives.

Saint-Pierre selected a chair that could accommodate his bulk and turned to Stephen. He brought the tips of his fingers together over the mound of his stomach. His daughters rolled their eyes at each other: their father, the magistrate.

'Take *mainmorte*: it requires a peasant to obtain his lord's permission before selling his own land. It also prevents him from bequeathing that land to anyone other than a direct relative who has shared his roof. And then there are ancient hunting rights which allow an aristocrat to keep game that may feed at will on a peasant's crops. When harvests are bad – as they were last year – that is especially resented.'

'Understandably,' ventured Stephen.

Hubert began rocking on his heels. 'You have a very imperfect *understanding* of the situation. There were attacks on property all over France in the spring. On my own estates,

31

rabbits and pheasants were slaughtered, buildings set on fire and cattle herded onto the crops. One of my gamekeepers was beaten with an iron bar and barely escaped with his life.' He eyed Stephen with distaste: a foreigner with opinions. 'I suppose you condone barbarism in the New World, but I assure you we take a very different view of it here.'

'To understand isn't the same as to condone,' said Stephen. He would have liked Claire to acknowledge his bravery; but she studied the empty fireplace with intent. 'Naturally, nobody has the right to carry out acts of violence with impunity.'

'Impunity didn't come into it,' inserted Saint-Pierre smoothly. 'My son-in-law had the ringleaders hanged after summary trial.'

'And if I hadn't acted decisively, we'd have had our throats cut as we lay in our beds. Which is what we're facing now – and our assassins urged on by those popinjays in Paris.'

'My dear Monferrant, you're confusing cause and effect. The spring riots were provoked by certain elements in the aris-tocracy insisting on the rigid application of their rights. The abolition of aristocratic privilege will be greeted with delight, not with further violence.'

'You're as deluded as the rest of them if you think we've seen the end of it. I'll be escorting my wife and son back to Toulouse tomorrow morning. Bands of brigands are already on the loose, pillaging and murdering as they go. The coun-tryside is as dangerous as Paris these days – even for those who live like peasants.'

Back and forth, back and forth rocked Hubert, and smiled at them all. He stood on tiptoe and crowed, and helped himself to more armagnac.

In the silence the gilt clock on the mantelpiece ticked unbearably. It never kept the correct time, chiming to unpre-dictable impulse, sometimes several times in the hour, some-times not at all for days; but it had belonged to Marguerite, so Saint-Pierre wound it with tenderness and would not hear of throwing it away. When was love ever conditional upon utility?

When the magistrate spoke, he directed himself again to

Stephen. 'The feudal cause is not a subject the marquis takes lightly. Two years ago, he hired a lawyer to investigate privileges that had long fallen into abeyance. He felt, you see, that Paris was making too many concessions to upstarts urging reform, and he reasoned that it fell to fellows like him to revive ancient obligations before all trace of them vanished forever.

'Well, this lawyer spent months with his nose in various archives and a pretty penny he charged for his trouble. And do you know what he ferreted out? He discovered that Monferrant here possesses the inalienable right to lead his peasants into the hunt in winter and, once in the woods, to make them open their bowels so he might warm his feet in their ordure.'

Stephen's laugh was heard in the kitchen, where Mathilde and Brutus had sought consolation in gingerbread. Sophie failed to suppress a smile. Claire gazed stonily out of the window.

'The right to warm your feet, Monferrant, shame that's gone forever now, the right to warm your feet.'

1

How could she have married him? He's unprepossessing in every way. And old – he must be thirty-five at least. He's rich and titled, of course, but she has given me to understand that these things weigh as little with her as they do with me.

Could it be for the sake of her sisters? Perhaps his connections will enable her to put suitable marriages their way – and Sophie is plainly getting on in years and in want of a husband. Yes, that would be like her, to have sacrificed her own happiness with a view to obtaining theirs.

It's obvious that a man like that could never care for Art.

2

No one has ever looked at me the way he looks at Claire.

But she's beautiful. There can be no comparison.

I wonder if he'll stay after they go back to Toulouse? It would be good for Matty. He makes her laugh and that's good for her, she's too serious for her age. There's a lightness in him that we lack.

He's young, of course, not yet twenty-two. Six whole months younger than me.

I should do my hair that new way Claire showed me.

3

On the side of his head, just below his ears – that's where he smells best. A warm smell, like baking.

When he has been in the river he smells different, like mud. But after a few hours his own smell comes back. And his paws always smell grassy – even in the morning, when he has been indoors all night.

He only bites people whose smell he doesn't like and I don't think it's fair to punish him for it.

He doesn't like the way Hubert smells. Who does?

*T*hat morning the sky above Castelnau was laid with creamy clouds lit up along the folds like crumpled satin. Joseph crossed the street to greet Sophie, raising his hat, and saw that for entire seconds she looked at him blankly.

And he had thought of little else since meeting her.

He took off his spectacles to wipe them, but remembered in time that his handkerchief was none too clean. Whereon she smiled and held out her hand: 'Dr Morel, good morning.'

'I trust the American gentleman – Mr Fletcher? – has quite recovered?' Trying not to stare, trying not to notice that her hair contained strands of light brown and dark, and another colour that lay between the two.

'Why yes, thank you. It was so fortunate you were at the Costes' farm. I'm sure the promptness of your response saved Mr Fletcher a great deal of discomfort. He was – we're all of us – extremely grateful.'

'Not at all.' He shuffled his large and dusty boots. 'I hope Dr Ducroix was able to examine the patient himself?'

'Yes, he confirmed your diagnosis and returned the next week to monitor Mr Fletcher's progress. But there was no need for anxiety – the ankle healed quickly.'

'Good, good.' Casting about for ways to prolong the encounter. 'Excellent news.' She must think him insane. 'And . . . and is Mr Fletcher enjoying his visit to our part of the world?'

Where did drivel like that come from?

'He returned to his cousins in Bordeaux a few weeks ago. He'll be in Paris now.'

Good, good. Excellent news. The American was exactly the

sort of charming idiot women found irresistible. 'Paris,' he said, 'well, that is the place to be.'

She smiled again. 'Then you're no different from all the other young men.'

Could she be teasing him? That would be a good sign, an excellent sign. 'And you?' he asked boldly. 'Don't you wish you were there, where they're making history?'

'That sounds so serious.'

'You don't take what's happening seriously?' He moved his head and light glittered fiercely on his spectacles.

'I didn't mean . . .' She shifted her weight onto one foot and he realised he had disconcerted her. 'Now you'll decide I'm frivolous and conservative, as well-bred young ladies are meant to be. History – I think of it as distant and dreary and impossible to fathom, like German philosophy. A reflection on my schoolbooks, perhaps. Or more probably on my capacities as a scholar. I always preferred novels.'

He heard *dreary, impossible, German*. Terrible words.

'But it's precisely a question of imagination,' he said, 'of being the first to conjure the world differently.' Cursing himself, even as he spoke, for a pompous fool. It was imperative to put an end to this conversation *at once*.

'I'm on my way to see a patient, so –' He thrust out his hand.

'You must call at Montsignac when you can. I know it would please my father.'

'I'd be delighted . . . Good, good . . .'

His tongue thick against the roof of his mouth, he watched her walk away.

Having in fact nothing whatsoever to do, Joseph found himself loitering on the waterfront. February and October marked high season on the river, when merchants sent their goods downstream to the Garonne, and so eventually on to Bordeaux, and you could walk across to the other bank on the glut of barges. Already, in September, the wharves were swarming with stevedores hoisting bolts of fabric and bundles of hide from wagons and conveying them aboard the boats

37

that lay two and three deep along the banks.

Clerks in tall hats were fussing over tall ledgers. A barge-man got in the way of two small boys leading a draught horse, which occasioned opulent swearing.

Joseph climbed the steps to the comparative calm of Castelnau's only bridge. It linked the town's respectable centre, where he had run into Sophie, with the district of Lacapelle, where he had been born. Its huddled wooden buildings housed the poor: workers who produced the textiles for which Castelnau was renowned, bargemen, stevedores, coopers and carpenters connected with the river trade, the usual flotsam of street-sellers, stable-hands, petty thieves, widows, the old, the desperate, scrapers and scrabblers of one kind or another. Since returning to the town in the summer, he had taken lodgings on the right bank, where once he had seldom had reason to stray.

He thought of the bridge as linking the two halves of his life, a brick-and-mortar embodiment of the transition he had effected. His mother had been a washerwoman who took in laundry from the imposing houses that fronted the river on the town side. In these mansions lived Castelnau's wealthy textile and flour merchants – the Nicolet clan, for instance, who enjoyed a monopoly on the manufacture of a stout woollen fabric stamped with the royal seal, which clothed the entire French army. Joseph's father carded wool in their Castelnau workshop, which employed more than three hundred people, not counting weavers; most weaving was carried out by women and children in the countryside, where guild regulations were difficult if not impossible to enforce.

When Joseph was seven years old, tragedy crawled in and curled itself about the Nicolets. Robert Nicolet, sole heir to the vast family fortune, was drowned in a boating accident along with his two young sons. One moonlit night not long after, his wife put on her wedding dress and threw herself off the bridge. They found her the next day in the usual place at the bend in the river, held fast by rocks and the roots of a willow tree, a confetti of bright yellow leaves stuck to her hair.

Old Mr Nicolet took to wandering around his mansion in a dressing-gown of peacock-blue silk, opening doors at random, stumbling along passages he hadn't known existed. Sometimes he spoke aloud, disjointed words or phrases that required no reply. In this way he came across Joseph, who was playing with an empty cigar box on the cold scullery floor. His mother, who had been gossiping with a maid, stammered excuses, rushed to haul her son out of the way. But the old gentleman paused and looked down into the child's upturned, frightened face; he said nothing, but reached out a brown-spotted hand and very lightly, with the tips of his fingers, stroked the little boy's cheek.

Joseph never saw him again and soon forgot the encounter. But when the old entrepreneur died eighteen months later it was discovered that his will provided for Jeanne Morel's son to be sent to school. Eventually, if the boy showed aptitude, he was to be trained, *as a physician*, ran the stipulation, *so that he might learn to ease the suffering with which this world is so rich endowed.*

Since returning to Castelnau, Joseph had often found his steps taking him to the river. He couldn't have said what had compelled him home after he had completed his studies. His parents were dead, both his sisters had married and moved away; it would have been easier and no doubt more prudent to stay on in Montpellier and exploit the connections he had made in the university. The decision to return, taken impulsively with the vague intention of honouring his benefactor, now hovered at his shoulder like a bird of ill-omen. The idea that he might have made an irrevocable error was novel and terrifying.

At first he hadn't recognised the dull unhappiness that accompanied him everywhere. How could he, when he had never been lonely? In Montpellier, there was always someone rapping at his door. He ached for those companionable winter evenings spent outdrinking each other in taverns, for the ease with which friendship comes when youth and common endeavour level out the craggy landscape of difference. He was homesick for the *garrigue*, the dry, herb-scented hills behind the southern city, where he had often walked off a hangover; once he had come across a ruined village given over to thready wildflowers, and birds whose tiny looping bodies stitched tirelessly at the air. Entering rooms where illness held sway, eating his solitary meals, trying to impose a shape on the succession of his shapeless days, he longed for the life that had fitted him like a shirt worn soft.

Now, standing on the bridge, he wondered whether it wasn't this vantage point he had come back for: this parapet under his hands, that crumbling mansion upstream, the workshop where his father had laboured, the laundry barges where his mother had scrubbed the heavy Nicolet linen.

People need the past, he thought, and for a moment everything seemed as clear as the view leaping into light along the river. They need to know where they have come from.

That reminded him of what he had said to Sophie about history, and embarrassment trickled like sweat down his spine. He was only a physician, he should leave pronouncements to other men and confine himself to the things he knew. *To ease the suffering with which this world is so rich endowed.*

right cold, after a week of rain.

Mathilde walked along a path where fat orange rose hips were strung like beads through the hedgerow. Brutus, running sideways ahead of her, looked around every so often to check on her progress, or paused to thrust his face into a clump of flat brown toadstools. Taking off suddenly, he disappeared into a field.

There were small yellow snails everywhere, with translucent, butter-yellow shells. A puddle as wide as the lane reflected the leaves overhead; she splashed through, soaking her boots and her grey woollen stockings.

In Paris the crowd followed her without hesitation, as she led the way fearlessly through the streets of a city filled with tall houses, taller and grander even than the houses of Toulouse. There was torchlight and singing. At the elaborate iron gates, a man lifted her onto his shoulders and she addressed the blur of adoring faces: 'Citizens! It is our patriotic duty to free these unfortunate souls, subjected to torture, victims of untold tyrannies.' Her fist was clenched over her heart. '*Vive la liberté. Vive la France.*' The people cheered and surged forward, courageous under the crackle of musket fire. Walls tumbled before their onslaught, bars melted before the heat of their passion. The wretched prisoners, clad in rags, their ankles still in fetters, knelt in front of her and kissed her hand. In the distance she caught a glimpse of – could it be Hubert's head on a pike?

Humming a tune, she skipped over ankle-turning ruts.

Brutus materialised a little way ahead of her, his paws in a lamentable state.

They turned a corner where a wild crab-apple tree grew and

there, at the far end of the pasture, stood the pigeon-house. Built of flat grey stones and half-timbered with oak, it still belonged to her family, although the land that surrounded it had long been sold. The *colombine* – the layered droppings that covered the floor of the pigeon-house – enriched the Saint-Pierres twice, fertilising their diminished holdings and fattening their pockets when sold to peasant farmers, who were forbidden the aristocratic privilege of keeping pigeons.

Mathilde had the sun in her eyes, so when Brutus began barking she couldn't see him. But running towards the sound, she saw arch-shaped darkness where the wooden door had hung.

She almost trod on the first pigeon, which lay on the threshold. There were many, many more inside, huddles of still feathers. She stood stiffly by the door, her toes curled within her boots. Some of the birds had had their necks twisted but most had had their throats cut. A few tiny, tiny feathers rose on a draught, twisting in a ray of sunlight.

Brutus had been swallowed by the shadows. She could hear his scuffling. Otherwise, only different birds, calling from the woods.

Saint-Pierre poured Sophie a glass of *floc*, the local herb-based liqueur. 'They did us no harm in the spring when their rage was far greater for having no sanctioned outlet. This is an expression of victory: they're letting us know that the scales have tipped, at last, in their favour.'

'You don't think we should be concerned?'

'Not at all. They didn't take the birds away to eat but left them for us to find. A profoundly symbolic gesture, don't you see? Here, my dear –' holding out the dish – 'do have some of these excellent walnuts.'

For a moment, anger flashed through Sophie: You haven't asked once about Matty, stop eating and *listen*.

'From what you tell me, the *colombine* was left untouched as well,' he was saying. 'That points to town-dwellers. Probably a band of young fellows from Castelnau out for some fun.' Detached, sifting the evidence, dispassionate, reasoned.

Sophie thought, Sometimes I am for unreason.

But said, reasonably, 'Jacques has been making enquiries in the village. That afternoon three days ago, when the rain cleared, several people saw a group of women, strangers, armed with sticks, come out of the woods and make their way over the fields in the direction of the pigeon-house. They were singing and appeared to have, as Jacques puts it, partaken of strong drink.'

'There you have it, then, there you have it. Castelnau is all abuzz with reports of the rioting market-women who constrained the King and Queen to leave Versailles and accompany them to Paris. One must always prove oneself equal to the challenges thrown down by mere Parisians: that is the entire drama of provincial life.'

'Pierre Coste told Jacques that they called him Citizen and invited him to join them. Of course he's anxious to make it understood that he had nothing at all to do with the pigeons, so according to him there were twenty or thirty of them, tall, strapping women with loud voices, who were plainly up to no good. Others say there were no more than a dozen, though everyone agrees they were boisterous and wild.'

'Tall women with loud voices?' Saint-Pierre cracked walnuts meditatively. 'There was a case, about ten years ago in the Beaujolais, much talked about at the time. A group of men decked themselves out in bonnets and long white shirts resembling female attire, and set upon the surveyors measuring their fields for a new landlord. Later, when questions were being asked, the men and their wives claimed complete ignorance of the events, insisting that the assailants must have been sprites come down from the mountains to spread their mischief among humans.'

'But why dress up as women?'

He shrugged. 'In many parts of the country, the full weight of the law is reserved for men.'

She said slowly, thinking it through, 'It's the symbolism I don't like. It turns us into symbols, too.'

But Saint-Pierre had finished his second glass of *floc* and his interest had shifted elsewhere: 'Isn't Berthe late with dinner? Are we to live on walnuts?'

1790

er nephew blew spit bubbles at Sophie from her knee, and chuckled. 'He favours you increasingly,' she said. And – thinking, Which is just as well – felt obliged to ask, 'How is Hubert?'

Since the birth of the child Claire rarely bothered to affect concern for her husband. The face she pulled now was made up in equal parts of indifference to Hubert, and annoyance with Sophie for pretending otherwise. 'How should I know? I scarcely saw him in Paris. He and Sébastien spend their days in conference with sympathetic members of the Assembly. A group of them managed to obtain an audience with Lafayette and put it to him that he and his National Guards should defect to the aristocratic cause. Only they call it the King's cause, of course, when they remember.'

'And . . .?'

'All Hubert would say when I enquired was that he forbade me to speak of that popinjay.' Claire smiled. 'But Anne had it from Sébastien that they had spoken scarcely three words when the general told them to get out of his sight before he had them all arrested for treason. And as they were trooping out, he asked why they weren't wearing his new cockade and made them line up while a guardsman fixed tricolours to their hats.' She caught Sophie's eye and they began to giggle. 'Can you imagine? Hubert forced to wear the tricolour.'

The baby, unused to merriment, began to grizzle. His aunt tried to soothe him, cuddling him into her neck; but Claire rang a bell and had him handed over to his nursemaid: 'No, really, Sophie, you don't realise – children must not be mollycoddled.'

That was another thing since the birth of Olivier, thought Sophie. To the list of all the things that she could not possibly understand as an unmarried woman had been added all those beyond her comprehension as a childless one.

Claire, having made her point, was as usual moved to conciliation. 'I'm so glad you could come straightaway. It was quite unnecessary for Hubert to insist that I leave Paris a whole month earlier than planned. He's convinced the mob will turn on us, set fire to the *faubourg* and cut our throats – it's quite an obsession with him. He alarmed Sébastien sufficiently for Anne to be banished to her mother-in-law in Blois. I wanted her here with me and we argued for safety in numbers, but she's in a delicate condition again and Sébastien thought the journey to Toulouse would be too taxing. He's hoping for an heir this time, so her wellbeing is a paramount concern.'

Really, thought Sophie, there's nothing like marriage for fostering cynicism.

She said, 'According to Father it's all rhetoric now, as they debate the Constitution. Surely there's no real danger?'

Claire rolled her eyes. 'Only of boredom. You wouldn't believe how dreary Paris has become. Even the theatre – all the new plays are about the fall of tyrants and the sovereignty of the people and have titles like *The Triumph of Liberty* or *The Patriot's Wife*. Can you imagine? Of course there were demonstrations and things, as well. Protests about the price of bread.'

Bored disdain: that was the line Madame la Marquise intended to take towards the Revolution.

'There've been demonstrations in Castelnau, too. Wigmakers complaining they've been robbed of a living since undressed hair became a sign of patriotism.'

'The leading man in a play we saw had had his hair cut short and combed over his forehead in a fringe.'

'How did he look?'

'Hideous. Like one of those awful Roman busts. You wouldn't believe the fashions, Sophie. Simple white shifts. Shoes fastened with red, white and blue ribbons instead of silver buckles. I suppose it's only a matter of time before we see them in the provinces.'

'Well, leaving can't have been too much of a wrench.'

'There are always amusing people about, of course.' Claire picked up her embroidery and frowned over a butterfly's indigo wings. She made up her own designs, disdaining to buy them ready-drawn on the satin. Insects were her speciality: lumbering bees, furry caterpillars. Aged eleven, she had pleaded to begin sewing her trousseau.

Sophie sipped tea.

After a while: 'Has Father had word from Stephen?'

'No.'

Separately, they contemplated the effects of blue-green eyes, a lazy smile.

Sophie was determined to remain calm. 'You saw Stephen, then?'

'Yes, the de la Mottes gave a reception for him. Louis de la Motte fought in the American war with Stephen's father . . .' Claire put down her needle and met her sister's gaze. 'He wants to paint my portrait.'

Sophie glanced involuntarily at the wall above the fireplace which was dominated by a portrait of Claire and Hubert – she seated, he with proprietorial hand on her shoulder – against a background of trees, hills, deer: Hubert's estate at Lupiac, unaccountably endowed in the middle distance with a few broken columns suggestive of a ruined Grecian temple.

'Oh, yes, yes.' Claire waved a dismissive hand in the direction of the portrait. 'But this will be quite different: Stephen favours the fresh new style, out of doors but not posed, not artificial. The thing is to be completely natural, do you see? And he'd also like to do a study after Raphael or . . . or . . . one of those Italians, of me with Olivier.'

'A Madonna and Child?'

'Exactly. He's turning down commissions all over Paris, you know – he's very much in demand . . .'

Sophie said nothing.

'. . . so it's a tremendous compliment. He has connections in the Assembly, thanks to his cousins, and it's likely he'll be offered a commission for a painting to mark the anniversary of the fall of the Bastille or the Tennis Court oath, I'm not sure which. He'll have to temper his style to suit official taste, of course, which is terribly conservative: he envisages a large allegorical work . . .'

'*The Triumph of Liberty*, perhaps?'

'Exactly.' Then she had the grace to laugh; she was Sophie's sister after all. 'You're teasing me, as usual. But he's really very talented, everyone says so, and he wants to paint me at Montsignac, in your garden. He was going to write to Father asking if he might spend June there with us.'

In winter, even the smallest of Claire's three drawing-rooms was draughty. A maid who had come in to clear away the tray was told to stoke up the fire.

'Don't you think it's a splendid idea?'

Sophie looked at the narrow back of the girl on her knees in front of the flames. This is how it is in Claire's life, she thought, everything can be arranged.

She said, answering the unvoiced question, 'I'm sure Father will agree.'

'I know why you're hesitating, Sophie. But Stephen has offered, with great delicacy of course, to pay for his board. He understands . . . well, the situation. There's no need to be anxious on that score.'

'I'm relieved to hear it.'

'You worry too much. Stephen has noticed it, too.'

They've talked about me. The idea was appalling.

'That little crease between your eyes grows deeper by the hour. I must show you the new apricot cream I bought in Paris, everyone swears by it. And I have some lace for you and a pair of evening gloves.'

She made an effort: 'No white shift? Not even a tricolour sash?'

'Heaven forbid. We must go through your dresses and pick one out for tomorrow night. We're invited to dine at the Linguets. Marianne's brother, the lieutenant, will be there – she mentioned it particularly. He was quite taken with you last year, do you remember?'

Heaven forbid, thought Sophie.

*S*pring came, and reminded him how lonely he was. The doctors with established practices, like Ducroix, could pick and choose their patients; he could not. Winter saw him trudging muddy roads to the outlying farms and hamlets – he couldn't afford a horse, although he would rent one from the stables if a case warranted urgency – or crossing the bridge to Lacapelle, where they could not pick and choose their doctors. He traced and retraced the familiar map of its streets, the filthy alleys and cramped houses where disease nestled up to the poor like a lover, sharing their food, clasping them as they slept.

There was a smell there, a sweetish, clinging odour compounded of river, cabbage soup, dye, excrement, tar, sawdust, sweat, the mud left behind by the unfailing annual flood. Undressing at night, he fancied it adhered to his clothes, and would sniff at his discarded linen, only half-repelled. The smell of his childhood, waiting always to reclaim him. Daily, he crossed the bridge and re-entered its domain.

He rented a room in a second-floor apartment from a locksmith's widow. It would have been more practical to have lodged on the other side of the river in Lacapelle, where he ran his practice. But he wouldn't sleep there.

As the days lengthened and the weather grew milder, loneliness crowded him out of his narrow room at night and he walked to the furthest reaches of the town, where gardens melted into fields and the world unrolled in unfathomable darkness before him. Prostitutes accosted him frequently on these excursions. But he was afraid of the infections he knew they carried, and so turned quickly away before longing could overcome fear.

He had called twice at Montsignac. On both occasions, she had been away. It seemed hopeless from the outset, anyway. The Saint-Pierres might be both impoverished and affable, but they were still the Saint-Pierres.

He took to stopping in the taverns that flourished on the edges of town, noisy places patronised by small-time shopkeepers and artisans – butchers, bakers, candle- and candle-stick makers – as well as a sprinkling of porters, servants, day labourers. They nodded at him, invited him to drink with them, or left him to drink alone if he pleased, their talk washing over and around him, quieting the tremor in his blood.

That spring, the talk was all of the recent municipal elections at which the Vicomte de Caussade had been elected mayor, along with a council made up of aristocrats, elite administrators, high-ranking clerics. Lacapelle had voted for the Revolution-minded Patriot party; but the rest of Castelnau – or at least that portion of its male population accorded a vote – had preferred the viscount's promises of full employment, an end to food shortages, the elimination of undesirables – in short, the restoration of the rightful order of things.

Joseph was twenty-three years old. He could read Latin and Greek. He had studied mathematics, physics and chemistry. He understood the finer points of Lavoisier's groundbreaking work on combustion and its bearing on respiration. He could have told you the number of bones in a human hand. He practised percussion of the chest, a modern diagnostic technique developed in Vienna where it had been observed that a healthy chest produces a noise like a cloth-covered drum when tapped with the end of a forefinger, while a muffled or high-pitched sound betrays the presence of pulmonary disease.

But he was twenty-three years old.

For instance: it surprised him that the underclass clientele of the taverns was by no means united in its politics. Arguments between Caussade's followers and those who had voted for the Patriots were frequent and fervent. On an evening when debates and tempers had been running particularly high, he expressed astonishment at the support Caussade was able to muster among people whose interests could scarcely be said to coincide with those of the privileged minority he represented.

The man sitting next to him sighed. 'What do you expect? These fools see no further than their noses. They're inflated with provincial pride, so Caussade tells them that the Revolution is being run by Parisians. They hate Protestants, so he assures them the Revolution is being masterminded by heretics bent on ensuring the triumph of their faith.'

With sudden force, Joseph's companion slammed down his tankard and roared over the din of voices, 'Have your heads been stuffed so full of lies by your priests that there's no room left over for your brains? The viscount and his cronies cared nothing for you before '89 and less now, for all that they smile and shake your hands on polling day.'

In the hush, all faces turned to him. He looked at Joseph and said, 'Well, shall we go?'

The indignant murmurs started up in their wake.

They walked along streets slick with rain. Joseph had exchanged a few words with Paul Ricard on previous occasions; had heard him voice his contempt for the viscount in the run-up to the elections; had seen how other men listened, inclining their heads, when he talked.

He knew that Ricard was a pork butcher by trade, with a shop in Lacapelle. He was an imposing figure, a tall, heavy-set, wide-shouldered fellow with a shock of reddish hair. For such a big man his tread was light enough, but he walked with a slight limp. People said this was the result of an accident he had had as a child, when a carriage ran him down in a narrow street.

Joseph was trying to recollect who had told him that story when Ricard spoke. 'Everyone talks of you in Lacapelle, doctor. They say you're not too proud to enter the poorest hovel. Antoinette Bergis, the rag-seller, says she owes her life to you; and there are plenty like her to testify that you ask no fee of patients who don't have the means to pay. A good man: there's no better reputation.'

He was intensely moved. At the same time, he felt the praise unmerited. Would he have chosen to work with those people if choice had been possible? Is there virtue in necessity?

'They say you grew up there?'

Who had last spoken to him with such kindness? At first he couldn't reply. Then he was talking, talking. About his parents, a man he had once seen beating a donkey, a cold scullery, the sleeve of a peacock-blue dressing-gown, two children who came to him in his dreams with starfish hands reaching to drag him down into their kingdom, a girl he had known in Montpellier, something his professor of anatomy had said, his dingy room, the warp and weft of his past, the tangled future.

They had reached the bridge. Before turning away, Ricard placed his hand on Joseph's shoulder. 'Some of us have started a club for political discussion. You should come along. I think you'll find it interesting.'

Once more, rain began to fall.

*T*he sheet was almost two hundred years old and had begun to wear thin. Someone had to cut it in half, turn it sides-to-middle and sew it together again. Which explained why Sophie was sitting beside an open window on an afternoon in early May, stitching furiously and without enthusiasm.

Furiously because it was one of those days when the yearning was acute.

She called it the yearning in an effort to render it ridiculous to herself, to diminish its power over her. She identified it as a sensation that was at once of the mind and of the body, a longing for ... for wideness, thought Sophie, coupled with a paradoxical craving for closeness, for a hand other than her own trailing over her skin.

The yearning might take the form of a restlessness that drove her from the house, that made sitting still a discipline, that set her humming and dancing around her bedroom, turning this way and that in front of her mirror, assessing herself coolly. Or it might manifest itself as a stupor inching through her veins, infusing her blood with inertia, weighing down her limbs, distorting time so that languid minutes eased past and the saucepans boiled over, roses wilted beside a vase, columns of figures stayed untallied.

The yearning would seize her and bat her about in its paws. Grow bored and let her fall. Return, stepping stealthily, when she was looking the other way.

Remedies (all of dubious efficacy):
• outdoor exercise – vigorous walks, digging in the garden

55

- indoor exercise – rearranging furniture, chasing a shrieking Matty up and down stairs
- improving the mind – playing chess, reading books that were not novels, working through the *Encyclopédie* (she had read to the end of Cartesianism, p. 726, vol. II; 33 quarto volumes and 200-odd pages stretched ahead)
- eating a quantity of sweet foods, quickly

So far that day, two hours of brisk walking (with hills) and a quarter-pound of preserved cherries had brought only moderate relief.

Twenty-seven days before Stephen arrives, thought Sophie, which is only two washdays. Then she corrected herself: Twenty-seven days before he is polite to me and asks Claire to walk down to the river with him.

Experience had not given Sophie cause for optimism in these matters. There were also the proverbs, fables and superstitions that cautioned against anticipating happiness.

A tremendous crash resonated up the stairs.

I wonder if that was the last of the good dinner-set, she thought.

Even when she was a child, as far back as Sophie could recall, in the mysterious way things are decided in families without any decision being taken, it was understood that Sophie could be called on. When the pig was killed, before carnival, heralding the annual flurry of carving, chopping and preserving, and someone was required to watch the fat as it melted down. When parcels had to be carried to the neighbouring farms for the ritual exchanges of black puddings, rillettes and chitterling sausages. When plums were shaken from their trees in summer, dried in the baker's oven, stoned and stuffed with prune paste. When endives had to be tied up, a fortnight before picking, to blanch the leaves. Claire was the eldest: sheets, plums, mismatched dinner-plates, these responsibilities might have devolved on her shoulders. But they were so slender, those shoulders, so white, they formed such an eloquently tender line; they shrugged, and obligations settled elsewhere.

Beyond the orchard wall a thrush was calling from the pear tree.

Sophie thought of a day not unlike this one, all blue air and the scent of hawthorn, her mother moving about the kitchen, preparing dinner because Berthe was late home from market. A chicken had been plucked. Sophie stood at the sink peeling onions. On the other side of the house Claire sang her way up and down scales.

But Signor Bertelli said I had the sweeter voice, argued Sophie, I remember that too. Claire didn't speak to me for a week. Yes, but who did he seize by the waist and try to kiss behind the drawing-room door? Not you, said Sophie to herself.

There came the terrible summer when Matty was born and their mother died. Saint-Pierre blamed himself for one as for the other, and was not to be counted on. The girls wandered red-eyed in and out of darkened rooms. Overnight, the house had lost its sickbed smell. The letter from Claire's godmother, a well-to-do, childless widow, lay unopened for days; finally, Claire broke the seal and wrote back at once to say she would be arriving in Toulouse within the fortnight. At fourteen Sophie inherited a garden, a collection of recipes, a colicky baby.

I didn't ask to be the reliable one, thought Sophie, her stitches growing mutinous, I never wanted to be sensible.

Then, because she had inherited her father's scrupulous weighing of possibilities, she conceded: But perhaps I did. In a way. Perhaps I was glad to be singled out for anything, even peeling onions. A conclusion no sooner formulated than it struck her with the terrible familiarity of a truth she had always known.

Immediately, her mind fled in search of consolation.

When Marguerite had been in the first flush of her enthusiasm for everything to do with gardens, and it was still taken for granted that money could always be found, she had sent away to Paris for the latest books and journals with a bearing on her schemes. These included serious works of botany that Marguerite fully intended to read. But they bristled with sentences that discouraged, even in French: *These fibres, however,*

57

never cut through one another, but make, even when they come together, no knots, but anastomose as it were among one another; and therein is this netlike structure wholly different from an actual net.

Not long after her mother's death, Sophie came across these old volumes stacked away in a bureau in Marguerite's bedroom, most of their pages uncut. Because she was still gripped by grief, anything to do with her mother was dear to Sophie. She opened a book, began to read.

It must be admitted that her reasons for returning to these publications over the months that followed were not always sentimental, nor yet entirely scientific. Certain passages from the great Linnaeus, for instance, could be relied on to produce troubling yet not unwelcome sensations: *On a certain day about noon, seeing the stigma absolutely moist, I removed an anther with slender forceps, and lightly rubbed it over one of the expanded portions of the stigmas. The spike of flowers remained for eight or ten days, a fruit developing in that flower from which I had previously removed the anther* ... Or there was the work of Joseph Gottlieb Kölreuter, Professor of Natural History at the University of Karlsruhe: *The knobbly dark-red stigmas, which hitherto had remained still quite dry, began from their long, fine and pointed papillae to secrete the female moisture, and acquired thereby a glistening, as though they had been painted over with a varnish or saturated with a fine oil.*

With time, Sophie amassed a considerable amount of botanical knowledge. In this, as in the other sciences, her century had made significant advances. The sexuality of plants had been asserted; also the role played by insects in pollination (previously ascribed to the wind). Botanists all over Europe had conducted innumerable experiments into artificial pollination and plant hybridisation to arrive at these conclusions. Naturally, this did not prevent their findings being attacked. Moralists pointed out that to write about promiscuous flowers was to incite depravity. More hurtful were the accusations of fellow scientists, questioning the validity of the experiments. Kölreuter fumed against 'stiff-necked doubters' who would just as soon argue, against the evidence of their own eyes, that bright midday was black midnight. But scepticism is integral to scientific enquiry, where knowledge itself is at stake. Gardeners, concerned above all with practical outcomes, were less interested in what the botanists' experiments proved than in what they yielded.

Sophie noted that Professor Kölreuter, going about other people's gardens in the Westphalian springtime with a fine brush that he used to transfer pollen from one plant to another, effected several successful crosses between species of Chinese pinks. Where a doubled flower was crossed with a single one, it was observed that the resulting crosses generally showed multiple petals; this suggested not only that characteristics could be transferred across species, but also that certain characteristics, such as doubleness, were stronger than others. This germ of genetic thought reappeared in further experiments, where the professor discussed the effect of crossing flowers of different colours. Red crossed with white produced a light purple, white crossed with purple gave a whitish hue streaked with violet, yellow and red crossed with each other resulted in a deep orange-yellow.

Throughout all his experiments Professor Kölreuter recorded a far greater degree of irregularity in the hybrid plants than in those occurring naturally. That was a professorial way of saying there was no way of knowing how things would turn out. On the other hand, Professor Richard Bradley of Cambridge University, detailing his forays into the manual pollination of tulips, ended with this thrilling promise: *a Curious Person may, by this knowledge, produce rare Kinds of Plants as have not yet been heard of.*

Am I curious enough, wondered Sophie, turning over her secrets, What if I'm not equal to irregularity?

But what did she have to lose?

Because otherwise there was only that interminable seam, and the unbearable thought that stalked the edges of her days: Will my life always be like this?

Shame-faced, he confessed to not having the twenty-four *livres* which represented the club's annual subscription. He charged fifty *sous* for a house call – the price of two pounds of beef or five masses. Ricard offered him the money at once, waving away Joseph's reluctance. He was of the opinion, he said, that the membership fees were ridiculously high, 'designed to exclude ordinary Frenchmen'.

The Friends of the Constitution, as the Patriots titled themselves, met once a week in the house of their president, Étienne Luzac, a rotund little man with a skipping step who, since the demise of the Nicolet empire, ran most of Castelnau's textile business. Two footmen – non-liveried, to show Luzac's disapproval of badges of personal servitude – served drinks and refreshments to the two hundred or so men gathered in the vast reception room. Joseph was taken aback by the elevated social tone – wealthy merchants, lawyers, bankers, two magistrates, a marquis who had relinquished his title and now slapped the newcomer on the back and thrust a tricolour in his buttonhole. The uniform of the National Guard was everywhere: straining over Luzac's high stomach, moulded to the elegant limbs of the ex-marquis.

Notable too, given the eminent company, was the deference everywhere paid to Ricard. Having introduced Joseph to a dark, sharp-featured young man, the pork butcher was moving from one knot of people to the other, his bulk making it easy to distinguish him in the room. Shown a sheaf of papers, he nodded approval. Men whose dress and manner marked them as his social superiors seemed to be asking his opinion; Ricard shrugged, said something that made his interlocutors laugh, moved on.

The dark man, a printer called Mercier, lost no time in quizzing Joseph. How long had he known Ricard? Where had he met him? Why did he want to join the Patriots? Did he know anyone else there? How long had he lived in Castelnau? What did he make of Luzac? All the while, the printer's narrow black eyes darted about the room. The only personal information he volunteered was that he had known Ricard 'for years'; staring hard at Joseph as if to impress the fact on him. Soon after, he hailed an acquaintance across the room and went to greet him. Joseph remained where he was, not far from the door, where the footmen were easily intercepted.

Formal proceedings were opened. The formality of the proceedings was another surprise. Joseph placed his hands in Citizen Luzac's plump palms and swore loyalty to the Nation, the Law and the King. He promised to do all in his power to uphold the Constitution decreed by the National Assembly and accepted by His Majesty. Luzac spoke of the importance of bringing together those who sought reason and justice, adjured Joseph to be ceaselessly vigilant on behalf of liberty, equality and the rights of man. There were cheers. Luzac's face glowed with sweat, emotion, the excellent wine served by his footmen.

Minutes of the previous meeting were read aloud by Ricard, who was one of the club's two secretaries. Someone summarised the correspondence received in the past week, most of it from pro-Revolution clubs in other towns. A banker just returned from the capital reported on the meeting he had attended in a disused Jacobin convent in the rue Saint-Honoré; his pedantic account of routine discussion in the Paris headquarters was received with hushed reverence.

Questions were invited from the floor.

Joseph summoned up his courage and asked whether the membership fee could not be reduced to extend a welcome to those who loved reason and justice on limited means. Luzac tugged on his yellow epaulettes and retorted that the question had already been debated and defeated in a previous meeting. 'Our expenses are considerable, Citizen, how considerable you will come to appreciate. Maintaining links with our brothers

61

all over the country is necessary but costly. And we subscribe to no fewer than sixteen newspapers from Paris alone.'

'Why?' asked Joseph and saw Ricard smile behind his hand.

It was the former marquis who answered, while Luzac, frowning, drummed his fingers on his thighs. 'Information, dear brother, information. A citizen's prime duty is to keep himself informed. The Paris broadsheets keep us up to date with events in the capital, notably the deliberations of the Assembly. As for the reactionary press, it's vital in alerting us to anti-revolutionary strategies. An invaluable window onto the mind of friend Caussade, don't you see?'

He saw, but persisted. If the annual subscription could not be lowered, why not make it payable monthly? Discussion, demurs. Finally, a not-unanimous vote settled on quarterly payments.

Joseph looked to Ricard for recognition but the pork butcher was on his feet with a proposal of his own: volunteers were required to read aloud and explain selected newspapers and pamphlets to the town's illiterate workers, 'bringing the Revolution to the people', as Ricard put it. This time, approval was general. Ricard smiled, sat down.

A man standing not far from Joseph spoke up. He proposed that women should be eligible for membership. Female citizens had played a significant role in the Revolution; he need not remind his brothers of the market-women who had marched on Versailles the previous October. Women had charge of children, were instrumental in the inculcation of patriotic ideals in these citizens of the future. And then, there was already news from Paris of clubs that admitted women, like the Fraternal Society for Patriots of Both Sexes – from a practical point of view, didn't the Friends of the Constitution risk losing ground to rival organisations if it continued to disallow female membership?

Joseph was nodding – the arguments seemed common-sensical, irrefutable – while noting dispassionately that he felt pleasantly tipsy.

Ricard's voice cut across the hubbub. 'If the Société Fraternelle wishes to admit women, that is entirely its affair.

But a club is one thing and a collection of skirts is quite another. By all means let them rustle elsewhere.'

Amid laughter, the proposal was defeated by an overwhelming majority.

With the close of formal business, the footmen returned to the room. More wine. Singing. More wine.

Ricard was over there, signalling to him.

As they were leaving, the former marquis leapt up onto a table to lead the chorus:

'Ça ira!
Tous les aristocrates, on les pendra!'

The stars canter across the velvet-black heavens. He can hear the music of the spheres.

He sings along to it: '*Ça ira! Ça ira! Ça ira!'*

Ricard steadies him. 'Easy now, easy.'

A low mist has risen over the river, is starting to slip over the parapet and into the street. They sit at the top of the flight of steps. Their feet and shins are invisible, shrouded in mist. He laughs and points this out to Ricard. The pork butcher nods, goes on filling his pipe.

After a while, things settle down.

Joseph yawns enormously.

'You're in for an aching head tomorrow, doctor. You're fortunate Luzac shows such impeccable taste in wine, or the prognosis would be worse.'

It's spoken lightly, but Joseph fancies he detects disapproval. He notices that his companion seems entirely sober. Although with that mass, Ricard could drink more than most without appearing any the worse for it. Are there any thin butchers, he wonders? Recalling close-grained flesh, dense bones.

'I'm pleased you found the Club so congenial. You know, it might prove useful to you, too – when our bourgeois friends find themselves indisposed, or their wives take it into their heads to find fault with their physicians, they might think to send for you.'

'They might.' He rather doubts it.

63

'I made a point of singing your professional praises whenever I could . . .'

'That was extremely good of you,' he says, touched.

'. . . and so, on other occasions, it would be advisable to keep a clear head.' The bowl of the pipe glowing into life. 'A physician with a taste for drink cannot be said to inspire confidence.'

He opens his mouth to protest. But Ricard forestalls him, getting up, holding out a hand to help him to his feet: 'It's late. You need sleep. And I have to be up at five.'

At the bridge, the pork butcher shakes his hand, then holds it in both his own. 'Shrewd of you to propose monthly payments. Well played, my friend.'

He loiters in the shadows until the small orange light appears on the far bank. Then he raises a hand that he knows Ricard can't see.

June brings roses.

Roses that show carmine in the bud and open to reveal petals of the palest shell pink.

Roses in every shade of white: ivory, cream, parchment, chalk, snow, milk, pearl, bone.

Roses with nodding, globular flowers, large as teacups.

Purple roses streaked with raspberry and slaty lilac.

Purple roses that fade to grey-violet.

The Alba Rose, the original white rose, is a very clear, pure white. It may be single (that is, five-petalled), semi-double or double. All three forms are found in Sophie's garden. They thrive in sun or shade, give a splendid display when trained up walls and rarely fall prey to mildew. Their scent is intoxicating, especially in the evening or after rain.

The Apothecary's Rose has light-red petals and bright yellow anthers. In Provins, to the south-east of Paris, an entire industry – oils, essences, conserves, powders, syrups – flourishes around this rose. Renowned for the intensity of its fragrance, it is celebrated in folklore, medicine, history, venerated for its power to heal, soothe, seduce.

There are roses that open flat and wide, their petals curving back.

There are incurved roses, their centres quartered like a crown.

Celsiana is a particularly graceful rose, thinks Sophie, its branches arching under the weight of silky, clustered, warm-pink blooms. Its buds are rosy-red, so the contrast with the open flowers is very telling.

Conditorium has loose, tousled, wonderfully fragrant

magenta flowers, heightened with purple as the season wears on. These are the flowers Sophie keeps beside her bed, the scent she escapes on in the long summer evenings, lying on her bed with the shutters half-closed.

A rose with deep-pink, papery petals, veined all over with purple and lilac.

Roses striped red and white.

Small, dark-pink roses.

The hundred-petalled Provence or Cabbage Rose has pendulous branches laden with nodding flowers. Its leaves are large, rough, deeply serrated.

There are crumpled roses.

Blush-pink roses blotched with red.

Robert le Diable can be a liability in the garden. It's decidedly lax, requiring propping up with other bushes, and very thorny. But it flowers late, providing colour at the end of the season, and its violet petals are splashed with cerise and scarlet. Later, they fade to a soft dove-grey. Sophie has a terrible weakness for it.

The Sulphur Rose is the only yellow rose known to European gardeners and therefore greatly prized. Sophie, perversely, doesn't think much of it. Its large, double, butter-yellow flowers may be beautiful but it is not a hardy plant, succumbing easily to frost or disease.

There are Summer and Autumn Damask Roses, strong, bushy growers, with pale-green downy leaves and highly scented flowers. Sophie looks at the Damasks and sees court-yards, nightingales, cool water running over sky-blue tiles. Legend relates that when Saladin recovered Jerusalem from the Crusaders he sent for five hundred camel-loads of Damascus roses to purify the Mosque of Omar, which had served the Infidel as a church.

There are roses in clusters, single roses at the end of arching canes.

Roses with short mossy stalks.

Pompom roses.

Irreproachable white roses folded around a minute green eye.

The thick, red-purple petals of Tuscany, a very old rose, suggest the rich glow of velvet; in fact it is also known as the Velvet Rose. A deeper purple spreads over the flowers as they age. It suckers freely, so has to be cut back hard in the summer.

There are lilac roses, pink-speckled.

Roses that smell like cinnamon. Like myrrh, lemon, balsam, musk.

Rose-scented roses.

So many roses. You'd think they would satisfy anyone.

But Sophie, tense as a cat, prowls her rose-crowded garden and sees only what isn't there:

Dark-red roses.

Impossible roses.

In eighteenth-century Europe, crimson roses do not exist. There are red-purple roses, of course, and rosy-reds, and a sumptuous deep pink overclouded with plum and mulberry.

None of which will do.

Watered, fed, cosseted, protected from frost, nurtured on sunlight, desire has taken root in Sophie and is putting out fat buds.

I will not think of him, thinks Sophie, eating rose petals, I will not think of him sitting there with one leg stretched out, watching Claire over the top of his book, I will not think of his clean smell or that curved scar on his forearm, I will concentrate on roses.

'Stay!'

He stayed, drooling heavily, his eyes fixed on Mathilde. When she dropped her hand, he dashed forward with a clitter of claws to the bowl she had placed on the ground.

'Dinner's the only time he does what he's told. It's more interesting when he acts independently.'

'Few would agree with you there. But such is the fate of all original minds.' Stephen, at a prudent distance, was patting his pocket for his pipe when he remembered that he had given it up as a bad cause and switched to cigars. 'He reminds me of one of those idols, the squat and terrible kind. Men prostrate themselves before him with ghastly vows.'

Fondly watching the idol, Mathilde chose to ignore this.

'What do you feed him? The pulsating hearts of his victims? Their still-warm livers?'

'Oxtail today, and a little extra fat, mixed in with finely chopped carrot –'

'Somehow I don't associate Brutus with vegetables.'

'Carrots prevent rheumatism, as everyone knows.'

Brutus, licking his bowl clean, was pushing it around the courtyard. Tin grated unpleasantly on stone. Having reached Stephen's feet and made sure his bowl really was empty, he looked up, smacking floppy black lips.

Stephen removed himself smartly to the kitchen steps. 'You should offer Brutus's services to the Assembly. One glimpse of him dining should be sufficient to bring the most hardened anti-revolutionary to his senses. Do you realise he has flecks of green on his tongue? Though why I'm alerting you to the presence of what might prove to be a fatal ailment I can't imagine.'

'Silly.' She giggled. 'I mix parsley in with his food, to keep his breath sweet. And it makes him smell nice all over. Haven't you noticed how wonderful he smells?'

'No.'

'Except when he's found something dead and rolled in it. But you can't count that.'

'Of course not.'

'Then he smells rather like Hubert.'

They snickered, like conspirators.

'Rinaldi told me what to feed him. And he was right – Brutus is never ill.'

'Rinaldi?'

'The pedlar. We told you about him, last summer.'

'Ah – the rose man, who's travelled in the East. Does he know about dogs, too?'

'About all sorts of animals. I think he's lived with gypsies – might be part gypsy himself. He gave me Brutus.'

'I've often wondered whose idea that was.'

'He was just a puppy. Rinaldi heard him whimpering in the woods. We enquired in the villages and put up notices in Castelnau but no one came forward to claim him.'

'Extraordinary.'

She leant against Stephen's knees and smiled at him. 'Are you still smitten with Claire? I suppose you must be, or you wouldn't have come.'

He laughed, and tweaked her hair.

The truth was, he had almost stayed in Paris. He had a huge, north-facing atelier overlooking the Seine where all sorts of people turned up, and said agreeable things about his work, and invited him to supper or concerts or the theatre. There was a girl at a café in the Palais Royal, the happy possessor of dimples, blue eyes and a friendly disposition. The chestnut trees burst into blossom in the gardens and along the boulevards. Great things were being decided in the Assembly; boys sold broadsheets on every corner, shouting themselves hoarse. He stayed up all night, drinking and talking and arguing; walking home one chilly May morning, he saw the sun rise over Notre Dame. He discovered an excellent tailor and acquired a new jacket in a shade that exactly matched his eyes. On the obligatory pilgrimage to Ermenonville, twenty-five miles outside Paris, everyone in his party had been moved to tears at the sight of Rousseau's grave. All his friends insisted he spend the summer on their estates. He was even offered a quarter-share in a particularly fetching concert-singer. He turned it down, of course; love should be freely exchanged, not bought and sold. But still – it was all part of the bright adventure into which his life had fallen.

A dozen times he had intended to write, pleading an urgent commission, a sudden but lingering indisposition.

But then he woke one rain-washed afternoon, and vowed to live differently, without distraction, devoting himself to his work. He remembered the calm of Montsignac, the river running beyond the garden, the rooms filled with light. He thought of sketching in the woods, picnics in the meadows, pictured the sisters laughing together and the smiles they would have for him.

And when he saw Claire again, he had felt that all the others – the girls in the cafés, the models who frequented his studio, the witty, elegant women who teased him in drawing-rooms – had been only so many pleasant ways of passing time.

Just as there are weeks when streaks and patches and even whole stretches of blue sky tempt you out of doors without a coat, so that the wind, snaking around a corner, slides down your collar and you realise that the sun, which was shining so steadily a minute ago, has been swallowed whole by clouds; and then, without warning, summer arrives, and you know the difference.

Brutus, blissful and sated, rolled over at Mathilde's feet, exposing his hideously mottled stomach. 'Frog belly,' she crooned, with infinite tenderness, 'dog spawn.'

*L*unch was garlic and herb soup, beef kidneys with fried onions, duck fricassee, a dish of marinated artichokes, green peas, a small roast sirloin basted with melted marrow and garnished with root vegetables, and a salad of chicory and ox-tongue. Dessert – lemon tart, biscuits, cherries, strawberries and plum jam – waited on the sideboard.

'Look at the carrots,' said Mathilde, 'and the turnips!' They had been carved into flowers, stars, something that could have been a ship or a hat.

Jacques said, 'Berthe thought they would appeal to a foreigner of artistic temperament.'

'They're delightful! You must convey my sincere appreciation to Berthe.'

'When I was young,' remarked Saint-Pierre, 'there was a fashion for chicken dressed to resemble bat. The thing was to truss the bird with the wings drawn up over the belly and the legs tucked beneath. Then you had to beat it and break the large bones. It was served grilled, with a herb sauce.'

'Is it true that potatoes are everyday fare in the New World?' Claire wrinkled her nose. 'I can't see them taking hold in France, for all they tell us the flavour compares with truffles and chestnuts.'

'But they're delicious, prepared correctly with butter and salt! And nutritious, they say. Isn't that so, Morel?'

'If Citizen Parmentier is to be believed, yes.' Seated on Sophie's right, it was difficult for Joseph not to be distracted by the neckline of her dress. 'At any rate, he defends the potato as animal fodder. And as a cheap and filling crop for the poor.'

'Well, I suppose they'll eat anything.'

'Not as readily as you might imagine. In Burgundy a rumour got around that potatoes cause leprosy, so no one will plant them. When superstition stirs the pot, hunger isn't always a good sauce.'

'When I grow up, I intend to eat nothing but vegetables.'

'*If I am given milk, eggs, salad, cheese, brown bread, and ordinary wine I am sufficiently entertained,*' quoted Stephen. 'So in matters of diet you're an orthodox Rousseauist, Matty?'

'It's got nothing to do with him and that nauseating Émile. It's cruel to eat animals – you'd think anyone could see that. But Sophie refuses to listen. She often thwarts the free expression of my nature.'

'Do you agree with Rousseau that men who eat meat are more inclined to violence than those who shun it?' Sophie's hair was done differently, ringlets falling softly about her face. His own hair had been cut short and combed forward in the new revolutionary style. Had she noticed?

'Well, as to scientific proof . . . But as you'll recall, he cites the barbarism of the roast beef-mad English in support of his claim – a cogent enough argument, don't you think?'

With their laughter, the constriction loosened in Joseph's chest. What did it matter if his best coat was worn at the cuffs? He adjusted his spectacles, grew bold. 'Perhaps Rousseau's preference for a meatless diet is an unconscious metaphor for his belief that the inequality of our society enables the rich to cannibalise the poor.'

In the silence, Sophie tilted her head and looked at Joseph. Really looked at him, as if seeing him for the first time, he thought, and felt his face grow hot. She looked away.

'Fascinating subject, the connection between social change and fashions in food.' Saint-Pierre dabbed at his mouth with a napkin. 'Two or three hundred years ago in this country, Oriental spices – ginger, malaguetta pepper, galingale and so on – were used every day in aristocratic kitchens. Then, in the last century, our cooks began to criticise the spicy dishes that were still being served in the rest of Europe. Our native herbs became all the rage. Now we eat food seasoned with chervil, thyme, tarragon, chives, basil – herbs as accessible to a peasant as to his master. One could argue that when the distinction between rich and poor kitchens diminished, a revolution was inevitable.'

'My father is writing a treatise on the history of French cooking,' explained Sophie. One of her eyes, the left one, contained a speck of gold in its dark-brown iris. There was a small vertical crease in the middle of her forehead. These imperfections struck Joseph as a superior kind of perfection. He emptied his glass again.

'Lately, I've been thinking about pies. Why did they fall out of favour? The Middle Ages covered everything with pastry. At banquets, large joints of meat were always served in a pastry crust, and on a poor man's table everything ended up in pies – dormice, badgers.'

'We count as the poor too, you know,' said Mathilde to Joseph. 'More than ever now, with the courts declared in indefinite recess and the magistrates obliged to live off their own fortunes. Since Father doesn't have one, we'll soon be eating nothing but potatoes. I shan't complain. I shall show cheerful fortitude in the face of adversity.'

'I hope we might yet be spared that.' But Saint-Pierre's expression was sombre.

'The old system will be replaced by elected judges and tribunals,' said Joseph. 'It'll be fairer overall. Justice shouldn't be venal –' Adding hastily, 'Naturally, I don't mean –'

Saint-Pierre waved a dismissive hand. 'You're quite right. The courts have been crying out for reform for the past century.'

'The weather's never been the same since those people started doing things with kites in thunderstorms.' Jacques stalked from the room accompanied by an ominous clatter of plates.

'He's becoming impossible,' said Claire to Sophie. 'You don't notice because you've grown used to it.'

'Will you be standing for election, sir?'

Joseph noticed that 'sir'. But what could you expect of a foreigner? And he himself had not been able to address

Saint-Pierre as Citizen, and so hadn't called him anything at all. There were these little hesitations these days, small snags around which conversation unravelled.

'I have no choice in the matter. They say we'll be able to recoup the loss of our salaries by deducting them from our taxes, but ...' Saint-Pierre shrugged. 'In the meantime I wouldn't want to put Mathilde's fortitude to the test.'

There was a bowl of roses on the table. Stephen drew one of them out, flicking the arrangement askew, scattering petals. 'Astonishing, the colours in a single flower. Look – dark pink suffused with claret and purple. And the centre a shade paler. What is it called, Sophie?'

'*Rosa burgundica.* But we call it Saint Francis's Rose.'

'Lucky Saint Francis. How does one set about being immortalised in a rose, do you know? Does it require being kind to animals? Even Brutus?'

'Being kind to rose growers would be more practical.'

'So it's your favour I have to win, Sophie. What would you ask of me?'

'Oh,' she said lightly, 'the usual things. Gold spun from straw, a leaf from the tree that grows on the summit of a glass mountain, a bridge to the moon. Only the impossible.'

'I stand a chance, in that case. Isn't that the proper business of artists and revolutionaries, the pursuit of the impossible?' And Stephen reached across the table to hand her the rose, with a little flourish.

Sophie turned the flower in her fingers, tucking it at last into the lace on her breast. She kept her head down. Her delight was plain to see.

If only I could throttle him, thought Joseph. I'd like to watch him turn dark pink, suffused – suffused! – with claret. And purple.

Why was it that even the most excellent women ...?

'Really, Sophie,' said Claire, 'that shade of pink clashes horribly with your dress.'

He was to leave for Bordeaux early the following day. So far they had talked a great deal about Art – that is, he had talked, she had listened – and gazed into each other's eyes. They had read aloud to each other from *Paul et Virginie*, a novel they both adored. Once, their hands had brushed. There had to be ... clarification, thought Stephen. He believed in the scrutiny and voicing of sentiments – how else was sincerity to be achieved? That was why he had asked Claire to walk with him in the garden before dinner. As usual she had yielded; as usual his nerve failed him. He talked about Art. He assured her he would devote all his time to her portrait as soon as he returned to Paris.

'But after Bordeaux there's your walking tour of Switzerland. It'll be months before it's ready.'

'It won't take long, with all the sketches. Although they scarcely do you justice.' There were clusters of ruffled white roses, ghostly in the half-light, overhanging the path. Reaching out at the same moment, their hands brushed. She drew hers away at once.

'We'll miss you.'

He had to bend his head to hear. On the side of her neck was a small birthmark that he longed to kiss. 'I'll think of you every day,' he promised.

She blew on the roses. Petals drifted around them. 'So you say. But you'll be distracted by milkmaids with blue eyes and golden curls.' There were many such references – teasing, testing – to the other women who came his way.

'I hope so.' His ready acquiescence in the adventures she

75

devised for him was essential to the charge between them. 'I believe cowsheds are perfect for dalliances.'

She laughed, but moved away when he tried to see her face. 'Meanwhile,' she said, 'I'll be in Blois. Where there'll be several small children, innumerable dogs, prayers before breakfast and a great deal of time devoted to exclaiming over what the world is coming to.' And by then she could look at him.

He thought, This is the moment it should end. Now, while everything is still possible.

Instead, he said, 'I know I have no right to ask . . .'

But of course she wanted him to.

*S*tephen's writing, widely spaced and innovatively punctuated, looped over two sheets of paper. 'He's only written on one side.' Mathilde had never seen such extravagance. 'I suppose it signifies an artistic disregard for wordly concerns.'

'It signifies that he's rich,' said Sophie.

He informed them that the inns in Switzerland were exceedingly clean, the food exceedingly bad. He had difficulty understanding what people said to him. The mountains were all he had dared hope for: *Daily, I wake humbled to Nature at her most sublime – a stern and splendid mistress.* He had swum in lakes laid out like blue jewels in narrow valleys, their waters *icy but utterly exhilarating. I feel my very soul purified, like a little child set down in a world made new.*

'I'll read that last bit out to Jacques,' said Mathilde. 'He's still grumbling about the quantities of hot water Stephen had him fetch. He says it's unnatural for anyone to bathe three times a week even if they come from a place where the savages walk around on their heads.'

'I think he has his savages muddled.'

'Do you suppose we'll ever travel? Rinaldi says a long sea voyage is written in my palm. I hope he's right: I long to see the ocean. And have my arm tattooed like Rinaldi, to prove I've been to the Pacific. I can't say I'm tempted by Switzerland – all those people feeling sublime in lakes.'

'Perhaps we'll go to Paris one day. If only it didn't take seven days in a coach drawn by four horses – think of the expense. And Father would grow gloomy from the moment it was suggested and predict nothing but bad weather and moral turpitude.'

'What about the victory of the republican virtues?' Mathilde was a great reader of newspapers. Their farrago of local and foreign news, essays, songs (music and words), puzzles, riddles, reviews, scandals, innuendo and debate was highly suited to her eclectic tastes.

'True. And to remind us of it, Stephen has sent you a present.'

'*The Death of Tyranny*,' read Mathilde. She examined the drawing: Brutus in chalks, crowned with a laurel wreath, lifting a hind-leg over a corpse whose features bore an uncanny resemblance to their brother-in-law.

'It's not a very good likeness of Brutus, is it?'

'Perhaps not quite stern and splendid enough.'

'Do you think Stephen's taken against Hubert because he's Hubert, or because he's married to Claire?'

Sophie, who had wondered the same thing, didn't answer. But after a brief debate with herself, she slid another sheet of paper across the table. 'He sent this, too.'

'*Sophie, from Memory* – oh Sophie, it's exactly you.'

'He's made my nose smaller and my eyes larger.' But Sophie was biting her lips to keep from smiling.

'He could have taken a bit more trouble with Brutus. His ears are altogether a different shape. But yours is good enough to have framed.'

'Of course.' Sophie reclaimed the drawing and rolled it up. 'Plain women are obliged to keep a single flattering likeness on prominent display.'

'You won't throw it away?'

She shook her head. 'But Matty – there's no need for . . . for Father to see it.'

'Don't worry,' her sister said kindly, 'I shan't say anything to Claire.'

*T*he woman stopped him in a street in Lacapelle, laying her hand on his sleeve. 'Joseph.' Her angular face framed in frizzy brown hair was not unattractive. Nor did he have the least idea who she might be.

Embarrassment made her laugh. 'You don't recognise me,' she giggled, covering her lips with bony, short-nailed fingers.

But with that gesture of putting her hand to her mouth, the years dissolved. 'Lisette Mounier.'

They stood smiling at each other while people swerving past them sighed pointedly or swore. He stepped back into a convenient doorway, drawing her with him.

'Lisette Ricard, now.' When he stared: 'Paul hasn't said anything, I see. I told him I knew you long ago, before you went away to study and become a doctor.'

'I knew he was married, of course.' Joseph fiddled with his spectacles. There was a gap in her mouth, on the left side, where one of her eyeteeth was missing. She saw him noticing it and her hand flew up to her lips. He said hurriedly, 'You look well.'

It was true: she was very thin, skin stretched tight over her bones, but clean, respectably dressed. There were small gold rings in her ears, a pretty brooch fastening her shawl. Ricard would have been an excellent catch for a girl like that. Her father was a tiler, alcoholic, filthy, quick with his fists if a woman or child got under his feet. Joseph had been afraid of him, crossing the street or slinking into an alley if he saw Mounier headed his way.

He asked after her family.

'Mother lives with my sister – you remember Marie? – just

outside town. Marie's husband owns a field, they're doing well. The boys ...' She shrugged. 'We don't keep in touch. Guillaume's in the navy, I think.'

'And your father?'

'He died just after you left. Fell off a roof. He must have been drunker than usual.'

'I'm sorry to hear that.'

'I hated him,' she said with unexpected vehemence.

That way she'd had of sparking up without warning: she had kept that, too.

'How long have you been married?'

'Five years. We have two daughters. Our son died.'

She must have been barely sixteen when she married, was still not much more than a girl. Yet she had that taut, slightly wizened look that made her appear older. He saw it everywhere in these streets: the unmistakable stamp of hunger, generations-deep.

'I suppose you were too busy with your books to find a wife?'

'Something like that.' He remembered, with great clarity, kissing her in the dank room where the Mouniers lived, while small children tumbled around them and she tried to stir the soup. He must have been seven? eight?

'And now?'

'Now there's not an abundance of feminine interest in a physician with no money and few prospects.'

'Oh, I don't know,' she said with utter seriousness, 'women can be very foolish.' Then she grew agitated and fussed with her shawl. 'I must go. We have a girl to help in the shop and the house, and she's supposed to keep an eye on the children, but –' with a toss of her head – 'you know what these girls are like. I have to do most of my shopping myself, for fear of what she'll bring home. The other day it was horse-dung ground up and sold as coffee – can you imagine?'

Her pride was self-evident: to have a girl to complain about!

He said, 'You've done well, Lisette. Paul is an exceptional man.'

Her light-brown eyes were exactly the same shade as her hair. They searched his face as if trying to decipher a secret inscribed there. Her hand lay lightly in his, like a small cold animal.

80

The concièrge handed Stephen his mail with a smile in which insinuation and unctuousness struggled for the upper hand. 'So much correspondence, Monsieur! Monsieur has worked tirelessly on his holiday.'

In his studio he lay on the divan with his boots still on and dropped off to sleep, surrounded by letters from Claire.

He had asked her to write and she had done so, almost every day. Anne, her sister-in-law, remained poorly after the birth of her fourth daughter, she hoped he was enjoying Switzerland, did his cousins resemble him, she was reading a novel set in Persia, there had been a violent storm, how many milkmaids had he met? In short, they were charming, empty little notes. What she wanted to say to him could only be gauged from their quantity. And the violet ink she had chosen.

His friend Chalier barged into the room, demanding to be told everything Stephen had 'got up to', then launching, without pause, into a description of the Festival of Federation which had marked the first anniversary of the fall of the Bastille. Chalier, as a National Guardsman, had sworn an oath of loyalty to the Nation, the Law and the King in a ceremony orchestrated by Lafayette.

'Such crowds, Fletcher! One hundred and fifty thousand citizens of all classes and countless women. I saw a duchess being trundled along in a mahogany wheelbarrow by her daughters, each of them prettier than the last, and all garlanded with roses. Lafayette rode his white charger. We raised our right arms, like this –' checking his pose in the mirror – 'and when the general had read out the oath, we all cried, *Je le jure*. Like

81

that, all together. *Je le jure*. Our company was so close to the royal pavilion I could have plucked the ostrich plumes from the Queen's hat.' Chalier shifted a stack of books, peered behind a dinted copper pot containing a fig tree, opened and shut cupboards. 'Don't you have any wine? Where are your manners?'

'Did it rain all day, like the newspapers said?'

'Poured down. An aristocratic plot, obviously. But nothing could dampen our spirits. We danced under lanterns on the site of the Bastille until dawn. I was drunk for a week, at least.' Chalier spoke absent-mindedly. He had come across some notes and was reading them with interest: *Mlle Thouars, rue du Petit-Pont, 23 bis – full figure, tall, models draperies; Mlle Corentin, passage du Maure, 6 – v. pretty girl, remarkably proportioned.*

'I made a drawing of the scene from the newspaper reports.' Stephen, scrabbling beneath the divan, emerged triumphant. He handed over the bottle, opened a portfolio, began hunting through its contents. 'There was nothing to do in Switzerland at night besides draw and drink cherry brandy. I made sketches from memory of just about everyone I know. The girls were so ugly that life drawing was out of the question. And there are only so many things you can do with mountains. Here – what do you think?'

Chalier stroked his moustache. 'I don't know about art but I know what I saw. The clouds didn't part like that above Lafayette's head.'

'That's artistic licence, you dolt. The shaft of sunlight symbolises the triumph of liberty as it pierces the dark clouds of oppression with its rays. The very elements, you see, conspire with the people of France against tyranny.'

'Well, but it didn't actually let up, you know. I was soaked through.' Rifling through the drawings, Chalier paused . 'Were you lying about the girls?'

That way Claire had of holding her head slightly on one side; it had translated as stiffness. Stephen frowned and looked around for a stick of chalk. Various surfaces yielded a plaster bust, siccative, a candlestick, a notebook, a bottle of paraffin, another of linseed oil, an assortment of rags, varnish, a clean palette cup, several dirty ones, a knife, soft soap for washing brushes, a shrivelled orange that had grown an exquisite blue-green mould – he examined it admiringly – a chipped saucer, an Oriental vase, a handful of coins and two lumps of coal. 'Naturally, a few adjustments are called for before I can begin painting.'

'I see, I see – your provincial marquise. Well, she's beautiful, Fletcher, I grant you that, unless it's more artistic licence. But is she virtuous?'

'Of course,' he said.

'A pity. There's only one sure way to deal with infatuation.' Chalier felt he had a tutelary duty in these matters. Wasn't Stephen six months younger, and an American? He studied his friend's head, bent over the table. 'Fletcher,' he said sternly, 'you do see it's infatuation, don't you?'

'The thing is . . .' Stephen sat very still for a moment. 'When I see her, I'm utterly certain of my feelings, and if she wasn't married everything would be straightforward. But she has a husband and a son, and when I'm away from her . . .' He stared into his glass, and a splinter of self-knowledge inserted itself into the silence. 'Perhaps I like her best when I'm with her,' he said, at last, 'and other girls best when I'm with them. Whatever's easiest, do you see?'

'Perfectly.' Chalier spun in front of the mirror, admiring his admirable figure. 'I haven't been idle, you know, I've been to the Opéra every night this week and have discovered a little dancer whose acquaintance you must make. I already have – and she expects us both to supper tonight. This wine is filthy, Fletcher, even for a foreigner. Is there nothing else to drink?'

'I'm afraid not.'

'Hurry up, then – we'll have champagne sent to our box and catch the last act.'

As he put on his jacket, Stephen's eye returned to his sketch of Lafayette taking the oath. 'I've half a mind to work this up into a painting and present it to the general. It could lead to commissions, couldn't it?'

'Why don't you present him with an intimate sketch of your

marquise instead? I know which I'd prefer.'

The sound of their boots woke the concièrge in her lodge. She lay in bed with the covers pulled up to her chin despite the mildness of the air and listened to their racket on the stairs tearing up the soft September night.

They had been born on a dark November day, a day of mists and low red sun, and when Sophie saw them they were seventeen hours old, asleep in the high feather bed beside their mother, who had insisted on mulled wine to celebrate their birth. Warm milk sweetened with sugar was the usual thing for a daughter, or even two, but the pretty girl lounging against the bolster fluffed up her chestnut curls and informed Sophie that she wasn't having any of that, no, she told Henri when the first pains came that he was to have wine waiting for her and no mistake, she had never liked milk, everyone knew it gave you diseases.

Her mother-in-law – toothless, rheumatic, irredeemably stooped at fifty-three – brought wine for the two young women without a word. In any case, what she thought was plain. She sat as far from the bed as possible, which wasn't very far, and cracked her knuckles in disapproval.

Sophie, handing over a silver coin for each of the babies, admired the thickness of their golden-brown lashes, put out a tentative finger to stroke their wrinkled faces, agreed that they were perfect, congratulated their mother on her feat.

'The midwife said they were the first twins she'd delivered.' Under the sheet, Jeanne was fingering the paper twisted around the coins, trying to guess their value before placing them on the pillow. 'They run in my family, of course: I have twin uncles and my father's mother was a twin.'

Her father kept an inn in a village on the other side of Castelnau. There had been no shortage of heads shaken over Henri, the best-looking boy in Montsignac, electing to marry an outsider.

'I knew it!' said her mother-in-law, from her stool by the fire. 'There's never been anything like that in our family.'

'Have you decided on their names?'

'Antoinette and Victorine.'

There was a snort from the fireside.

'Why shouldn't I name them after my parents? Henri was in complete agreement, after all they've done so much to help us. If it wasn't for them –' Jeanne raised her voice – 'we wouldn't have the means to feed useless mouths.'

'Useless, am I? When she spends hours gossiping at the stream and I break my back in that so-called field she likes to make such a fuss about, fit for nothing but rocks and weeds, useless you might call it, and see if everyone doesn't agree, I'd have been ashamed to have such a thing in my dowry.'

'Though who'll christen the little angels I can't imagine.' Jeanne glanced sideways at her visitor and the tip of her tongue flickered between her lips. 'Have you heard? About Father Valcour? Isn't it shocking? It would never have happened in my village.'

At his last mass Father Valcour had informed his open-mouthed parishioners that the Church was nothing but a tool for propping up privilege and spreading ignorance, and that as far as he was concerned he was getting out and intended at the first opportunity to marry the widow who had cleaned his cottage and cooked his meals for the past forty years.

'At their age, too! It's disgusting. They're both over sixty.' Jeanne leant closer to Sophie. 'Of course everyone's suspected it for years.'

'I think it was brave of Father Valcour,' said Sophie, in whom eighteen centuries of dogma had been distilled down to two articles of faith: severity towards monks and bishops, held to be dissolute and worse; respect for hard-working parish priests, getting on with life on earth. 'It's touching, don't you think, that they loved each other secretly all that time?'

About to sniff, Jeanne changed her mind and twirled one of her ringlets around her forefinger instead. 'Of course a young lady like you can't possibly imagine ... but those of us with husbands know that men are after only one thing.' She glanced at the fireplace and whispered, 'You wouldn't believe it, but even in my eighth month ... Naturally I wouldn't let him, but it just goes to show, doesn't it?' She settled back against the bolster and smiled. Henri was mad for her, something poor beaky-nosed, bosomless Mademoiselle de Saint-Pierre couldn't be expected to understand.

'You must be exhausted,' said Sophie, 'after all you've been through.'

'Exhausted!' hissed the old woman. 'I had eleven children, and not two at a time either like an animal, and I was always back in the fields an hour after giving birth.'

'Yes, but I'm not an ugly scarecrow with a good-for-nothing husband looking to charity to feed the brats I keep spawning year after year.' In a different voice, Jeanne said, 'Please, don't go yet, I'd like to know what you think about the land.'

'I'm no judge of these things, but I'm sure your parents meant very well when they bought you and Henri that field.'

A cackle from the fireside.

'No, no.' Signalling for Sophie to bend closer. 'The land that used to belong to the priests. When will we be getting our share of it?'

'I don't think it works like that.'

'Oh?' Jeanne frowned up at her. 'But everyone's saying that the government is taking the land from the Church to distribute to people like us. That's the Revolution, isn't it?'

'Property and land confiscated from the Church are being sold off to the highest bidders.'

'But that's not fair.'

Sophie shrugged.

The moment they were alone, Jeanne turned to the old woman: 'I don't believe a word of it. The Saint-Pierres are probably out to get their hands on everything themselves. You can't trust aristocrats, everyone knows that. And just look at these, will you?' She had unwrapped the coins, and now tested them one by one between her teeth. 'That's all she gave us, the stingy cow – I wouldn't be surprised if they turned out to be worthless.'

Her mother-in-law spat into the fire.

As wind and rain broke autumn up into winter, he made a resolution: he would not forget he was a man of science. Anniversaries unsettled him, calling him to account. The end of the year threatened with its reckonings, and it would be eighteen months since he had returned to Castelnau.

Now only two seasons stood between him and his quarter-century. He had to do something before youth trickled away altogether. You thought you'd seized life in your hand but one day you folded back your fingers to discover they'd been clenched over emptiness.

In Montpellier he'd known steadiness of purpose. His days were oriented towards the future, which was a set of attainable goals: knowledge absorbed, skills acquired, examinations passed. Then suddenly it was over and the present crushed in on him, a series of demands, emergencies, symptoms that required his attention, all his attention, immediately, now.

To ease the suffering ... But why had that been reduced to setting a broken arm or treating old men for gout? When he was a student he had dreamt of finding a cure for smallpox or identifying the origins of malaria. One day he would return to the faculty to lecture to rows of upturned, admiring faces. In their text books, an ailment would bear his name: Morel's Syndrome, *so-called because the brilliant young physician Joseph Morel isolated the cause of this hitherto incurable and fatal affliction. Morel went on to develop the treatment which has brought the disease under control and saved untold thousands of lives.*

It made him smile, the nonsense he'd spouted back then with his friends.

He scoured his plate clean with a piece of bread, shoved the empty dishes away. He had to recover that sense of the future – intact, uncreased, waiting to be folded into the shape of his choosing.

So naturally, he turned to the past. He would become a student again, observing, recording, analysing, hypothesising.

Now, unless he was called out on a case or due at a meeting, he stayed home after dinner. His room was cold. Firewood was dear and anyway he had never known adequate heating. With his overcoat slung around his shoulders, he sat at the table writing, writing, as the year stumbled to its close and rain slid like silk down his window.

He was preoccupied with bad smells.

From earliest times, an influential school of medical thought had held that disease was the product of disorder between man and his environment. Hippocrates himself had urged physicians to study the milieu in which diseases presented. The student of medicine was to investigate climate and weather, site, soil, all the characteristics of a given locality which influence its ailments. Not that the environment could be modified: the Hippocratic tradition viewed milieu fatalistically, as a factor to be taken into account when diagnosing individual cases, not as something that was itself open to treatment.

In Joseph's century – the Age of Remedies – medical emphasis had shifted from aetiology to therapy, from the causes of disease to the search for cures. Advances in science and technology had turned manipulation of the environment into reality. For instance: the association between swamps and disease had long been observed, but it was eighteenth-century hydraulic engineering that made it possible to drain the country's marshlands. Steps could be taken. So he had been taught.

If a stranger tarries in boggy places, he is certain to fall ill. The virulence of the stagnant waters is indicated by their noxious odours: a sure indication of the presence of disease-carrying miasmas.

It has been shown that these emanations are the product of the putrefying animal and vegetable matter present in the swamps. Where such places have been drained, a corresponding decrease in intermittent fevers, mortality rates and general insalubrity has been recorded.

He poured out the last of the wine.

If air corrupted by putrefaction is the most fatal of all causes of illness, its cleansing and purification should be foremost among the physician's concerns. I would point out that marshlands are not the only site where putrescent odours may be detected. In the urban environment too, stench is a sure indication of a disease-ridden milieu.

He had promised himself he would make a difference. He would go out of the world having improved it.

I note in passing a few of the means by which responsible municipal authorities might seek to remedy this situation: the periodic collection of filth from our streets, and its disposal by burial or at sea; the construction of public latrines; the relocation of polluting manufactories and refuse pits outside and downwind of human settlement; or where this last is not practical, the treatment of such sites by chemical means, such as the application of strong vinegars.

He had already sent the town council a letter expressing these views in some detail along with his willingness to advise on the implementation of public sanitation measures in Castelnau. *The wealth of a state lies in the health of its citizens*, he had concluded, rather pleased with the formula. No reply had been forthcoming.

'If there was nothing in it for Caussade,' said Ricard, in whom he had confided, 'what did you expect?'

But Joseph refused to be deterred. He had arranged a meeting with his colleague Ducroix, who presided over the administration of the town's hospital: a crowded and, in Joseph's view, hopelessly unsanitary institution where the sick and the dying were piled indifferently together to suffocate in each other's malodorous emanations. If Ducroix could be persuaded to agree to his proposal, he would observe its effects on the patients, keep careful records, write up his findings into an article for the Royal Society of Medicine.

Someone sneezed on the staircase. He lifted his head, listening to a man's heavy tread.

Over and over in the margin he had written: *Sophie Morel. Sophie Morel.* Crossing out these scribbles, he attended to science.

When the site under consideration is an enclosed one, we find ourselves in the presence of a paradox: buildings protect man from the elements but within their walls they frequently hold stale, disease-bearing air. I would argue that ventilation is the most efficacious means of combating the noxious odours that linger in enclosed spaces. Dwellings, meeting halls, hospitals, prisons, ships – any place where people are gathered in an enclosed area will benefit from regular airing. To this might be allied the simmering of vinegar, the burning of sulphur or tar, or any other chemical means which will serve to absorb or reduce the stench of putrescence. In extreme circumstances I would advocate the installation of mechanical equipment designed to force fresh air into the mephitic site – in a prison, for instance, where other forms of ventilation might not be feasible.

He paused, and tapped his pen against his teeth. It was answered by a rapping on his door. Ta-ta-ta-*taah*. His landlady's servant, presumably, come later than usual to collect his dirty dishes.

But it wasn't.

'You're not Clémence.'

'That's right.' She shut the door and turned the key, seeming unperturbed by the stupidity of his remark. 'I'm her niece. I'm staying with my aunt for a day or two, to break my journey. I'm on my way to take up a situation in Albi –' proudly – 'assisting my cousin in his bakery. I might even marry him. But whatever happens, people always need bread.'

'Yes.' He stared open-mouthed at her, her clear skin, rounded cheeks, small, bright eyes. She was short but – his gaze moved downwards – no, you wouldn't say her figure was deficient.

'I saw you in the street. My aunt says you're kind-hearted and partial to roast parsnips.' She set the pitcher down in front of him. 'I stole us some wine. The old witch will never miss it.'

She had a very nice laugh.

'What are you doing?' She was pressed right up against the table. There was an overpowering smell of violets – she must have sacrificed half the bottle – and behind it her real smell, sweetish, musty, faintly overlaid with the reek of fried onions.

He swallowed. 'I was writing about the need for . . . for ventilation.'

'Ah, yes.' She began to undo her dress.

The wind had risen again. It slithered down the chimney, flung handfuls of flinty rain against his window, slid through the ill-fitting casement. The girl standing in front of him had goose bumps on her flesh.

Steps had to be taken.

He took them.

1791

erthe would have preferred Rinaldi to eat his cabbage soup in the scullery. Or better still, in the kitchen courtyard.

'But Berthe, it's snowing.'

'He's a gypsy. They don't experience the weather as we do.' She sighed a little, wearily, for would Sophie never grasp this simple point? 'They're not like us.'

But Sophie had insisted, so there was the pedlar ensconced in her warm, clean kitchen, dunking rye bread in her soup, snow still in the creases of his pack and now dripping on her freshly scrubbed floor. And Sophie sitting down at the table with him. Next, she'd be inviting him to dine with her father. That was what had come of this Revolution, a lot of Parisians putting ideas into respectable people's heads. In Castelnau the Sisters of the Little Flower had had their convent seized, their order dissolved; and where did that leave her, now that she could no longer look forward to ending her days with them, lending a hand from time to time in the kitchen, the nuns' voices soaring in her ears at the last?

'Berthe, I believe the stairs need sweeping. Perhaps . . .?'

She sniffed, and flounced from the kitchen, taking care not to shut the door behind her. That way she'd hear Sophie cry out when that fellow attacked her and be able to come to her aid.

'I've offended her,' said Sophie, 'but if she stays, she clatters so.'

'A thin cook is a household misfortune,' observed Rinaldi sententiously. 'Although this one's soup is full of flavour.'

She took the hint and refilled his bowl. 'Where have you been these months past?'

'North,' he said, concentrating on sucking his bread, 'and east.' Which effectively applied to most of the country. Rinaldi was never very keen on divulging his itineraries; he had an outcast's fear of giving away too much. He searched for something with which to divert Sophie's attention. 'I have some gloves impregnated with attar of roses. The finest calfskin.' Now his shiny, coal-black eyes sought hers and the tip of his tongue appeared in the corner of his mouth. 'Exactly like those the Queen's Swedish lover procures for her by the boxful.'

'They'd be of as much use to me as I imagine they are to her these days. I don't suppose she has occasion to go about in society any more than I do.'

'A young lady like you would be surprised,' he said darkly, 'at the things that go on in the Tuileries palace.' He beat a small brown hand on the table for emphasis and hissed, 'Parties.'

'Have you been in Paris, Rinaldi?'

At once he busied himself with his soup, ducking his head over his bowl. Sophie took pity on his discomfort and said, 'My China rose is thriving. And I've been able to propagate almost twenty new plants.'

'That was a fine bargain you struck. I knew that rose would bring you a fortune.'

'When you congratulate me on my shrewdness I know beyond doubt that the transaction has been to your advantage.'

He smiled. 'There's a gentleman who grows roses on his estate near Poitiers. He's very keen to acquire some plants. I told him to write to you.'

'Thank you.' She beamed at him and he thought, not for the first time, that she was one of those women who did not expect to be found attractive and so usually weren't.

He said, keeping his eyes on his plate, 'Wouldn't it be a fine thing to cross that China rose with one of the old varieties. The result could fetch a great deal of money.'

'Isn't it cold!' said Sophie gazing out of the window. 'All this snow.'

I was right, of course, thought Rinaldi. He poured the dregs of his wine into the last of his soup and picked up the bowl to drink from it.

A low black shape pushed the door wide, shot across the room, leapt onto the pedlar's knees, licked his face with loving munificence. 'I knew you were here,' said Mathilde, in its wake, 'because Berthe has got all the silver out and is counting it.'

'*Bellina! Che bellina!* As beautiful as the morning.' Rinaldi put out a monkey-paw to pinch Mathilde's cheek, behaviour she wouldn't have tolerated in anyone else. Reaching deep into a pocket, he produced a pink sugar almond and popped it into her mouth.

'Thank you, Rinaldi.' She shifted the sweet to her cheek and said, scarcely more distinctly, 'Brutus has broken a tooth. On the right side, at the back.'

Rinaldi looked, slipping his fingers into the dog's mouth to ease its jaws apart. 'It's nothing. His gums are healthy, that's the thing to be concerned about.' He scratched Brutus behind the ears and set him on the floor.

'I was afraid he'd have to have his teeth out, like Berthe. Sophie tried her on lavender water and cloves, but she said the ache was dreadful so she had them all pulled at the Michaelmas Fair. We're hoping her temper will improve in the spring.'

'Oak leaves boiled in rainwater,' said Rinaldi, 'that's the thing for the toothache. Or dragon's blood and myrrh – a remedy much used in the East with astonishing results. As it happens, I could show you ...'

'That won't be necessary,' said Sophie hastily. Once let him open that pack in Matty's presence ...

He turned a reproachful gaze on her. 'The gentleman from Poitiers bought a vial.' He paused to let this reminder that she had reason to be grateful to him take effect; Sophie's conscience was a sensitive instrument long since mastered by Rinaldi. 'Besides, such things are educational. I also have a dear little cup, the finest china, with a portrait of General Lafayette. Or a cotton dishtowel printed with the Declaration of the Rights of Man.'

'I don't think we need a dear little cup. Or more dishtowels.'

But Mathilde was already struggling with the buckles on the pack and Rinaldi got to his feet. 'A few patriotic objects might come in useful one day in a household such as this.'

'Really?'

He shrugged. 'For myself, I take care to wear the tricolour in my hat at all times.' With a flourish, he unrolled a length of magenta ribbon and wound it tenderly around Mathilde's head. 'A present for my little lady, *per la píu bella*, a present from Rinaldi.'

He liked her sister well enough. But he loved Mathilde. And now Sophie would feel obliged to buy something from his pack.

*J*acques informed Joseph that Saint-Pierre was in Castelnau – as he had hoped – and that Sophie was in the garden: 'She takes after her mother, who was always a great one for flowers, although it's a terrible shame she's nothing like as pretty.'

The door in the courtyard wall was open. She was standing with her face tilted to the sky. He scraped his boots and cleared his throat, not wishing to startle her.

She opened her eyes, and smiled to see him: 'I thought winter would never end.'

The east wind was chasing shreds of cloud across the pale sky. But the sun shone steadily and there, near the wall, its hoarded warmth could have been mistaken for May if not for the smell of grass and leaves, the watery green smell of early spring.

He unbuttoned his new lemon-yellow jacket.

'Is someone ill in the village?'

'No, not exactly, that is ...' He settled his spectacles more firmly. 'I was passing,' he lied, 'and thought I'd look in on old Laval, he's had difficulty shaking off that cough ...'

'I heard him shouting the other day, cursing his daughter-in-law because her soup tasted like cow's urine. He sounded very well.'

'I see, yes, of course, he's quite recovered now, no sign of the cough, not any longer.' In desperation he pointed at the nearest plant. 'These flowers – what are they?'

She broke off a mauve spike and handed it to him.

He sniffed. 'Lavender?'

She nodded, laughing.

'I know the red ones in the courtyard,' he said. 'Geraniums.

People keep them on windowsills. They're nice.'

'Do you have a sunny windowsill?'

He had to think. 'Maybe.'

'I could pot up a cutting for you.'

'Would you . . .?'

'Of course. A scarlet one, if you like. Or Berthe has plenty of pink and white at the back of the house.'

'The scarlet are my favourites,' he assured her, never having considered the matter.

'I won't forget.'

'I've never . . . What if I kill it?'

About to say, 'It's not one of your patients,' Sophie bit back the words. Something about those spectacles was overwhelmingly earnest. 'Geraniums are very hardy,' she reassured him. Noticing that his waistcoat was obviously new, his cravat stiff with starch and blued to a dazzle. People always needed doctors, she thought, because they always needed hope – or the illusion of it.

'Shall we go inside?' she asked. 'You must be thirsty . . .?'

He wriggled his shoulders, revelling in her kindness. 'I'd rather stay here.' And added, greatly daring: 'With you.'

Birds pecked at the damp earth, and the roses were putting out their first tender leaves. When had he last known utter contentment? All that came to mind was the time when his dissection of a cadaver's left arm had gone particularly well, flesh and muscles falling away cleanly under his knife, and that didn't seem quite right.

A gust of wind brought a handful of white blossom whirling in from the orchard. A wet petal clung to the back of her head. He thought, I could just put out my hand, very gently, and take that petal on my finger and she wouldn't know I'd touched her.

Small brown birds were making a fearful racket overhead. 'A farmer told me that if you go into a barn at night with a lantern under your coat, so the light is half screened, the sparrows will fly at it and settle on your shoulders. He said you can pick them off by the dozen – which you'd need, to make a meal of them.'

'I don't much like eating birds, any birds, even the kind which seem to exist only to be eaten, like geese. There's something about a dead bird's feet. And the little ones, when you think of their songs and the way light falls on their feathers .... It's not so different from eating flowers,' said Sophie, 'and imagine what people would say if they caught you at that.'

'When I was a student my friends made a cat pie for my birthday and told me it was rabbit until I'd eaten it.'

'And ...?'

'It wasn't bad at all – not unlike rabbit, in fact. I've acquired a taste for it. Now I always have a cat on my birthday.'

Her eyes slid sideways at him.

'And a dish of dog cutlets, on a Sunday.' He flung up his chin when he laughed. Sparrows scattered to the furthest reaches of the garden.

'Do you ever find yourself wondering which day you'll die on, your death-day?' she asked. 'It's so strange, the months coming and going, and nothing to mark the day that'll be your last.'

Joseph knew that the villagers were fond of her and sorry for her because she didn't have a husband. But as one woman had said, you couldn't blame the men, she was taller than most of them and had her own way of putting things.

They were coming up to the gate in the brier hedge. 'What's on the other side?' he asked.

'Only a few beds where I grow roses to sell. And the park: trees and so on.' She looked around: 'You know, I could find you a geranium now, it wouldn't take a minute.'

But she was too late. He had opened the gate and stepped through to row after row of small, bony bushes. Dark earth sloped down to another hedge. Beyond that a strip of pasture lay open to the wide, deceptive, pale-blue sky; and then there were birch trees and the river.

Sophie said, 'There's nothing to see. As you can see.' Frowning beside him, standing first on one foot, then the other, like one of those grey birds you saw stalking their way along the edge of the water.

101

He had bent to examine a scrap of colour on the nearest plant: two strands of cotton, one purple, one mauve, twisted around the stem. And on the next bush, and the next and the next.

'The white ones are popular because they do well even on north-facing walls. But I'm lucky if I sell two dozen a year.' Sophie hung about by the gate, one hand on the latch.

He was walking about, peering at the bushes as his spectacles slid down his nose. 'But you grow so many.'

She said, in a rush, 'I experiment with new varieties. Most of the plants come to nothing. But you need a great many, you see, to choose from.'

He turned back, delighted: 'A scientific endeavour.'

'It's largely a matter of chance,' said Sophie firmly, reminding herself as she did twenty times a day. 'An entire year's efforts can be wiped out by frost. I can hardly expect to be successful.'

'And the cotton?'

'The two strands represent the parent plants – a different colour for each one. It's a way of recording the origins of the seedlings.' She pushed away the hair blowing across her face. 'We might as well go back. It's windier here.'

A conversation from the previous summer was coming back to him with terrible precision: the American, lolling about at lunch, asking Sophie to name a rose after him. Resentment rose in Joseph like sap in springtime. He would be happy to suggest a suitable appellation: Bombast Recollected? Fragrant Fool? With murder in his heart, he glared at rosebushes.

Sophie thought of Professor Kölreuter, whom she imagined stocky, peppermint-scented, a little severe. The professor was quite a favourite of hers: he visited her often at night, and although he was elderly and all his endearments were German, his plump, pink fingers manipulated stigma with astonishing delicacy. Not, of course, that one could draw a parallel with Dr Morel.

Safely back on the other side of the hedge, it occurred to her that there might be a new law – there were so many, these days – requiring anyone who grew roses for sale to register with a central, Paris-based authority. There would be permits, a fee to pay no doubt. The doctor would know all that – she associated him, vaguely, with progress – which would explain why he looked so disapproving. 'I've neglected the paperwork,' she confessed. 'But it comes down to a few sales in Castelnau, that's all. I'm sure I could sort it all out.'

He opened his mouth to ask her to marry him –

'Sophie, Sophie!' Mathilde careered down the path and pulled up in front of them. 'Berthe's put preserved duck in the lentils.'

A promise had been made to the effect that lunches would contain no meat, at least if their father wasn't at home. Berthe had allowed herself to be talked around but rallied from time to time.

'Is it too late to ask for an omelette?'

Mathilde considered. 'She was muttering when I left.'

'It's too late. I'd better talk to her. She might let me make you one.'

'With chives?'

'With chives.'

Hanging on Sophie's arm, Mathilde said, 'There's a letter for you. From Stephen.'

'Do you like lentils, Dr Morel? You'll join us, won't you?'

But he knew it was impossible.

When he heard the musket fire, he picked up his black leather bag and ran. Hat and jacket were left behind, along with the woman who had come to him complaining of pains in her chest. He had already examined the lump, smelt her breath, heard out the litany of her symptoms; she would die from the tumour and there was nothing he could do for her.

For weeks, months he had been waiting for that sound. At meetings, the Patriots had raged against Castelnau's unpatriotic municipal government. Caussade had still not carried out instructions from Paris to sell off the holdings of the Order of the Little Flower, sequestered before Christmas. Worse than this stalling, the mayor was arming a company recruited from the peasants who worked his lands and headed up by his aristocratic cronies. They wore a black cockade surmounted by a white cross and claimed to be fighting a holy war against the infiltration of power by unbelievers – or worse, Protestants.

The Assembly itself handed them their most potent weapon, the decree subjecting all clergymen, as good citizens, to the Constitution and requiring them to swear an oath of loyalty to the nation and its laws. A petition was circulated demanding that the Catholic faith be acknowledged as the official State religion; to the fury of the revolutionaries, it attracted almost two thousand signatures.

Ricard, who remained calm through most debates, however heated, lost his composure at this evidence of 'religious fanaticism'. He thundered his conviction that Catholic zeal among the poor and uneducated would bring down the Revolution, 'exploited by aristocrats to serve their own retrograde ends'.

Reason dictated that clergymen should be subject to the Constitution. Wasn't that far more logical than owing allegiance to 'that jumped-up Italian priest, that Roman turkey-cock' now threatening excommunication to bishops and priests who took the oath?

The meeting decided that a detachment of local guardsmen would begin inventorying the contents of the convent, preparatory to their sale, without further delay.

It was one of those perfect April days, the sky high and blue. People had their windows open. Joseph ran past the smells of midday meals and recalled that Caussade's followers were derisively known as Onion Eaters.

The bridge was jammed with people. He pushed his way past, shouting, 'Let me through. I'm a physician. Let me through.'

A fat woman in a red-flowered blouse said, 'No need to shove!' and rammed her elbow into his ribs. He stumbled on.

At the head of the bridge a dozen Onion Eaters barred access to the far bank. 'I'm a physician,' he said, to the nearest. 'Let me through.'

'No one is to cross the bridge. By order of the mayor and the municipal council.'

'There are people dying in those streets. Your friends and neighbours could be among them.'

The man brought his pitchfork up to Joseph's nose. 'I doubt it. And no one is to cross the bridge.'

But then Joseph saw a face he recognised. 'Pierre Berger! You were glad enough to see me when your son fell from the barn. Let me through!'

Berger rubbed one bare foot against the other. 'Perhaps, sergeant . . .' he began.

A boy who had climbed up onto the parapet chose that moment to hurl a turnip at the sergeant's hat and hit Berger full in the chest instead. Shouts went up from the men in front of Joseph and a cheer from the crowd behind.

Then there was a shot and the boy screamed. Moments later, they heard the splash.

The officers came riding up to the ragged line of guards.

105

'Trouble?' enquired the one who had fired. Casually, with a smile. He levelled his pistol in Joseph's direction, without bothering to look at him.

If not for the crowd at his back, he would have fled. He would have begged, if he could remember the words.

It was Berger who spoke, rubbing his breast. 'It's Dr Morel. He's asking to be allowed through in case a physician is needed.'

Now the officer looked at Joseph, a long, unhurried scrutiny: coarse hair combed forward, spectacles, a crumpled shirt, a leather bag clutched in both hands, large, dingy boots. He smiled again, gestured with his weapon, wheeled his horse sideways. 'By all means. Let him pass. Why not?'

And Joseph realised that from the other side of the bridge there no longer came the sound of gunfire.

A toddler was sitting in a flowerbed, his plump legs stretched out in front of him. His nursemaid was flirting in the pantry and the balustrade hid him from his mother, so he was taking the opportunity, hitherto denied him, of conducting an experiment into the taste of daisies.

In the garden the little girls were shrieking as they chased each other. On the terrace, a baby slept in a wicker cradle in the shade. There was coffee on a silver tray, along with cream, sugar, and a blue-and-white dish of crimson strawberries.

Claire, watching her sister-in-law heap berries onto a plate and coat them with sugar and cream, was thinking about what she had just been told. 'Do you think it's wise,' she asked, 'so soon after . . .?'

Anne continued spooning fruit into her little pink mouth, lodged like a plump berry in the creamy expanse of her face. 'The sooner I have a son,' she said, 'the sooner it'll stop.'

'It's not fair!' The child's voice floated over the golden air, high and indignant. Wait ten years, thought Claire, and you'll find out all about not fair.

Hubert strode out onto the terrace and tossed a piece of paper onto the table. 'Duval, again. Last time it was stealing wood. This time they've been grazing their cattle on the estate. The fences have been trampled down and the tenant farmers are in an uproar over the herds being driven over their fields. Duval has filed a complaint with the magistrate but that's less than useless these days. I'll have to go myself.' He poured out a cup of coffee and began pacing up and down.

'You're always rushing about,' remarked Anne, wiping cream from her lips. 'Why can't you leave your bailiff to deal with it? Isn't that what such people are for?'

He paid her no attention; they had long fallen into the habit of addressing only critical remarks to each other. 'I can't say how long I'll be away.'

Claire said, 'But Sophie and Mathilde will be here tomorrow.'

'You aren't suggesting that my absence will distress them?' A thought struck him and he swung around to face her. 'They're not bringing that dog?'

'No, Hubert, Mathilde knows you won't allow Brutus in your house.'

He looked at her with suspicion. 'But you told me that she said she'd never want to go where it wasn't welcome.' Then, hopefully: 'It hasn't died, has it?'

'You know, my dear,' said Anne, 'I think I'd prefer chocolate to coffee, after all.'

'Father insisted on her coming to us.'

Claire went into the house, where she spoke to a servant. On her way back down the terrace she paused beside the cradle, stooping to look inside. The baby sighed and made small sucking noises in her sleep. 'Such an adorable baby, Anne! Those dimples – and I've never seen such long eyelashes.'

'Yes, she takes after Sébastien's family.'

Hubert had drawn up a chair and was helping himself to a plate of berries. 'I wouldn't have believed your father capable of insisting on anything. That child runs wild. She should be in a convent, having some discipline drummed into her.'

'You forget there are no longer any convents. Or nuns to do the drumming. Father thought it more prudent for the girls to leave Castelnau until things quietened down. Although according to Sophie, everything is already more or less back to normal.'

He snorted. 'Caussade fled, most of his councillors imprisoned, troops from all over the place occupying the town. Is that what you call normal?'

A grey-haired woman appeared with a jug of chocolate, spoons, bowls, more cream. Claire frowned: 'Where's Marie?'

'A fit of dizziness, Madame.'

'I don't know what's come over that girl – she's been quite peculiar lately. If things don't improve I'll have to let her go. Sickly servants are intolerable.'

'Oh, she seems a pleasant enough little thing,' said Hubert, applying himself to spooning up strawberry juice.

'Would there be any of those exquisite little vanilla tartlets left over from yesterday?' asked Anne.

But Claire was staring at Hubert, who kept his eyes on his dish. After a few moments she said, 'I shall invite Stephen down, as well. He's finished my portrait, and says he'll be delighted to deliver it in person. What a pity you won't be here.'

Well, that's bold, thought Anne.

Hubert turned to his sister. 'For heaven's sake! Do you ever do anything other than eat and spawn brats?'

They're like two birds, thought Claire, Anne sitting plumply on her nest and Hubert a quarrelsome cock sparrow.

Overcome by the magnitude of his undertaking, her son suddenly set up a fearful roar in the flowerbed.

While all this was going on, a girl with puffy red eyes was sitting on the bed she shared with her cousin in a narrow room at the top of the house. She was trying to imagine what her life was going to be like.

*P*ollination occurs naturally where roses are grown outdoors, for bees will pollinate the flowers. But if you wish to make a controlled cross – if it is your ambition to bring a rose into the world, to add to its multiple phenomena – here is what you must do.

The basis of all plant breeding is selection. You must begin by choosing the traits you would wish to reproduce: the musky scent of this lilac-flowered cultivar, perhaps, the parchment-to-pink tones or striking double form of that one. The roses selected for these traits will be your parent plants: the male or pollen parent and the female or pod parent. You will aim to combine the parental characteristics you favour in their resulting offspring.

Choose a young bud – one that barely shows colour – on the rose you have selected as the pod parent and, very gently, remove all the petals. This will enable you to reach the unripe anthers, which you must now cut off to prevent the plant from self-pollinating. Bees will usually ignore a flower without pollen-bearing anthers, but to ensure that no unwanted pollen creates seed in the female plant you would be wise to cover the stripped-down bud with a small bag tied in place. In a few days the stigma will ripen, becoming slightly sticky. In this state it is receptive to pollen from the male parent.

While the stigma is ripening, collect just-opening buds from the pollen parent. Carefully cut out the anthers and set them on a sheet of paper to dry. Once that is done, place the dried pollen in a clean receptacle – a small box, a glass jar. Beware of humidity: if your box or jar is less than perfectly dry your pollen might turn mouldy.

Now you are ready to place your pollen. Using a fine-haired brush, collect up the dried pollen and dust it gently over the ripe stigma. If the pollen germinates, it will send a long pollen tube down the style into the ovary of the female plant, and seed-pods – known as hips – will eventually develop.

Once a hip begins to form, be sure the mother plant is well fed and watered. In four or five months the hip will turn orange and be slightly soft to the touch. This indicates it is ripe for picking. Open up the hip, pull each seed from the flesh and dry the seeds on paper placed in the sun. Take precautions against mice, who are inordinately fond of rose seeds.

Plant the seeds in a shallow tray containing a light propagation mix, water the soil and place the tray in a cold place for four to six weeks. This chilling period will cause most seed to germinate when the tray is later transferred to a warm location.

Seedlings will bloom in a few months' time. However, you should wait for a second flowering to appraise the plants more accurately. And you should be prepared for considerable variation in these cross-bred offspring: roses, like people, are liable to disconcert you, rarely running true to type. You will have to discard most of the seedlings, but any that appear to conform to your specifications should be tagged and potted for further appraisal.

You must repeat this entire process hundreds – no, thousands – of times to have any chance of producing the rose that flowers only in your imagination.

As you will appreciate, late spring is a crucial season for breeders of roses. So you will understand why Sophie worked late into the long evenings with scissors and brushes and muslin bags. Why she was bone-tired but slept badly, roses breaking in on a confusion of dreams.

He loves his daughters, but days without them drift downstream, easy navigation in unruffled water. He takes his meals in his study, which adjoins his bedroom. His old brown dressing-gown, the one Marguerite embroidered with yellow suns the first year they were married, hangs around him in silky folds. He eats as much as he pleases, without Sophie, under instruction from that fool Ducroix, frowning at his plate.

He thinks about Sophie. He fears she's growing fussy, old-maidish. He ought to devote some time to finding a husband for her. He ought to write to Claire, ask her advice, enlist her help.

Instead he goes for walks in the green summer lanes. For these excursions he has dug out his ancient black felt hat, his one relic of his days in the Toulouse courts. Its broad brim where moths have feasted is lacy with holes. They let in the air, which blows gently around his face.

There's a field on the far side of the village which to all appearances is no different from those which surround it. And yet the skylarks single it out, and day after day their song pours out of the blue sky in that one place.

At night, silence curves itself around him like a wing. When sleep comes, he curls himself into its softness.

An owl calls from the beech tree by the open window and he jerks awake. He notices that one of his sleeves is flecked with gravy.

This growing desire for solitude that leads him to neglect old friends, old colleagues, his children; the difficulty with which he simulates interest in the affairs of the world. When did they begin? When his wife died? When Claire went away to Toulouse? When she married that intolerable fool?

He has been elected to the new judiciary, but even his work, once a passion, can no longer be said to compel his attention; he goes through the motions. He remembers believing that the law existed to civilise men. And he supposes that he still does, only he can't bring himself to care very much about it.

He is aware of his fondness for small rituals, his coddling of himself. I'm growing old, he thinks, appalled. And, for a long minute, nothing is more difficult than breathing.

But is that possible, when the past noses at his heel, when childhood keeps him company like his shadow? The ring of boys hold him down in a dark, marble-floored corridor, their bony fingers digging into his arms. He still knows by heart the catechism for courtiers with which they tormented him while keeping a cold penknife pressed against his gullet: *How many kinds of nobility are there?* And he would have to reply, Two, that of the sword and that of the robe. *Which is the more esteemed?* That of the sword because it is acquired only after frequent risk of life ...

The clock on the mantelpiece strikes the hour. Soon Jacques will arrive with his *digestif* and something to eat, something ... small and delicious.

Anticipatory saliva spurts in his mouth.

He bends once more over his books and papers. When the door opens, he says, 'Did you know that large fowl were once served complete with all their feathers? At the great banquets it was commonplace to remove a bird's skin without tearing it – devilishly tricky operation, I should think – and then roast the fowl over a slow fire. When the bird was done, it was put back in its skin and brought to table. That couldn't have done anything to improve what I imagine was the already dubious flavour of swans and storks and herons.'

'Nasty great things. Why would anyone want to eat them when they could have a nice tasty thrush instead?'

'You're an exemplary product of our times, Jacques. Some two centuries ago, large wildfowl fell out of favour and people began eating snipe, warblers, thrushes, larks, ortolans. I argue that the substitution of small tasty birds for large decorative

113

ones marks the shift from our ancestors' concern with the appearance of a dish to our own preoccupation with its taste.'

'Berthe goes to a lot of trouble with her pie crusts. She wouldn't like to hear you say otherwise.'

'Indeed, indeed, Berthe's crusty efforts are delightful. But she doesn't add inedible colourants – powdered lapis lazuli or red tin-leaf – to our food, and so much the better. That's what her great-grandmother would have done, as a matter of course, with the sole aim of producing a visually striking dish. Today we discriminate between brown and white sauces or red and green currants because we appreciate their distinctive flavours above all – whatever visual pleasure they might afford is a secondary consideration. I shall go on to suggest that our modern emphasis on taste in the literal sense is paralleled in our discussions of art and literature by an increasing concern with good or bad taste in the figurative one. Listen –'

He rummages among the clutter on his desk, overturns a brass paperweight, scatters a sheaf of papers, seizes the volume he requires –

'Here's Voltaire: *Just as bad taste in the physical sense consists in being gratified only by overly piquant or excessive seasonings, so bad taste in the arts is a matter of being pleased only by affected ornament and of not responding to natural beauty.*' Gratified, he looks up at Jacques. 'What do you think?'

'I don't see how you can possibly know that about her great-grandmother. Berthe was abandoned in the porch of the village church as an infant – she told me so herself.'

For a moment Saint-Pierre is dumbfounded. Then he laughs, and closes the book. 'Historians forget what interests people,' he says, 'that's why most history is unreadable.'

For answer, Jacques sets a dish patterned in pink and gold – a survivor of the Sèvres dinner-set – on the desk. 'Blancmange,' he announces. '*White* blancmange with a *red* raspberry sauce.'

Saint-Pierre leans forward.

Conveys a trembling spoonful to his lips.

Opens his mouth.

Closes his eyes.

114

*T*he boy who ran errands for Joseph brought word that Luzac had been elected mayor and that Ricard had a place on the council. After days of drizzle, the combination of good news and June sunshine was irresistible. For once, the waiting room was empty. Why not? he thought, and locked the door before he could change his mind.

He felt lighthearted and full of goodwill: exactly like the time he had gone boating when he should have been cramming for an exam. What was the name of that Swiss student with the crimson birthmark on his neck who had fallen in and later almost died from the fever?

A striped cat dozing on a sunny wall purred when he tickled its ears. He was thinking of a girl who smelt of violets and onions, remembering her blowing out the candle beside his bed. He whistled tunelessly, and a canary on a balcony whistled back at him.

Ricard's charcuterie was in one of Lacapelle's few respectable streets, a neighbourhood where artisans and tradesmen lived and shopped. Joseph passed an ironmonger's and a confectioner's, both shuttered for the midday break, which lasted until half-past three. Two young children, dressed identically, were playing in the street with a hoop. In their fair colouring and solid limbs he could discern no trace of Lisette; although perhaps the smaller one's carroty locks tended to frizz. He smiled at them and they stared up at him with their father's flat blue eyes.

The charcuterie too was still closed up. But the girl seated on the step, keeping a listless eye on the children while shelling peas into a blue enamel bowl, assured him that the family had

115

long finished their meal and went to fetch her mistress. It was Ricard who appeared, however, in the covered alley that ran down the side of the shop, crowding the narrow space with his broad shoulders. He received Joseph's congratulations with a wide smile and the insistence that he come in and raise a glass to the occasion.

Inside, there was an overpowering smell of cooking. It grew stronger still as he followed Ricard down a short passage tiled in green and white, and into a room behind the shop. But the room itself was pleasant enough: a green jug of yellow flowers stood on the table, which was covered in dark-brown oilcloth, and the walls, papered over as had recently become usual, were striped yellow and green. A plaster bust of Cassius? – one of those antique republicans back in vogue – gleamed in a corner. The floorboards, oilcloth and walnut sideboard shone. If the family had eaten here, not a trace of their meal – a crumb, a smear on the table – remained.

Ricard was telling him, with casual pride, that most of the food sold in the shop was produced on the premises. He limped over to open another door and stood aside for Joseph to peer in. The far wall of the huge kitchen was taken up by an enormous cast-iron stove. He saw forks with long handles, knives, an array of saucepans, a basin brimming with something dark, the scored surface of a massive table, a jar of golden fat, tiles the colour of dried blood, two buckets by the door that gave onto the courtyard. A tall boy with severe acne stood at the table cramming parsley-flecked butter into a snail shell.

Ricard was slicing up a coarse-grained dry sausage onto a plate. He had made it himself, he said, pork and bacon, salt and green peppercorns, all stuffed by hand into the sausage skin; Joseph had to try it. And then there was this ham, cooked *au foin*, a speciality of the house: only the top of the pig's thigh was used, steeped in brine for four days, wrapped in a mixture of dried sainfoin and clover, and cooked in a *court-bouillon*. It was the finest ham in all Castelnau, he could guarantee that.

The kitchen looked as spotless as such a place could look and fresh air came in through the courtyard door. Yet the heat was terrible and the smell overwhelming. Joseph thought he understood now why Lisette was so thin: he himself would have no appetite left if he sat down to eat with that odour in his nostrils every day. No wonder she scrubbed her rooms as if removing all vestiges of a crime. He murmured the admiration that was evidently expected, took the plate he was handed, and was thankful when the door closed at last on that infernal place.

From the sideboard, the pork butcher brought out two glasses and a bottle of colourless liquid. Plum brandy, he said, made by his mother who lived in a village a few miles south with her married daughter. His sleeves were rolled up, revealing muscular forearms that ended in slim, well-shaped hands – as if he had woken in a hurry and fastened the wrong pair to his wrists.

They clinked glasses and drank to the Revolution. Joseph knocked back the brandy, then fiddled with his spectacles as Ricard refilled his glass. But the pork butcher only observed that they had reason enough to celebrate: 'Barely two months ago I was in prison, and Castelnau belonged to Caussade.'

They drank to each other's health. This time Joseph sipped circumspectly, then tilted his glass towards the dull red mark above his friend's left eye. 'You're quite recovered? No headaches?' Confident of the answer but needing to hear it anyway.

Ricard fingered the scar. 'I forget it's there.' Taking out pipe and tobacco, he smiled at Joseph. 'For which I have you to thank.'

'Not at all,' he said, delighted, 'it was a shallow wound. It would have healed anyway.' He rolled the liquid around in his glass. 'Luzac, now – that was a near thing. The bone was shattered. If gangrene had taken hold . . .' He ate some of the ham; it was, indeed, delicious.

After a little while Ricard said, 'Luzac might be poorer by an arm but he's managed to enrich himself in other ways.' At Joseph's look of incomprehension: 'Didn't you know? He bought the farms and all the land that used to belong to the convent. Why do you think he raged at Caussade for delaying the sale?'

117

'Well . . . because it was anti-revolutionary.'

'People like Luzac look on the Revolution as an unparalleled commercial opportunity. He's buying up Caussade's land as well.'

Joseph blurted, 'But I thought Luzac was on our side.' Downing his plum brandy defiantly when Ricard smiled.

The pork butcher leant forward. 'You're quite right and I was wrong to laugh. It's the brandy, you see: I have no head for it, particularly in the middle of the day.'

For a while there was silence. Then Joseph said, 'Everything was so much simpler two years ago, wasn't it?' Wondering if that was naive too, he risked meeting Ricard's blue gaze.

'Yes, but '89 was only the start. In difficult times it's easy for a man to lose his way. If the outcome is worth fighting for, the struggle is bound to be long and complicated.' Ricard often spoke softly like that, gathering you up in the intimacy of his thoughts.

A floorboard creaked above their heads. The pork butcher said, 'My wife is indisposed.'

Joseph had assumed she was out. But he should have enquired after her, anyway. He was always getting simple things like that wrong. He moistened his lips with his tongue: 'If I could do anything . . .?'

'Thank you, but . . .' Ricard waved a hand. 'The usual women's troubles.' Adding, after a moment, 'I hear things have been looking up for you professionally. Luzac tells me his daughter-in-law talks of nothing but the clever new physician who rid her of her cough and is recommending you to all her friends.'

'A lucky diagnosis.' Joseph traced an invisible pattern on the oilcloth. 'Sometimes I think I spend my days telling people what they want to hear: I prescribe sirloin in rich houses, garlic in poor ones, prayer to the devout, brandy to sinners.'

'If that's true – but I'm certain you're underestimating your talents – it's nothing to be ashamed of. There's no greater art than reading men's minds.'

In all the intricate world, who else cared enough to talk to him like that?

He ate slice after slice of excellent sausage, watching fragrant blue pipesmoke spiral in a shaft of light, and everything was all right again.

The pork butcher said, 'Tell me – what do you make of Saint-Pierre? Is he sound, do you think?'

'Saint-Pierre? Why, yes – of course. He was on the tribunal, remember? They sentenced that officer to death for shooting the boy on the bridge.' Joseph grew agitated, thinking of the splash, the pistol levelled in his direction, eyes the colour of weak tea looking him up and down. 'I was at the trial, I had to give evidence. Of course Saint-Pierre's sound.'

'I think so too,' said Ricard smoothly. 'But I value your judgment of character. And it's his family I was thinking of, really.'

Sophie? Mathilde? 'They are ... *girls*,' he said, bewildered. But then realised: 'Monferrant?'

'Letters from him were found among Caussade's papers. Have you ever heard him speak of our former mayor?'

'I've never met him – only his wife.' He took off his spectacles, looked at them as if he didn't recognise them, put them back on. 'I had the impression she wasn't very fond of her husband. Are the letters incriminating?'

'Not particularly – expressions of support, pledges of assistance ... The usual thing.' Once again, Ricard's voice had grown soft and caressing. 'But it's convenient that you're acquainted with the Montsignac crowd – you can alert us to anything we ought to know.'

Footsteps sounded in the passage. Ricard's daughters came trotting in, the older one carrying a fluffy white kitten. On their heels was the dark, good-looking printer from the Club.

'Papa,' said the smaller girl, 'there is a man.'

Mercier nodded at Joseph and thrust the broadsheet he was holding into Ricard's hands. 'Have you heard?' His black eyes were snapping. 'Citizen Capet and his Austrian whore were arrested in Varennes, trying to flee the country.'

The older child stood in front of Joseph and deposited her kitten on his lap. 'My name is Julie and this is Sugar.' Tiny claws dug into his flesh and the kitten swayed on his knee in fright.

119

ate October, and a mother-of-pearl early morning sky.

Sophie took care to stay in the middle of the path, avoiding the dew that still clung to the long grass. Her mind was half on her errand, half on the yellow-green dress she was wearing for only the second time. It had been passed on from Claire, who had decided the colour didn't suit her, and who had her dresses made with generous hems that could be let down for Sophie. But did this one show too much of her boots anyway? Was it too late to cut it down for Mathilde?

The lane curved to the left and the church tower came into view. In the foreground, a grey horse cropped from the green ditch. Near it, a man sat slumped on the damp grass.

'Dr Morel?'

He got to his feet as if he could not quite remember how to do so. She noticed that he hadn't shaved and that his hair was wet, and it occurred to her that he might be drunk. The sun, breaking through a cloud, turned the tops of his ears pinky-orange.

He said, 'Félix Morin is dead.'

'Félix? But I'm on my way there,' she said, as if that made it impossible.

He looked at the basket on her arm. 'You can save your soup – or is it a flask of brandy? Whatever it is, he's past needing it.'

She had not thought him capable of harshness. His manner, as much as his news, shocked her into platitude: 'Such terrible things happen.'

He stared at her boots. Asked abruptly, 'Will you walk with

me?' And turned away before she could reply.

She set her basket down behind the hedge and hastened after him, catching up as he turned onto a path which struck out over the bare brown fields. For several minutes they walked in silence, Sophie hurrying to keep up with him, the toes of her boots turning black from the grass.

They skirted a spinney of young oak trees and emerged on the sunny flank of a hill where the path ran along the edge of a narrow, deep-green coomb. Like a river of grass, she thought, and paused to catch her breath.

He stopped when she did. 'There's scarcely a house in Laca-pelle where a child hasn't died in the past few weeks. The first cold weather, and the fever appears and spreads like fire. Night after night, I've watched them die. Félix had been visiting his cousins in town and returned with a cough. Two days ago, he complained of a sore throat. His father came for me last night – this morning. As soon as I saw the child I knew I was too late. The whole back of his throat was like white velvet. The disease had invaded the larynx. I stretched the skin over his trachea, anyway, I had to try. But my hand was shaking so much that I couldn't make the incision. He stopped breathing. His father swore and shouted at me to save his son. So I cut into the boy's windpipe and inserted the tube. It gave him some relief, for an hour or two. But the false membranes continued forming, deeper and deeper, where the tube couldn't reach them. And so he choked, and died. I took the tube out and went outside and the sky was starting to grow pale. I went down the street to the well and put my head in a bucket of water. When I came back, Morin was sitting on a chair, holding the child in his lap. The lamp was still lit.'

He took off his spectacles and Sophie saw his wide grey eyes, the colour of the river in winter. 'He was six years old.' He put his hands over his face.

She picked up his spectacles, wiped them on her sleeve, said as gently as she could, 'You're exhausted. You must sleep, have something to eat. Please – you must come back to the house with me.'

He dropped his hands.

121

Then he moved a step closer to her.

He can't be – I must be imagining – he is looking at me as if . . . Sophie said in a rush, 'The Morins have two other children and Agnès is still young, they'll have others. It's terrible now but it'll pass, you will see.' She meant his own anguish, as much as anything.

He snatched the spectacles from her and jammed them into place. At once the morning filled up with thick, unforgiving glass.

He said, 'That's very typical of your class. I suppose it's convenient for you to believe that the poor don't care much, at heart, for their children. It soothes your conscience about the conditions in which they live – and die.'

'That's not what I said,' she protested. 'I didn't think – but I didn't mean – No . . .'

That dress – what a vile colour. Like pus, thought Joseph. He pushed past her without a word and, walking rapidly, made his way back down to the village.

is yellow gaze never leaves her face. Head on one side, he listens intently:

'*How you are changed and you alone, within these two months!* Mathilde intones. *Where now is your languor, your disgust, your dejected look! The Graces have again resumed their post; your charms are all returned; the new blown rose is not more fresh and blooming* . . . and so on, et cetera . . . Here's a good bit: O, *how infinitely amiable you were when less beautiful! How I do regret that pathethic paleness, that precious assurance of a lover's happiness, and hate that sprightly health which you have recovered at the expense of my repose!*'

The book slides off her lap and onto the rug. Brutus inches closer and wags his tail. She picks up the book and keeps reading, so he springs onto her knees.

'*How I do hate that sprightly health!*' says Mathilde, scratching him behind the ears.

He licks her chin.

'*Those sparkling eyes, that blooming complexion* . . . But now you must get down . . .' At once, he curls up on her lap. 'Down, I said!'

He sighs and closes his eyes.

'*I am weary of suffering ineffectually* . . .' And she shifts in her seat, as if to rise.

Landing heavily at her feet, he looks at her with deep reproach; when this has no effect, he gathers himself up, leaps onto the bed, turns around three times, tucks his nose under his tail and falls asleep.

The key is kept in the carved wooden box which also contains her ribbons, the brooch with a blue stone that belonged to her mother, a tiny silver spoon, a sea urchin's lilac-striped case (a present from Rinaldi) and a lump of greyish rock (he swore it had been part of the Bastille). She unlocks her desk and fishes out her journal.

Thursday
Rainy afternoon. Goose for dinner again, that makes three days in a row.

Friday
Rainy morning. Sophie cut down Claire's yellow dress for me. The colour reminds me of when Brutus vomited on the sofa. But she said I'm growing fast and need a new dress for the cool weather.

Saturday
Can't remember.

Sunday
Dr Ducroix and Isabelle to lunch. I wore my new dress; not a success. Now that the King has accepted the Constitution, Father and Dr Ducroix think the Revolution is no longer necessary and should be declared ended. Sophie says what has been accomplished when children are still dying for lack of clean water to drink? I should be sorry not to have the Revolution when I grow up. Roast goose.

Monday
Brutus was limping, he had a thorn in his paw. Rain.

Tuesday
A letter from Claire. Someone has taught Olivier to say *Vive la Révolution*. Hubert is questioning the servants.

Wednesday
Sophie distracted. I beat her easily at chess.

Thursday
Snow!!!

Friday
I have a cold and Sophie won't allow me outside. Read *La Nouvelle Héloïse* to Brutus. Worse than I'd imagined.

erthe had skinned and gutted the hare before taking to bed with one of her headaches, brought on, she grumbled, by snowlight. Sophie jointed the carcass – dividing the saddle – and set the head aside for stock. She coated the meat in flour seasoned with pepper and salt, melted beef fat in a pan and, when it was sizzling, added a diced onion and two cloves of finely chopped garlic.

Mathilde had a cold and fever. It was useless trying to sweat it out of her, she refused to lie still and kicked off her quilts.

Sophie added the meat to the pan, along with dried herbs – parsley, marjoram, sage, thyme – two bay leaves and a blade of mace. She had gone out at daybreak with Jacques to brush snow from the canvas canopies that protected her seedlings in winter, and had been unable to get warm again all day.

If she had spoken unthinkingly, Dr Morel had been unjust, imputing the worst significance to words intended as comfort, however clumsy.

The browned meat was packed into a tall earthenware jug, with two cups of red wine, and beef stock thickened with the blood of the hare. Finally she crammed muslin into the neck of the jug and wound more over its mouth.

That's very typical of your class. Oh unfair, unfair to lump her in with the Huberts and the Caussades.

A pot of water was already bubbling. She lowered the jug into it.

They had welcomed 1789. Even if Father would like the Revolution neatly rolled up, bound with a ribbon and stored away for safekeeping. It was his legalistic mind: he liked tidiness, was intolerant of loose ends.

126

Stephen was wrong to claim a connection between artists and revolutionaries: their approach to the world was precisely antithetical. Art insisted on particularity: all that mattered was this woman, that sky, those trees. Contrast that with *your class*.

She longed to point out all this, and more. She had considered writing to Joseph. She had even envisaged lying in wait for him when he called on a patient in the village, seeing the scene in some detail: his grey horse trotting up the lane between twiggy hedgerows, and there she happened to be, emerging from the woods with a basket of chestnuts, wearing her green jacket that was only two winters old. She imagined him apologetic and humble, while she displayed calm, forgiveness and just a touch of *hauteur*.

The hare would cook over the next three hours, and be eaten with carrots and boiled cabbage. No one who was hungry was ever turned away from their door. So what right did he have to judge them? *And get it wrong?*

The ache behind her eyes was becoming insistent.

Lisette undid the cloth-wrapped bundle. The hare lay stiff and cold on the marble counter.

'They often pay me in kind,' Joseph explained. 'And at this time of the year ... It's only Thursday and I've had a hare, half a goose and a saddle of rabbit. I thought of you, I thought you might like some game for dinner.'

Her body was flat and rectangular as a playing card. 'Thank you,' she said. 'You're very generous. Paul will be so grateful.' Her husband was out, she told him, 'on official business'. They had been obliged to take on a second apprentice, the council claimed so much of Ricard's time.

The sleeve of her dress fell back a little way as she prodded the carcass, and he pointed to the mark above her wrist: 'What happened?'

At once she placed her hand behind her back, like a child. 'Nothing. An accident in the kitchen.'

She had always been ashamed of shortcomings, he thought,

she was one of those people who equate imperfection with weakness.

The street door opened. Within seconds Lisette had bundled up the hare, whipped it out of sight, reached for a spotless cloth and wiped the already gleaming surface of the counter.

While she attended to the customer, he wandered about looking at the food for sale: terrines, rillettes, hams, jars of mustard, ropes of fresh and dried sausages, a rosy tongue on a bed of fern leaves, hens' eggs in aspic, *foie gras* in pastry, pigs' trotters, pork chops, veal cutlets, galantines, capers, gherkins, stuffed cabbages, baked cauliflowers, a dish of preserved pork, a crock of lard, a plate of snails. Everything looked fresh and wholesome and was daintily presented; yet, remembering the smell in that dark kitchen, he turned away hurriedly.

The woman buying blood sausage had smooth brown hair and a russet shawl. He spied on her in the mirror. There was something about the tilt of her head ...

All I could think of was my failure to save the boy, and my harshness sprang from a sense that the profession to which I have dedicated my life is mostly powerless to alleviate the suffering which confronts it daily. I have nothing but the deepest admiration and respect for you. He touched his breast and felt the letter in his pocket shift against his shirt.

He became aware of a small flurry at his back and looked around. The customer must have queried her bill: Lisette shook her head, pointing at the short column of figures, clarifying something. The woman in the red shawl excused herself prettily, gathered up her parcels, smiled at them both and apologised again before going out into the darkening afternoon.

'They can't add up around here,' Lisette told him. 'I might not be able to read but I know my figures, I can do the sums in my head.' Her cheeks were flushed, her hazel eyes bright with victory.

One winter evening when his family had been sitting down to dinner, there had come a scratching at the door. His father opened it and there was Lisette. She said nothing, merely cowered on the threshold and stared at the children around the table. His father shut the door and turned back to his soup: 'Once you start . . .' he'd said.

I have nothing but the deepest admiration and respect for you.

But what did he know of Sophie after all? He might have spoken with unwarranted severity, but hadn't she provoked him? With her little charitable airs that couldn't quite carry her over her ultimate indifference to that boy, his parents, the way thousands of people lived and died.

The streets around were full of girls like Lisette.

On the quai des Grands Augustins a man was selling roast chestnuts. Business was slow: it was so cold that no one wanted to stop moving long enough to carry out the transaction.

The letter in Stephen's hand was dated the 9th of September. It had made good time, reaching him a fortnight before Christmas.

He told himself that he had meant to go. He had meant to sail in March, in May.

George wrote that the end had been sudden and peaceful: *When Hatty went in to Mother in the morning she couldn't wake her. We sent for Belleville but there was nothing he could do and she never regained consciousness.*

He had meant to go.

He couldn't stop thinking about her hair, which reached to the backs of her knees when unbraided. He used to sit on her lap and she would let her hair fall all around him, a crimped, golden curtain that kept him safe. He stroked it and it flared under his hands, he shut his eyes and breathed in its warm, flesh-scented fragrance.

She never complained and we had no inkling of the pain she must have suffered.

His father, John Fletcher, had been an architect of some renown, the only son of an old Virginian family known throughout the colony for the solidity of its investments and the eccentricity of its pursuits – architecture, for instance. In his youth he possessed undeniable talent, boundless charm, a classical profile and a personal fortune. Logic and civilised society ensured that the invitations he received from ladies with marriageable daughters filled three mantelpieces and overflowed onto a gate-legged table.

One day an entrepreneur named Edward Clay visited the architect, seeking to engage his services; Clay was to be married the following year and wished to begin wedded life in a mansion designed by the man whose star looked set to outdazzle the firmament. Fletcher declined; he already employed a clerk just to turn down commissions, and he had no need of the hefty fee Clay proposed as inducement. But he declined charmingly and evasively, as was his way, for he hated not to please; so Clay was left with the impression that the young man might yet be persuaded to change his mind, and he set about this task by insisting that Fletcher attend an intimate dinner for thirty organised in honour of the bride-to-be. Thus it came about that the architect found himself sitting at the right hand of a seventeen-year-old girl with ropes of light-gold hair. She smiled at him; lives swerved, collided. Early the next day, Fletcher accepted Clay's offer. After which it was necessary to call on Mlle Caroline Gallier to apprise her of the fact; and before she returned south with her uncle and aunt, it was imperative to solicit her opinion on all manner of architectural urgencies, from the dimensions of the octagonal drawing-rooms to the choice of raw materials for the foundations. The scandal that inevitably ensued sent aftershocks through commerce, agriculture, shipping, finance and – indeed – architecture, and animated after-dinner conversations on two continents. John Fletcher and his wife lay in their bed amid the bright disarray of her hair, and laughed between kisses.

'Do as your heart tells you,' she would advise in later years, whenever her sons hesitated over alternatives, 'do as your heart tells you and be happy.'

So rather than sail home, Stephen had spent the summer in Italy. In Toulouse, after a delicious fortnight, Claire had voiced her scruples; he had allowed himself to be persuaded. The virtuous drama of love renounced sustained him through everything that followed: frescoes, nightingales, diarrhoea, belltowers, opera, cardinals, pickpockets, marble, lemon trees, chiaroscuro, tombs, vistas, misunderstandings, moonlight, sunburn, cherubim, landladies, mortadella, cypresses, delays, drains, grottoes, martyrdoms, triptychs, terracotta. He took solitary walks beside antique rivers and experimented with melancholy.

When he returned to Paris his mother's letter was waiting for him. She said she was sorry he had changed his plans as she longed to see him again. No word of her illness, of course. She told him she worried for his safety, that she had lost her husband to one revolution and didn't wish to lose her son to another.

She had been dead two days when he had read that, smiled and tossed the letter aside. Had he even replied?

We are perturbed by the alarming reports of slaves rebelling in Saint-Domingue and fervently hope that the troubles will not spread to us here. And later, *When will you be returning to assume your responsibilities on the plantation?*

He had meant to go. To walk into his mother's embrace, to explain to them all that he could not do as they expected, that his ambitions were not the brittle dreams they had hoped a boy would outgrow, but the resolute intentions of a man who would not be swayed from his purpose. Why, only the previous week he had found himself outside the shipping office, and if he had not already been running late for a lunch-eon appointment with Chalier he would certainly have enqui-red about a berth in the new year.

Love was always urgent. How could he have thought it could be postponed, set aside on a shelf and occasionally taken down for dusting?

Among the great redemptive ideas that had revolutionised his century was the belief that everyone had the right to hap-piness. People were essentially good, and everyone, not just a privileged minority, had the right to profit from life. Stephen believed these things, certainly. Think carefully before you dismiss him as wrong or foolish.

Darkness had filled up the room behind him as the winter sky turned tender pink and mauve above the Seine. He left the window, lit candles, sat down at the table and began to write: *My love, I know we agreed it would be best never to meet again.*

1792

*T*he evening had been taken up with a party to celebrate Marianne Linguet's forty-fifth birthday. Sitting at her mirror, Claire congratulated herself on avoiding the colour that half the women in the room had been wearing, *boue de Paris*: it did nothing to flatter the complexion. Instead, she had chosen a delicate mushroom-pink shift. When she ceded to her hostess's entreaties and stood up to sing, she was aware of the way the men gazed at her and the women watched the men.

She yawned, and wished that the girl, who was new and slow, would hurry up and finish brushing out her hair.

Marianne had worn diamond earrings, a present from her husband. 'There are no better jewels for an ageing face, my dear – not that yours will need any ornament even when you're twice my age.' Was that true? Claire studied her reflection, put a hand up to her cheek. Lately she had fancied she detected . . .

Hubert came in and ordered the maid to leave them.

'Really – can't it wait until tomorrow?' Claire seized the brush, dragging it through her curls.

He was moving about, picking things up and putting them down again. Fingering the velvet ribbon she had worn in her hair, he said casually, 'We leave for England in a fortnight.'

She swung around to face him. He opened the blue-and-white Chinese jar she kept on her mantelpiece and peered inside. When he set it down again, he left off the lid. 'It's all arranged.' He smiled at her; he had reason to exult. 'Sébastien and Anne too – but they'll travel separately, of course. The permits have arrived. You're the wife of Citizen Laurent, a

135

textile manufacturer, travelling to Lancashire to study the latest advances in machinery. Rather good that, don't you think?' Courage, discernment, taking control: blood told, every time. He examined himself in the mirror and lifted his jaw.

'I hadn't realised you were so very drunk.'

He continued to sway above her. But at least he had stopped grinning.

'It's utterly ridiculous ... You know what happens to émigrés. We'll lose everything: this house, the estates, everything we have.'

He shrugged and resumed walking about. 'It's only a matter of time before they find an excuse to take everything from us anyway. As for the estates – I've talked to Duval, he's a good fellow. We've drawn up the papers: I make him a gift of La Brousse and Lupiac, in return for faithful services, which should be enough to keep them out of the Revolution's clutches until we come back. None of this will last – you'll see. There'll be war in a couple of months, the Austrians won't keep dragging their feet. Any insult to the Queen is an insult to the Hapsburg blood.'

'They've been slow to take offence so far.'

'You'll see. They'll declare war before the summer, and the Revolution will be over by the end of the year. You'll see.'

'It's preposterous. Where are we to go? How shall we live?'

'Sébastien's aunt is married to an Englishman. They're expecting you.' He picked up the string of pearls she had worn that evening and dangled it just out of her reach. 'Don't forget to pack these – and all the others.'

She shrank from his breath as he bent over her.

He misunderstood. 'Oh, there's no cause for concern. It's all arranged. Considerable sums have found their way across the Channel. Enough to keep you in knick-knacks until we return.'

'You tell me now, a fortnight before you expect me to leave ... everything. How long have you been planning this?'

'Since the summer,' he said proudly. 'Since Varennes. Sébastien and I put our heads together. Why do you think I've spent so much time in Blois of late?'

'And I suppose the two of you intend enlisting with the royalists.'

'Most of the officers in our regiment are already across the border. Condé's army is a professional one.' He saw himself on a caparisoned horse, giving and receiving orders. 'Our first cannon shots will sound the Revolution's death rattle. Paris will fall by Christmas at the latest. You'll see.'

'*Stop* saying that.'

'We should have gone in '89.' He stuck his finger into one of her creams, rubbed the pink lotion into the back of his hand and sniffed the result.

'There's a death warrant out on all émigrés.'

'By the time we're back in France there'll be a death warrant out on all revolutionaries. You'll see.'

'I can't ... I won't ... Olivier is so delicate – England is damp, it'll be the worst place for him.'

'Nonsense. Anyway, we're going – it's all arranged.'

'What about Father, and my sisters: what will happen to them?'

'Nothing. Nothing that wouldn't happen if we stayed.'

'I won't ... I can't ... The journey will be too much for me.'

He laughed. 'We're talking about England, not the Antipodes.'

'It would be dangerous. I'm not well.' She got to her feet. 'I'm expecting a child.'

He stared. He stood still.

'You know how ill I was with Olivier.' Claire's voice was defiant. But she wouldn't look at Hubert.

'How long have you known?'

'A few days. A week. I wasn't sure, at first.'

'When ...?'

For some seconds, she hesitated. Then she told him the truth.

She watched him make the calculation. She held her hands together in front of herself and waited for him to speak.

Hubert opened his mouth. But almost at once, he closed it again.

*S*unday afternoon in April.

Sophie and her friend Isabelle Ducroix are strolling in the park, the gravel crunching softly under their feet. The elms have turned a tender green. They stretch in long, pleasing avenues towards the fountain, and beyond to the steps and marble balustrade that affords fine views of the countryside around Castelnau. Pigeons preen themselves on forbearing statues. There are nursemaids with babies, and a woman selling lemonade. An old man has come to an inexplicable standstill in the middle of a path, his hands folded on his stick. Entire families are airing themselves. Small boys chase each other with ear-splitting whoops. A soldier bends over a girl, whispering. All over the town, all over the country in fact, soldiers are making reckless promises; France has just declared war on Austria.

Isabelle is wearing red-, white- and blue-striped shoes with elegant low heels, and her white cotton skirt is printed with posies of poppies and cornflowers. Sophie, in old-fashioned green, is all admiration.

Two young men lounging under the trees nudge each other. 'I wouldn't mind tucking that in my buttonhole,' declares one of them. 'Nor in my trousers,' replies the other.

The young women – though Isabelle, at thirty-four, can scarcely be described as such – stare stonily ahead. Once safely past, they exchange glances and smile.

'Last week, in that draper's shop,' says Isabelle, 'the one on the rue Royale –'

'You mean, the rue Nationale.'

'Of course, the rue Nationale. The new assistant called me Madame. He didn't think twice about it, didn't hesitate. I suppose it's a while since I've passed for Mademoiselle but the others know to pretend.'

'You should have threatened to have him arrested for not addressing you as Citizen.' And, as they turn into an alley that runs at right angles to the first, 'Look at that!'

A toddler sitting in the middle of the path is being buried by her brother, a fat child with red curls. Kneeling beside her, he heaps generous scoops of dirt and gravel over his sister's legs. The toes of her tiny white shoes, streaked brown, stick up out of the dusty earth; she contemplates them with interest, waving her hands and cooing.

'I always feel sorry for ugly children,' says Isabelle, 'I know what's in store for them. Just like a piglet, poor thing.'

A stout woman arrives in a flurry of lilac silk and exclamations. She hauls the piglet to his feet and smacks him, picks up the baby, tries in vain to dust her off, scolds both children.

Sophie and Isabelle move on.

'How is Claire?'

Sophie sighs. 'Like with Olivier, but worse.' She foresees months of trays and being at fault.

'She must be worried for Hubert,' says Isabelle, fishing.

'I suppose so,' says Sophie without conviction. 'A great cartload of their furniture arrived yesterday from Toulouse. Two of the satinwood chairs were damaged. Jacques's hidden them in the attic. We haven't dared tell Claire, she loves those chairs.'

'Should we be knitting undergarments for our soldiers?' asks Isabelle.

'Anything knitted by me would constitute an unpatriotic act.'

'They say it's only a matter of time before Prussia comes to the aid of the Austrians.' Isabelle peers up at Sophie from under her parasol. 'Will you be glad – if the royalists win the war and everything goes back to the way it was?'

'It can't go back to the way it was,' says Sophie. 'Anyway, there's a lot that hasn't changed – just as many people go hungry now as in '89.'

'Even the Assembly can't determine the harvests.'

139

'But it could control the distribution of grain or set the price of flour.'

'Next you'll be tucking up your skirts and sacking the grocers' shops.'

'Why not? We must strive to be modern,' says Sophie, stooping to trail a hand in the fountain. 'It's expected of women without husbands.'

Isabelle says nothing.

A pigeon is drinking from the basin: not with quick dips of its beak, like other birds, but drawing in a constant flow of water. It rolls its eye at Sophie and she flicks iridescent beads in its direction.

Wide shallow steps take them to the balustrade where Castelnau falls away: first tiles, chimneys, walls, then trees in their arpeggios of green, the boughs still visible between the leaves. To the south-east, beyond the river, the church tower at Montsignac can just be glimpsed.

Isabelle, short, thin, plain, places her hand next to Sophie's on the marble. 'I have something to tell you.' Her nails are pretty, pale-pink ovals with little shiny half-moons. 'I'm engaged to be married.'

'You can't be,' says Sophie before she can stop herself.

'His name is Louis Peronne. You don't know him. A cousin – well, one of those people you call cousin, although they're not really. A pharmacist. Father would have preferred a professional man but I'm not exactly spoilt for choice. Louis is a widower. Two sons, both married and living in Cahors. He's from here, he returned about eight months ago, after his wife died.' Isabelle says steadily, 'He's fifty-six.'

'It's wonderful news. I hope you'll be tremendously happy, I'm sure you will.' Sophie runs a finger up and down the back of her friend's hand, pats her wrist. How extraordinarily warm it is, more like July than April.

'I'd like to have children,' says Isabelle, 'before it's too late.'

'Yes.'

'He seems kind.'

She bends to kiss Isabelle. 'He'll have to answer to me if he isn't.'

A man standing nearby is instructing his son: 'When looking at a view,' he explains, 'one finds the symmetry and admires it.' The boy, who must be about eight, has exactly the same earnest face as his father. He stares at the statues, the alleys, the people, the birds, the glancing light, the fresh-leaved elms. 'Is that it? Over there, by the water?'

So the moment rights itself, and Sophie and Isabelle look at each other and smile.

'I wanted to get married as soon as possible,' says Isabelle, 'I've waited long enough. But Louis will have a grandchild soon and his daughter-in-law doesn't want to travel in the hot weather, so we've decided on September. Just think, Sophie – I'll be a grandmother before I'm a mother.'

They make their way back down into the park, where the soldier is walking arm-in-arm with his girl, on whose bright hair the light falls like honey. Sophie looks away. Now I'm the only one, she thinks.

'I have a confession,' says Isabelle, drawing closer. 'You must promise not to laugh.' Kind Isabelle, who wishes to make Sophie the present of some small folly. 'All autumn and winter, I imagined – well, I found myself thinking of Joseph Morel. Sometimes before breakfast. When I had that fever, you remember, he called almost daily and I ... Did you suspect anything?'

Sophie shakes her head.

'I kept finding reasons for mentioning his name. I was sure you'd noticed.' Ecstatic sparrows are fluttering in the dirt at the foot of a tree, chirping wildly. 'Not that I ... I knew he looked on me as nothing more than his patient. It was ... I don't know, a kind of madness.' She takes Sophie's arm. 'It's quite different with Louis. With Louis,' she says firmly, 'there's nothing like that.'

Then, because her friend still says nothing: 'Do you think it was very foolish of me?'

'No,' says Sophie, 'no, not at all.'

141

efore Brutus, she had been afraid of the dark. Her sister would leave a candle burning in her room at night, and then worry. A blurred picture at the edge of Mathilde's memory showed Sophie tiptoeing into her room to check that the bed-curtains hadn't caught fire; her hair was spread out over her shoulders, which were wrapped in something blue.

Sophie insisted that moths had got at the Indian shawl and that it had been given away far too long ago for Mathilde, who was only a baby at the time, to remember. And in any case she had never worn it, said Sophie, it had belonged to Claire, it had been sent to her from Pondicherry by her godfather. Matty had no doubt heard the story of how he always sent Claire a present for her name-day until, when she was twelve, a sandalwood box had arrived and in it a note, in his spiky, near-indecipherable hand, announcing that he had met a sadhu, a wandering holy man, and intended to close down his warehouse and set out on a pilgrimage to a cave that lay high above the world in the northern snows at the other end of that country. And that was the last anyone ever heard of him.

But Mathilde was sure she had seen the blue shawl . . . Only, when she tried to look directly at the picture, it refused to stay still. All the same, she was sure.

Beside her, Brutus shifted and groaned. She put her hand on his warm flank, feeling its slow rise and fall.

Sometimes he frightened her, waking her with a howling bark, leaping down to growl furiously at the window. Whenever that happened she forced herself to get out of bed and look outside, standing to one side of the window and peering out at the garden's assorted shapes, velvet-dark or lit by the moon's lemony glow.

Usually after a few minutes his tail and ears would sag, and he would leap back into the middle of the bed so that she had to push him aside to climb in. But sometimes he would scratch at the door and pad away when she opened it, returning long after she had clambered back in under her quilt, so that she didn't always succeed in staying awake for him.

Rats, she told herself, or owls, or a village cat. You had to go up into the mountains to find wolves, there were none around here, she was no longer a little girl to be frightened by the stories Berthe told over the fire in winter.

But one night, a moonless one, she supposed, and at the deepest, stillest hour, it wouldn't be rats or owls or cats. Not even wolves.

Brutus would warn her, of course, well before they entered the courtyard, perhaps even at the moment they turned into the lane. She would look out of the window and as soon as she saw the torchlight she would know what to do.

In one corner of her room was a low, dark-panelled door. It opened to reveal not the expected cupboard, but a steep flight of stairs that led up to one of the big attics. That was how she intended to escape, snatching up the candle from beside her bed, pausing only to lock the staircase door behind her; she had transferred the key to the other side, in readiness. Brutus and she would be safe in the attic by the time they pounded on the front door. Long before they had finished downstairs.

Would they look for her? She rather thought they would: they would know she was missing from their count. Both attics were even more cluttered these days with Claire's things, which was convenient. There were trunks, a wardrobe, a bureau with a broken leg, innumerable chairs, tables stacked one on top of each other, two firescreens, a sofa covered with a dust-sheet, paintings heaped face down on the floorboards.

Or would flight be easier if she remained concealed on the staircase, slipping out through her bedroom once they were occupied elsewhere? The stairs were low and narrow, even if they broke down the door they would have difficulty climbing up, they would have to bend double and they might not bother.

But somehow she thought they would.

She pulled her bolster over her head. Better the far attic. She had considered one of the trunks, but was afraid of not being able to breathe, and the lids were heavy, what if she dropped one, fumbling in her haste to open it, and they heard? But there was a large basket, ancient and with its wickerwork coming undone along one edge, but still sturdy. It had contained china figurines wrapped in an old curtain, a wooden tray and a pair of brass candlesticks. She got rid of everything except the curtain, half-filled the basket with more curtains, a tablecloth and an old quilt which trailed feathers. She dragged the basket to a corner away from the window, where shadows lay and the roof sloped down. A roll of carpet – heaved into position with considerable effort – two upturned chairs, a music stand, and a birdcage balanced on a footstool made it decidedly awkward to reach the basket. If you hadn't practised.

Before climbing in with Brutus and drawing the quilt over them, she would cross the attic and open the door. They would think she had fled that way, running down the back stairs and somehow slipping past them into the night.

And afterwards? She wouldn't be fooled by the stillness of the house into going downstairs at once. They might have left a guard outside the attic door or in the passage at the bottom of the stairs. She would stay where she was all night, the next day too if necessary; she had placed a bottle of water in the basket, and a bag of walnuts.

When she was absolutely sure it was safe, they would creep down the stairs. They wouldn't look in any of the rooms. They would let themselves out by the kitchen door, and run. They would live like outlaws in the forest. Brutus would catch rabbits, she would eat berries and nuts, and steal grapes when they ripened in the vineyards. In winter, they would find a woodsman's hut; she would take the quilt with her for warmth, and build a fire with twigs and pine cones.

Perhaps they would make their way to the sea.

Rinaldi would find them, one day. They would travel together, all three of them, to distant lands, where men had skin like yellow silk and roses bloomed all year round.

Claire, Olivier, Jacques, Berthe: she sacrificed them with a shrug, she couldn't save the entire household. Her father she hesitated over, but her father slept downstairs, he couldn't run, he was big, there would be no room for him in the basket.

Which left Sophie. Sophie's bedroom was next to hers. There would be time to warn her. But her sister would be slow with sleep and when she finally understood she would want to rouse the others, and by then ...

Whenever Mathilde reached this point in her deliberations she squirmed and shifted under her bedclothes. But there was nothing she could do: she was the youngest of three sisters, so she was the one who would be saved. That was the way it happened in every story.

Brutus rose and arched his back, releasing a gust of his smell – nutty, grassy, indefinably warm – and resettled himself with his head on her stomach.

She was asleep before he began to snore.

*I*t was a breech birth and that was not the only complication. The midwife sent for him just after midnight. He fell into his bed at five, exhausted, exhilarated, the woman and her baby asleep three streets away.

The knocking woke him from a dream in which he had found a swan in the street, its entrails spilling out into the mud. These entrails were soft and glowing, and not entangled but forming discrete strands of pearly, mauve-pink cord; at the end of each one dangled a tiny ivory playing card, and he bent anxiously over them, because if he could only . . .

He opened the door to Ricard, who had to duck his head to enter. 'Lying abed on the Lord's day? Isn't that a sin?'

'What's happened?' He was still half in the meshes of his dream – the glowing colours, the message in the cards – and reaching for his jacket.

'An emergency, doctor: it's past eleven and we're in danger of missing the trout.'

He poured water into a basin, splashed his face, rubbed his eyes.

Ricard slapped him on the shoulder: 'Hurry up, hurry up.'

The china rattled on the washstand.

On Sunday afternoons he usually went to the former guildhall where volunteers from the Club met to read aloud from the newspapers or the Assemby's decrees for the benefit of the patriotic citizens gathered there. He reminded Ricard of this, as they wandered up and down the bank of the river, choosing their spot.

'It's June,' came the rejoinder, 'let some other bugger do the work.'

Ricard, whose language was as prim as a spinster's, who frowned when other men swore! But it was obvious that the pork butcher was in high good humour, whistling his way past the last straggling houses and small market plots, across shoulder-high fields of wheat, meadows crowded with marsh marigolds, and so to a bend in the sunlit river.

They settled near a line of poplars, not far from a spot where willows came down to the water. 'The fish make their home there, in the banks in the shade –' Ricard cocked his thumb – 'but when the mayfly rise they come out into the sun and gorge themselves.'

They took off their boots and stockings, rolled up their trousers and waded out into the clear, brown-green river. Something tickled Joseph's toes: he looked down and saw tiny darting shapes, and silver beads attached to his calves, one to each floating hair. His feet on the dark gold sand were broad white fish feeding belly up.

Ricard, a few yards downstream from him, hooked the first trout: a swirl of bubbles, a tremendous rush, a twist of silver-brown. By the time they wanted to eat they had four fish. Joseph had caught one of them. Before wrapping it in leaves and setting the basket in the shallows, he ran a proud finger over its cold, mottled-green back, the pink spots on its plump sides. 'You landed the biggest of the lot – well over half a pound,' applauded Ricard, hefting it on his palm.

They ate bread, garlic sausage ('a mixture of pork and beef, lightly smoked'), a pot of rillettes, and thyme-dusted goat cheeses that had melted despite the shade. They shared a bottle of sharp, yellow-green wine.

Ricard leant against a poplar and smoked his pipe.

Joseph, mooching barefoot further up the bank, decided that he spent too long in rooms where sunlight penetrated not at all, or parsimoniously, in pale, grudging lozenges that flared briefly on a floor, a dingy wall. He came across a plum tree and returned with his shirt full of sweet golden fruit. He tilted his head back, and the juice ran down his throat.

Afterwards, he lay on his back, took off his spectacles and stared up into the green and silver blur. Perhaps he slept, a little.

Ricard showed him the place upstream where the river-bed shelved away from the shore. Having stripped down to his knee-length drawers, the pork butcher launched himself with a shout, arms raised, sending up long tatters of leaping water. Joseph, who could not swim, lay on his elbows in the shallows where it was deliciously warm and watched Ricard splash strongly out across the river. His bad leg seemed not to impede him in water; he turned on his back, waved to Joseph, floated in the sunlight.

Joseph found himself humming under his breath, that new song calling Frenchmen to arms. The stones on the riverbed were the colour of his trout. He watched Ricard, in mid-stream, blow waterspouts. There were dragonflies like enamelled light.

He rolled over onto his stomach and moved his limbs about gently. Clenching his jaw, holding his breath, he plunged his head and came up spluttering. The pork butcher scooped up handfuls of water and flung them at his face. He tried to retaliate, but Ricard dived under and away to emerge dripping, beaded in light, tawny, massive, magnificent.

They ate the last of the sausage and finished off the plums.

Ricard told him he had grown up in the country, only moving to Castelnau when he was nine and apprenticed to an uncle. Tamping tobacco into the bowl of his pipe, he talked, not as Joseph would have expected, of grinding hardship or hunger or exploitation, but of the delights of his rural childhood. He and his brothers ranged over the countryside, chasing each other through the woods, bird-nesting, setting illegal traps for rabbits. He learnt to swim and fish. Sent out into the fields all day at the age of six to guard the crops, he taught himself to identify birds, their various songs. There were five children, and his father was a day labourer with no land of his own. Yet Ricard smoked his pipe and spoke, with a half-smile, only of hazel-nutting in the autumn, of rooks in the elm-tops, of the mole he had captured by a stream, its huge pink hands and tapering snout. It came to trust him, would waddle squeaking up to him and take worms from his fingers.

Shadows shifted, lengthened.

A moorhen drifted by.

Joseph's flesh smelt differently: of river water, river mud.

Afterwards, when it was all over, and for the rest of his life, he would remember that day, how it had begun with a dream.

Its colours were gold and green.

It tasted of plum juice, licked from the wrist.

A friend's voice was detailing happiness.

Stephen appeared, holding a rose. Its purple petals were freckled with mauve: Belle de Crécy – she identified it automatically. He was incapable of setting foot in the garden without picking her roses. Whenever that happened, like all gardeners she was half flattered, half resentful.

'I've been meaning to ask,' he said. 'Whatever happened to your China roses?'

The Schoolmaster's Rose had exceptionally large double flowers of a soft, deep pink shading into lilac. Sophie went on removing the faded blooms, cutting cleanly through stem after stem with her knife, jagged with absurd happiness. He cared enough to remember.

'I sold a dozen plants last year. And the same grower took twice as many this spring. He says he has buyers clamouring for them from as far as England and Holland.' Adding, 'Although the war will put an end to that, I suppose.'

She was telling herself that he was only there to fill in time. Claire, claiming dizziness and a headache, had refused to come downstairs. I'm the one he takes an interest in when he has nothing better to do, said Sophie, striving for calm.

He stroked her chin with the soft purple flower. 'I've decided to move to Castelnau in September.'

'Don't do that,' she said. 'I mean – with that rose.' Her hand was unsteady. She slid the knife into its sheath and dropped it into her basket of brown petals.

He sighed. 'Don't be angry with me, Sophie, everyone is angry with me. My brother rails at me in letters, Charles advises me to go home, Claire won't talk to me. Last week, just before I left Paris, two soldiers stopped me in the street insisting I was a spy – did I tell you?'

'Yes, twice.'

'They might have killed me there, you know, outside my own studio. If not for my concièrge, who came out and shouted that she'd tell their mothers. That sort of thing wouldn't happen here. Your family is known in Castelnau. And my association with you.'

'Why not Bordeaux, in that case?' asked Sophie. She had decided, months ago, that what she felt was bearable as long as he didn't know she felt it.

He tossed the rose into her basket. 'Because my uncle will hunt up shipping timetables and talk about duty, while my aunt will feel compelled to find me a wife. She has innumerable god-daughters she'd like to see settled.'

'Oh?'

'At least three gawky girls who giggle whenever they set eyes on me. Each one plainer than the last.'

'I can see that would be very trying.'

'Sophie, I'd never have guessed it, but you're heartless.'

'But what will you do in Castelnau?'

'I'll work hard.' There was a faraway look in his eyes. Sophie felt in imminent danger of gawking. 'I could give drawing lessons. I would meet people, become part of the life of the town. It'll be quite different from Paris.'

'Yes.'

'And I'd be close to ... to Montsignac.'

'I see.'

'I'd be delighted to give Matty lessons.'

'Have you seen her drawings?'

'With guidance, there's no one who can't improve.'

A rose that overflowed from the corner where it had been planted, arching long canes into the light, reached out and plucked at his shirt.

'Stay still.' Frowning, she worked the thorn free.

'Dear Sophie – I know you'll always be good to me.' And before she could turn away, he kissed her.

Because Claire wouldn't answer the question that haunted him.

Because he knew, anyway.

Because, obscurely, he sensed the balance of power between them shifting and sought to assert himself.

Because it's always agreeable to give pleasure where no effort is required.

Because Sophie was there.

Because of the sunlight, the roses.

Really, it was the lightest of kisses.

When she drew away and looked at him he began talking about a play he had seen in Paris.

The rose Sophie was still holding was a variety at least three centuries old: vigorous, branching, informally shaped, long-flowering, sweet-scented, many-petalled. Its flowers show muddled centres, and are a soft yet warm pink on opening; later, the petals bend backwards and fade to a delicate cream-pink, the deeper tint remaining always, however, in the heart of the bloom.

In French this rose is known as *Cuisse de nymphe émue*. After its characteristic colouring, of blood under creamy white skin, suggestive – why not? – of the subtle flush spreading up the inner thigh of a nymph in a state of arousal. A typically French conceit: erudite, erotic, excessive.

The English, preferring a more decorous metaphor, calls it Maiden's Blush.

*I*n the upstairs room at the Café de la Victoire they sat around the table drafting their letter to the King. Occasionally, a customer with time on his hands would enquire after the origin of the café's name. No one could say with any certainty, least of all Bonnefoy, the lugubrious proprietor, who spoke only when speech was unavoidable. Nevertheless, as the Prussians advanced that summer with Prussian steadiness, the Victoire did good business; as if sympathetic magic might reverse the fortunes of the revolutionary army. Or perhaps simply because it was hot, or because Bonnefoy's eldest daughter was exceedingly pretty, or because with a war on, and *la patrie* officially declared endangered, people were looking for distraction. Takings at the municipal theatre were also up.

It was Mercier who insisted on having the window closed, despite the heat. He was given to secrets, adored the whiff of conspiracy. Joseph, sweating in shirt-sleeves, wondered irritably why Ricard indulged this absurdity – the window gave onto a fifteen-foot drop, a strip of foul-smelling, rat-infested courtyard and a sheer brick wall. Anyway, their business was scarcely clandestine: the letter would be read aloud and formally passed at the meeting the following night. But the pork butcher nodded at Mercier, and latched the window himself.

It was Mercier, too, who had the sheet of paper in front of him and was scribbling. '*Your duties are our rights. We shall take whatever steps are necessary to protect the liberties we have fought for; we shall tolerate no opposition; we shall punish any traitors, whoever they are.*'

Tes devoirs. Your duties. Joseph knew it was childish, the pleasure he took in the use of the familiar form to address the King, but he couldn't help smiling. He rolled the phrase on his tongue, relishing it like a sweet: *Tes devoirs.*

'Did you say something?' Mercier didn't bother hiding his impatience. There was always that sense that at any moment the air between these two might strain and snap apart.

'*Liberties we have fought for?* I would write *gained.*'

The others nodded approval. Mercier shrugged, crossed out his phrase and replaced it with Joseph's suggestion.

Luzac, sitting opposite Mercier, craned his neck to read what had been written. 'Wouldn't *your people's rights* sound better? That's what I'd put: *Your duties are your people's rights.*'

'Would you really? That's interesting. But the point is, surely, that we're not his people, he doesn't own us, whatever he or –' here Ricard inserted an infinitesimal pause – 'the reactionary element might choose to think.'

Luzac's pale moon features turned paler, moonier. He drummed his fingers on the table.

'I agree. No change.' Mercier read over the letter. 'But perhaps, yes, *eliminate* instead of *punish*, don't you think?' His pen raced, making the amendment.

Drafting was inevitably a lengthy process. Prodded perhaps by this reflection, the lawyer Chalabre spoke for the first time. 'We should make it quite plain that we're accusing the King directly and personally. Write something like, *By your actions, you are paralysing the Constitution.*'

Tes actions. Joseph smiled, under cover of wiping his mouth.

'Excellent.' Mercier continued, reading aloud as he wrote: '*We, the patriotic citizens of Castelnau, will do everything in our power to resist such sabotage.*'

'*Your* sabotage,' corrected Chalabre.

'*Your treacherous* sabotage.' Joseph went on: '*We have –* no, *the people of France have confounded your schemes; we shall not hesitate to . . . to overthrow you.*'

'*Overthrow* is weak,' said Luzac. 'It makes us sound timid. What about . . . *eradicate*?'

Ricard, filling his pipe, caught Joseph's eye, and smiled. Luzac, the radical!

'*Destroy*,' said Mercier, writing furiously. '*We shall not hesitate to destroy you.*' He had added a newspaper, *Le Citoyen*, to his printing business and now devoted most of his time to it. Castelnau devoured his inflammatory editorials and the articles he wrote under a variety of pseudonyms. Working from the Assembly's driest pronouncements he transformed politics into a quivering, ineluctable passion: you looked into your heart and found the Revolution already ensconced there.

Chalabre was eating gherkins, of which he was inordinately fond. 'That'll do,' he said, licking his fingers like a cat, 'that'll do very well indeed.'

Overweight, charmless, Louis XVI wandered around his prison-palace like a slow-moving, slow-witted animal while the chestnuts put out tentative green leaves beneath his windows. He vetoed the Assembly's death sentence on royalist émigrés suspected of conspiring against the fatherland. He vetoed the decree requiring priests to swear loyalty to the Constitution, or else; then he opposed the demand that offenders be deported at the request of twenty parishioners. Compounding stupidities, he vetoed a proposal from his Minister of War that an armed camp of several thousand revolutionaries from the provinces be set up in Paris to defend the capital from enemy attack.

Like the other provincial clubs, Castelnau's Patriots were reduced to venting their outrage in ink. The letters came from all over France that summer, tense with righteous indignation, trembling with thwarted purpose.

Parisians wasted no time invading the Tuileries. Louis le Faux – le Faux-Pas, in Mercier's memorable phrase – was made to wear a red bonnet and drink to the health of the sovereign people. A way of life vanished down the round white royal throat.

Chalabre opened his knife and sliced up a gherkin. He pushed the plate into the centre of the table. No one helped themselves. He was going to Paris and would be carrying their letter with him. They thought of boulevards, crowds, men running into each other in vast corridors and speaking urgently, their heads close together. They couldn't help hating the lawyer, a little.

A cat yowled in the courtyard, startling Mercier into blotting his fair copy of the letter.

Ricard said quietly, 'It'll do very well for the moment. But we shouldn't deceive ourselves into thinking that it'll achieve anything. As long as the King lives, he'll serve as a focus for anti-revolutionary sentiment.'

He wasn't looking at anyone in particular, but Luzac began drumming again.

'Don't do that – it's bloody irritating,' Mercier flared instantly. Joseph, noting the shadows under his eyes, wondered how much sleep the printer was getting.

Luzac spread his left hand slowly on the table. They watched him, waiting to see what he would say. Then they found themselves looking away from the other sleeve, pinned up to the stump at the mayor's shoulder. Luzac smiled. Petitions protesting the invasion of the palace and the manhandling of the royal family had been circulated in Castelnau. He knew Ricard suspected him of being behind at least one of them. But he had given his right arm to the Revolution; which of them could claim as much? His pale plump fingers hovered over the plate of pickled cucumbers.

Having knocked first, Bonnefoy's daughter came in. She smiled at them all, gathered up dirty glasses on her tray, asked if they had everything they wanted, wasn't there anything she could bring them? Leaning towards Mercier, she wiped down the table in front of him.

Joseph tried not to stare. But was mesmerised by a drop of sweat trickling into the exquisite crease running down into her blouse. Without thinking, he took off his spectacles; hastily replaced them.

Mercier said something to the girl, who had come round the table and was standing very close to him. She shook her head, laughing. His hand slid up to rest on her buttocks, and her body turned at once towards his, opening, inviting as a flower.

She must be ... fifteen? sixteen? Her skin had not yet lost that quality of simultaneously absorbing and reflecting light.

Joseph willed himself to look away, concentrated on refilling his glass.

At the door she turned one last time and blew Mercier a kiss. The printer waved at her, smiling, his sharp-featured face unclenched.

It wasn't the first time Joseph had witnessed the effect of Mercier's sloe eyes and dark, unruly hair on women. Good looks: where was the revolution to right the unfairness of that lottery?

Ricard's voice was even, uninflected: 'Well then, if we're all satisfied ... Time we were getting home to our wives.'

Chalabre and Luzac murmured, nodded, began gathering their belongings. The lawyer picked up the last gherkin, ate it in two bites and wiped his fingers on a napkin.

Mercier and Ricard stared at each other across the table. After a moment the printer looked down and shuffled his papers together. 'I think I'll have something to eat,' he said to no one in particular, 'before going back to the press.'

Joseph recalled that Mercier's wife had given birth to their first child some four or five months previously. And hadn't someone – Ricard? – told him she was pregnant again?

The pork butcher got to his feet. 'You work too hard,' he said to Mercier, 'there's nothing to be gained by driving yourself into the ground. You should look after yourself – what would we do without *Le Citoyen* to speak our visions?'

Mercier shrugged. But glanced up, appeased. 'There's always so much to do. Next week's edition is not even half ready.'

'Which reminds me.' Ricard stepped across to the window and paused with his hand on the catch. 'Didn't you tell me our friend here had offered to write something for you? Sanitation and Disease wasn't it, doctor?'

Joseph had been counting out coins to add to the pile on the table. His cheeks grew hot, he muttered an unintelligible phrase, dropped a coin and dived thankfully under the table to retrieve it. Some time in the winter he had suggested the article to Mercier, who had frowned and said, 'I'll let you know.' That was the end of it, he had thought. But obviously the printer had mentioned it to Ricard: sneering, no doubt, at Joseph's temerity, at the idea that he could . . .

'A pertinent subject, don't you think? Just the sort of thing *Le Citoyen* needs to keep it grounded in everyday concerns. Practical advice along with discussion of the connection between illness and unsanitary living conditions. You could match it with an editorial denouncing landlords who shirk their responsibilities.'

Joseph put the coin in his pocket, reached for his bag, kept his head down. Mercifully, Chalabre and Luzac were already halfway down the stairs. He crept towards the door.

Ricard flung the window wide, stretched his arms out into the warm evening, then turned back towards the printer. 'I take it you have no objection?'

All Mercier's attention seemed to be fixed on the piece of paper he was tearing up into smaller and smaller shreds. Without looking up he snapped, 'It'll need editing, of course, that has to be understood.'

'I was referring to the window,' said Ricard, and left the room.

*H*er room, a corner one, has two windows: one overlooking the courtyard and park, the other opening eastwards to the village, stubble fields where geese have been put out to feed, near and far hills. There, beneath the wider view, is where Sophie is sitting. Has been sitting for – can it really be half an hour?

She forces herself to turn the drawing face down and slides it under the catalogue from Poitiers that lies open on her desk. Roses, at least, can be evaluated, sorted, classified.

The grower advertises thirty-eight varieties. The cheapest plants, a pink-and-red *Rosa mundi* for instance, cost twenty-four *sous*. The most expensive, at twelve *livres*, is a new rose, described as a Moss Provins: '*Égalité*. Handsome, rosy-red blooms, very double, well disposed on bush. Neat, upward-pointing foliage. Strong fragrance. Open growth. To four feet.' A rose that combines the spectacular blooms typical of Moss roses with the upright foliage of its Provins ancestor ... But at that price, Égalité is well out of Sophie's reach. Anyway, it's bound to be mildew-prone like all Mosses, and 'open growth' is another way of saying it requires propping up.

Twelve *livres*! She wonders what Tassin is charging for her China roses, too few to be advertised in his catalogue. She had accepted thirty *livres* per dozen and congratulated herself on her acumen. I should have asked Rinaldi's advice, she thinks gloomily. As it is, I've nothing left over. And at once, because she's worried about money, she considers spending more by way of consolation: a Blanche de Belgique is very reasonably priced at two *livres* ...

'What are you doing?' Claire, sway-backed, wanders in

159

without knocking. She lowers herself with exaggerated care onto the bed, sighs, and after a little while, sighs again.

Sophie tells herself that she's not going to spring up, fetch cushions, rearrange pillows.

'Sophie,' says Claire faintly, 'my back ... Would you mind ...?'

Sophie springs up, fetches cushions, rearranges pillows. Recognising a pattern isn't the same as altering it; acquiescence merely comes at a higher price.

By way of thanks, Claire repeats her original question. 'What are you doing?'

'Looking through a rose catalogue. How are you today?'

'As usual – bloated, tired, ugly.' Then, truthfully, 'Bored.'

'Would you like me to read to you? Or I could get some mending and we could talk.'

'Oh, would you? But not a book – all those tales of virtue happily rewarded or tragically punished.'

'It doesn't have to be a novel. Sometimes the *Encyclopédie* can –'

'I should make an effort to finish embroidering that vest. Not that I really believe there'll be an end to this – I can't remember what life was like before this baby. My sewing's in my room. Or somewhere downstairs, perhaps. Would you ...?'

When Sophie returns, her sister is frowning. 'Is that Olivier crying? Have you seen him today?'

Sophie listens. 'Someone driving pigs up the lane. Angélique's taken Olivier for a walk. Down to the river, I think.'

'Was he wearing his warm shirt? I was right not to let him go to that terrible country, wasn't I? Poor Anne.'

Anne's last letter had brought the news that her new baby, the longed-for son, had died of a fever. They're saddened, of course, by this small, faraway tragedy but not in the least surprised. England is damp, miasmas, fog, disease invading your body with each breath; the wonder is that anyone manages to survive. And then, the food ...!

From Hubert or Sébastien, fighting with the anti-revolutionary forces, there has come no word. But Anne's letter said

160

that according to a French acquaintance, 'living like a pauper on a neighbouring estate, where he's employed as an under-gardener', their regiment was destined for Verdun.

But that was months ago, early in summer. Since then, the war has escalated. Treachery within its gates has seen Verdun fall to the unstoppable Prussians. The French artillery bombards the town daily, desperate to retake it. Panic skitters westward down the road to Paris. Chickens, grandmothers and sideboards have been loaded onto carts, everyone knows what will happen if their village falls to the enemy, the arteries leading to the capital are clotted with fear.

Claire never refers to the war, except to complain, like everyone else, of the shortages, the inconveniences, the prices. If she wonders about Hubert – under siege in the garrison at Verdun, floundering about in a field where the air is the colour of rust, lying somewhere on a wooded hill with leaves scorching overhead – if Claire thinks about these things, she doesn't say. Her dark head is bent over a small white garment, where tiny, exquisite stitches are describing a sage-green arabesque.

For no apparent reason, the thread in Sophie's needle tangles.

Claire launches into a story about her dressmaker in Toulouse, who claims to understand the significance of dreams. 'She told Marianne that dreaming of snakes meant a death in the family, and her mother's goldfinch died just two days later. Or was it eels, I can't remember.'

Of late, as the earth tilts away from the sun, the yearning has been dreamy, shot through with introspection. Sophie finds herself returning again and again to Stephen's drawing of her face. As if by studying herself as he envisioned her, she might at length learn ... what? the syntax of dignity? the grammar of consolation?

She has absorbed a good deal of literature about love and acknowledges that she doesn't exhibit any of the conventional symptoms. Stephen isn't her first thought on waking or her last as she closes her eyes. If he were to go away forever she knows she wouldn't die or go mad with grief. For whole stretches of time, she doesn't think of him at all. She finds him

161

charming, affectionate, eager to please; for all that, she recognises that he's self-indulgent and whimsical.

He is handsome, of course.

People who are not good-looking may react to physical beauty with envy or awe or dismissiveness. But never with indifference.

An inarticulate longing for perfection, as old as the race.

She knows, without turning her head, when he has entered a room or left it. She is aware of the rise and fall of his breath, she senses the movements of his eyelashes. Ten thousand invisible filaments run out from her body to his.

He reaches for a glass, a book, an apple.

She leans into space.

'Sophie, I wish you'd stop thinking about roses.' Claire is holding out two skeins of silk: 'Which one?'

'The violet.'

'Really? Oh no, I prefer the blue.'

A brand-new law had done away with the need for priests, churches, sacraments. Marriage was henceforth a civil contract. All that was required was a notice outside the town hall:

Announcing the marriage of Monsieur Louis Peronne (widower) and Mademoiselle Isabelle Ducroix (spinster) who intend to live together in lawful marriage and who today will present themselves at the municipal offices to reiterate their promise and have their intentions legalised by the laws of the State.

The room – like all municipal rooms – smelt of furniture polish, ink and sweat. It was dominated by an enormous statue of Hymen brandishing a wreath of flowers and a torch. Hand in hand, bride and groom stepped up onto a dais where a minor functionary wearing a tricolour sash informed them that marriage was like a conversation between two people, and he trusted theirs would be a long and happy one without any pauses.

How tiring it sounds, thought Sophie. She caught the eye of the groom's younger son, but he frowned and looked away.

The official, an earnest young man who sat up late thinking these things out, was telling the couple that the love of a man for his wife paralleled the love of the State for its citizens. After a pause, for the solemnity of the comparison to sink in, he put the traditional question to the bridal pair; together, they affirmed their intentions.

They were husband and wife.

The next couple stepped up. The young official scanned his jottings: *Duet. Couplet. Merging streams.* He wrote poetry on weekends and knew himself to be more than the sum of his municipal duties; still, he strove to carry them out as befitted one who was sensible to the beauty inherent in all things.

The day had been overcast, with a fine rain falling all morning. But as the bridal party stepped out into the square, the sun broke obligingly through dirty white clouds and the little knot of onlookers under the yellowing plane trees cheered. Brides in everyday attire with bonnets on their hair instead of orange blossoms took some getting used to. But at least the sun shone, keeping up tradition.

'Not exactly spring chickens, are they?' a woman remarked.

'Let's hope she doesn't find it's rusted up. He doesn't look the sort who'd be much use at picking a lock.'

Joseph nodded to Sophie from the other side of the room, where he stood with his back to the wall.

'This is ridiculous,' she said to herself and put down her glass, determined to set things straight.

But first, Isabelle: 'Dearest Sophie! Everyone's been exclaiming over my bouquet. Come and tell them about your China roses that flower in autumn.'

She breasted wave after wave of talk: the weather (unseasonable), foreigners (unnatural), Paris (unbearable), the cost of living (unspeakable), what things were coming to (unimaginable). By the time she reached Joseph, he was no longer alone.

'Sophie was there,' said Stephen, 'she witnessed it all. Love in a few legal phrases. Was he allowed to kiss her or did they just shake hands like trading partners at the conclusion of business?'

'Well, marriage is a kind of transaction, isn't it? Women gain security, men fidelity. And both are assured of respectability. Perhaps the new system is more honest: it lays the mechanism bare.'

She addressed the last remark to Joseph, with a smile. He stared at her – those spectacles! – and said nothing.

'You don't believe that, I know you don't.' Stephen selected

164

a tartlet from the plate he was waving about. 'What about the animating spark between two souls – ' indistinctly, through a mouthful of cheese and ham – 'what about love?'

'Love? Weren't we talking about marriage?'

'Now you're being sophisticated and I won't allow it. Cynicism is all very well in Paris but I refuse to entertain it in Castelnau. It has no part in my new life here.'

'Do you mean you've moved to Castelnau?' Joseph jammed his spectacles back into place. 'Settled here?'

Stephen nodded, chewed, swallowed, spoke. 'Three weeks ago yesterday. Wasn't it kind of Isabelle to invite me to her wedding? I've found four pupils already and been invited to address the Society for the Appreciation of Art.' Head on one side, he contemplated Joseph. 'I wonder, Morel: have you ever considered drawing lessons? With your knowledge of human anatomy . . .'

'Well? What's the verdict on Peronne?' Mathilde, appearing in their midst, helped herself to a tartlet. 'I asked his opinion of the notices setting out the Laws of Divorce and he said he hadn't observed them. Which I understood to be his way of telling me it wasn't a suitable topic for a young person of the fair sex.'

Joseph, unused to Mathilde, snickered into his drink.

She turned to him. 'What do you think of the new laws?'

'They're convenient. The municipality provides both the poison and the antidote.'

'Is that really how marriage strikes you?' asked Sophie. 'As a poison?'

He looked down, into his empty glass. 'Poison or prison, it often seems that way. Although there must be exceptions.'

'Of course there are!' Stephen, distressed, ran his fingers through his hair. An odd fellow, Morel, bleaker than he remembered. He cast around for an explanation and seized on one with relief. 'Naturally, as a physician you must be exposed to a great deal of unpleasantness.'

'I wonder,' said Mathilde, 'whether Claire will divorce Hubert?' In the crystal silence that greeted this remark, she looked at Joseph: 'Why don't you visit us any more? Is it because of Hubert fighting for the enemy? We don't approve either, you know. Although to be honest, we can't say we miss him.'

Joseph had turned brick-red.

'Stephen, Joseph, you're not to monopolise the prettiest girl in the room.' The bride, shiny with happiness, placed her hand with its bright new ring on Sophie's arm. 'Louis's nephew is here, he's longing to meet you.'

Mathilde said, 'We were just talking about your husband and wondering if he's good enough for you.'

Before Isabelle could draw her away, Sophie turned to Joseph: 'Please come and see us.'

He smiled and looked into his glass. The heart was only a muscle, he refused to accord it undue significance. But Dr Ducroix's wine was excellent. He intended to drink quite a lot of it before the evening ended.

On the night Isabelle goes to her pharmacist's kisses, the killings take place.

For weeks the former convent – which now serves as a holding jail – has been filling up ominously. The arrests are made on warrants issued by a tribunal presided over by the lawyer Chalabre. It has been created for the specific purpose of trying traitors – that is, those who have perpetrated crimes against the besieged nation. Refractory priests who persist in refusing to swear the civil oath have been dragged out of the seminaries, colleges and country churches where they were lying suspiciously low. The royalist press has been effectively closed down, its printers and journalists rounded up. Relatives, friends, dependants and known associates of Caussade and his supporters have been arrested. Suspects are not difficult to come by: a playwright whose very bad, very long verse-drama about the royal couple's flight to Varennes was booed off two days after it opened the previous winter; a Prussian watchmaker; a nonagenarian duchess; a waiter who has been reported for dubious witticisms.

The morning after Isabelle's wedding is clear-skied and mild. Saint-Pierre has breakfasted late on yards of bread, sweet cherry jam and purple figs in the company of Dr Ducroix at whose house he spent the night, staying on after Isabelle's husband gently but definitively drew her from her father's embrace.

Autumn has always been his favourite season. His grandfather used to tell him that as he grew older he would long for springtime, for blossom and quickening green. But spring promises so much, how can it help not living up to expectations? Autumn is unexacting, dependable, its leaves like so many responsibilities discharged and now unloosed, drifting quietly earthwards.

He finds himself taking streets that will bring him to the river. Why is that, he wonders, why are people drawn to water? Time and again he has seen it, people exhausted by hard work and hunger going out of their way to the quays, where they'll stare and stare at the river.

He thinks of the child who will soon be born, of Claire turned inwards as the time draws near and waiting, waiting.

Claire, his tiny, unimaginably perfect daughter. When she was born he wanted to hold her forever, wrapped up like that against the gale that was hurling roof-tiles into the streets, safe always, his beautiful, unfathomable girl. Only to discover, one day, that she had slipped unnoticed from his arms.

He suffers a momentary breathlessness, pain that vanishes as rapidly as it jolts him.

His inadequate heart.

He leans against a honey-coloured wall, and smiles because for once Ducroix drank more armagnac than he did.

Then he sees the bodies.

He has reached the place where a door in the convent wall gives onto the quays. The carts have been brought round here, where water sucks greedily at stone and wood and there are fewer passers-by – although the inevitable cluster of onlookers has formed to stare at what is being carried out into the sunlight.

There is a boy of perhaps fifteen whose genitals have been hacked off. A man with one very bright blue eye and a sticky hole where the other should be. A thing with curling black body hair and neither head nor limbs. A woman whose throat has been cut, another whose mauve tongue spills from her mouth like an obscenity. Several corpses lack arms, legs, hands – Saint-Pierre finds himself wondering where they could be and scanning the heaped carts for these missing parts, wanting to fit them together, make them whole.

He recognises and doesn't recognise a smashed-in face still oozing pulp: the Oracle, a malodorous old man with wild, flecked eyes and matted hair who bellows in the grain market in all weathers, detailing the nightmare hags and blood-splattered beasts that torment him, clawing at people until someone buys him a glass of gin and then another and then another.

There is the river smell, and overlaying it a different one, not unfamiliar. He thinks incongruously of doctors and sick-beds, before he sees the barrels the woman in the red cap is trundling in through the gate, and understands: they are washing the courtyard down with vinegar, disinfecting it.

Who for? he wonders. There can be no one left alive behind those walls.

His hands, like a baby's, are sketching small movements in front of his chest.

An official in a tricolour sash is supervising operations. 'Citizen Saint-Pierre' introduces himself, adding that he is 'an officer of the law'. 'What's happened here?' he asks, and his hand shoots out and clings to the other man's arm. 'What's happened?' he repeats, although what has happened is plain enough, and the fourth and final cart is now being loaded up.

The official is a young man – They are all young men! thinks Saint-Pierre, clutching more tightly at the uniformed arm – and not easily flustered. He looks at the man whose face is an odd, greyish hue and recognises the magistrate in whose courtroom he has stood often enough unremarked against a wall. Saint-Pierre is all right, as far as he knows, courteous to minor functionaries who run across him in the course of their duties. So the young man is polite and calm, politely and calmly disengaging his sleeve from the brown-spotted hand that has fastened itself to the fabric.

'An incident,' he explains. 'Some prisoners being escorted here last night were set upon by a group of armed men, who later found their way into the prison.'

'But this . . .' Saint-Pierre gestures at the carts, the terrible cargo. 'There are so many . . . Who . . .?'

The official has no orders to gloss over events, nor does he see any reason to do so. 'Traitors,' he says patiently, 'they were traitors. Plotting a royalist outbreak now that our soldiers have left for the front.'

'But you said there was an escort. And the prison guards – where were they?'

The young man sees that the carts are ready to move off. 'I wasn't here,' he says. 'Now if you would excuse me . . .'

Another official has emerged from the gate, and the two confer, checking something against a list. There is a discrepancy, a minor hitch. The second official disappears once more into the convent.

'How many dead?' asks Saint-Pierre.

'One hundred and eighty-seven,' replies the first official promptly. He has seen the tally on his colleague's list.

'How many people were being held here?'

He knows that too. 'One hundred and eighty-nine. We found a priest alive under some corpses and another fellow threw himself from a window. They'll be able to stand trial.'

'And the men who did this? Have they been arrested?'

The official looks at Saint-Pierre and feels a spurt of mingled pity and irritation. These old men, with their endless questions, nothing would ever get done if it were left to them. Then he sees, with relief, that his colleague has returned and is giving him the thumbs up. He issues the order for the carts to leave and takes a moment to savour the release of anxiety as they creak into motion. He is keen to display his capacity for the smooth and efficient execution of his duties. He has applied for promotion. He wants to get married in the spring.

'But the murderers?' cries Saint-Pierre. 'What are you doing to bring the murderers to justice?'

The official is moving off. But he turns to contemplate the old man with the beaky nose and dusty black coat whose time is so obviously over, there on the sunlit quay with the river at his back. 'I wouldn't say murderers,' says the young official politely, patiently, 'they were ordinary citizens. And as to justice, they were executing traitors.'

A cheer goes up from the bystanders as the last cart rattles past. The officials ride away. An invisible someone shuts the door in the wall.

Saint-Pierre lurches to the river.

A face wavers in the water.

The *Encyclopédie* was not considered suitable for pedagogy because it treated all knowledge with scientific impartiality. Thus, while it devoted page after page to useful considerations such as the declension of verbs and how to grind corn into flour, it dealt with subjects such as Generation in equally full and frank detail. Hence, for the core of her sister's formal education Sophie tended to fall back on works familiar to her from her own schooldays, like *The True Principles of Reading, Spelling and French Pronunciation, followed by A Little Treatise on Punctuation, the First Elements of Grammar and French Prosody, and by Selected Readings Suitable for Providing Simple and Easy Notions of All Branches of Our Knowledge* (Paris, 1763), by Nicolas-Antoine Viard.

It was no wonder Mathilde took matters into her own hands. The house was full of books and silverfish. Buffon and Jussieu could be relied on for natural history, Saint-Simon for gossip. Philosophy was amply represented – Montaigne, Erasmus, Diderot, Montesquieu, Voltaire, d'Alembert, Rousseau; it had quite usurped religion, which was reduced to a copy of Bossuet's *Sermons*. Her father's study yielded literature (Molière, Cervantes, Rabelais, Shakespeare, Ronsard, Dante), sturdy editions that were old when Saint-Pierre was young. Her sisters' bedrooms contributed novels, their flimsy pages bound in cheap sheepskin or simply folded into sixteen-page signatures and boxed. There were also oddities, such as popular hygiene (*Easy Instructions for the Care of the Mouth and the Conservation of the Teeth by Mr. Bourdet, A Dentist, followed by The Art of Looking After the Feet*). As for the

Encyclopédie she acquainted herself in private with certain articles, since naturally it didn't occur to anyone to take precautions against her doing so.

Above all, Mathilde took care to read newspapers. She never missed *Le Citoyen*, even though it skimped on murders. For instance, the latest edition carried only a paragraph about the cobbler who had strangled his landlady, the merest outline and not a single adjective. Political coverage, on the other hand, was detailed and Mathilde liked to be informed on all levels. 'The Assembly's been replaced by the Convention, the Patriots are calling themselves the Jacobins, and now half the villages around have given themselves new names. Why do we need different words for everything?'

'Because everything's changed,' said Stephen, looking up from his sketchbook, smiling at the cradle that stood next to Claire. In a moment he would have to leap up to hang entranced over the baby as she slept, and draw the coverings closer around her. More than anything he longed to be of use, to serve her in some way. Claire had already had cause to point out that children were best cared for by servants.

'Has it really changed?' Sophie straightened up, dusting her hands from putting another log on the fire. 'Or are we hoping it will if we find new names for it?'

Mathilde considered this for a little while. 'The rue des Droits-de-l'Homme is just as smelly now as when it was the rue Louis XIV.'

'What I refuse to get used to are these democratic forms of address.' Claire was downstairs for the first time since the birth of her daughter. 'Did I tell you about the day that awful girl who's married to Henri Lebrun accosted me in the lane? She simply wouldn't stop calling me *tu* and Citizen. I'm sure she knew it made everything she said sound twice as impertinent.'

'Jeanne's not so bad, really,' said Sophie. 'She only asked about your symptoms so she could tell you she's expecting her fourth and commiserate with you on woman's common lot.'

'Will we have to drop the Saint part of our names? You know, like those villages that are plain Antoine and Denis now.'

172

'She told me they plan to call the new baby Liberté. Can you imagine?'

'Better than Tenth August, like Isabelle's cook's grandson.'

'Why Tenth August?'

'Oh, Claire!' chorused her sisters.

'The storming of the Tuileries,' explained Stephen. 'The Triumph of the People.' Tenderness towards all things vulnerable had invaded his marrow. 'Are you tired?' he enquired of his model. 'You must say, the minute you would like to stop.'

Claire shook her head. Carefully, so as to maintain its angle.

Brutus sat up in front of the fire and scratched his ear, groaning. Then he sniffed the paw he had used and licked it a little.

Mathilde came to kneel on the seat beside Sophie, who began redoing her sister's plait. Mathilde's curls sprang from her head in all directions, out following strategies of their own. Ribbons, braids, clips clung in place for a while, then abandoned the struggle. 'Gypsy hair,' Rinaldi would say, stroking it with the tip of an admiring finger.

'Have you decided yet, Claire?' asked Mathilde. 'Are you going to name her after me? That would be proper, since I'm to be her godmother.'

Claire's eyes were cast obediently down.

Hunched on the mantelpiece, Marguerite's clock began striking the hour: one, two, three ... they all counted silently to seventeen, when it ceased.

They breathed out again.

'Claire?' persisted Mathilde.

Stephen concentrated hard on smudging a line with his thumb.

'Perhaps ... Caroline.' Adding at once, 'Caroline Marguerite.'

'Why Caroline?' Mathilde wandered over to the fire, where Brutus had curled himself into a circle, his tail over his nose. He half-opened a yellow and red eye, half-raised a skinny black leg. Squatting beside him, she stroked his belly. 'Is that from Hubert's side?'

173

'Lots of people are called Caroline,' said Claire sharply. 'There's nothing remarkable about it. Do stop asking questions, Matty, it's exhausting.'

'Brutus and I are going out now.'

They left, with considerable dignity.

Olivier sat on the floor in his nursery, which had grown crowded with unfamiliar objects, strange smells, a fat woman whose large mottled hands frightened him.

'What are you drawing?' asked Angélique. Any moment now the baby would wake up and cry, and she would go downstairs for her and bring her back to the nursery and hand her over to the wet nurse, a coarse lump of a creature like all these village women, but docile enough. 'The little boy's very talented,' she remarked, feeling it her duty to point out the family's accomplishments, and by extension her own pre-eminence, 'just like his mother. You should see her embroidery.'

The wet nurse sniffed and was about to wipe her nose on the back of her hand, when she remembered, and wiped it on a corner of her apron instead.

Angélique shuddered.

Olivier drew steadily, thick black strokes of charcoal filched from Stephen. A small hole appeared near the centre of the sheet of paper. He began to work his way outwards, systematically blackening the entire page.

'What is it a picture of, my cabbage?'

'My sister,' said Olivier, with satisfaction.

It was cold in the mayor's office and they all kept their coats on. The mid-century architect responsible for the town hall had avoided the obvious choice of local sandstone for its construction, insisting instead on grey-speckled marble which had to be imported from Italian quarries, depleting the municipal treasury for decades to come but adding considerably, so the architect had argued, to the town's prestige. He was eager to make a name for himself as an innovator and left for Paris as soon as his masterpiece was completed – thus cannily avoiding summary justice at the hands of the outraged Castelnaudians, or so the story ran.

It was true that on a dismal October day the sullen grey building struck a chill in those who had business there, which its draughty interior, overburdened with gilt and green-spotted mirrors, did nothing to dispel. Nevertheless, Luzac was always in favour of meeting at the town hall, rather than at the Victoire; the territory presented various small advantages to which he was not insensible. The other men had been kept waiting in an antechamber, for instance, while a clerk explained that the mayor was attending to important paperwork that required his immediate attention. After a suitable interval they were shown into Luzac's office, where the mayor half rose from behind an impressive expanse of gleaming oak and made no further effort to receive them. They were left to dispose themselves about the room as best they could.

There were only four of them that afternoon. Mercier had pleaded a temperature, and a newspaper to get out the following day. Ricard, manoeuvring his bulk into a spindly municipal chair, remarked that he too was troubled by aches and pains. Upon which Chalabre shifted his own chair as far away from the pork butcher and as close to the dispirited fire as possible.

Joseph, looking around with mounting dismay for a decanter or glasses, couldn't help smiling. Chalabre and his wife enjoyed almost perfect good health and were inveterate hypochondriacs. He called on one or the other in his professional capacity at least once a week.

'I thought yesterday's meeting was regrettable in the extreme.' Ricard, not looking at anyone in particular, was concentrating on his pipe. 'Dissent among us only strengthens our adversaries.'

Joseph flared at once: 'Dissent is the only honourable course when defenceless citizens are murdered in cold blood –'

'Yes, we heard you on the subject last night!' Luzac's whey face rose from the barricade of his desk. 'We're here to discuss what measures the municipality should take to rectify the . . . the situation.'

Luzac knew, as they all did, that the municipality would enact whatever resolutions were voted in by the Club. As usual, the business of what the mayor called their 'informal gatherings' was to determine what those resolutions might be. But appearances had to be kept up. Besides, invoking municipal authority was a way of reminding Joseph that, unlike the rest of them, he didn't hold office on the council.

Ricard intervened. 'There's nothing to be gained –' glancing at Joseph – 'by rehearsing grievances. The general temper of the meeting was plain enough.'

The previous night, speech after impassioned speech had denounced the massacre of the prisoners. There were those, Luzac among them, who spoke of royalist plots, necessary purgings and 'the intemperate but well-intentioned actions of patriotic citizens'. But the motion – proposed by Joseph – condemning the killings had been passed by a clear majority.

'I abstained from voting because I have no wish to encourage divisiveness,' continued Ricard. 'Nevertheless, something must be done to allay fears that the Revolution condones indiscriminate slaughter.'

'Wait a minute.' Luzac leant as far forward over his desk as his stomach would permit. 'The week before the ... the incident you were the one making speeches about our prisons being full of conspirators waiting for the opportunity to rise up against virtuous citizens. And what about Mercier's editorial calling for vengeance on the traitors within our gates? *The tree of Liberty thrives on impure blood* – wasn't that how he put it?

'I hope you aren't suggesting we're responsible for what happened at the convent.' But Ricard was looking at Chalabre.

The lawyer stirred. 'A commission of investigation – that's what I advise. Interviews with eyewitnesses, statements from survivors, house-to-house searches, interrogations of suspects, warrants, reports, cross-references, recommendations.' He looked across at Ricard and smiled, showing his inward-sloping teeth: 'The paperwork alone will take months.'

'Excellent. Excellent, my dear Chalabre.' Luzac's head bobbed above his desk like a fairground goose dodging the wooden rings hurled by spectators.

'I attended that man who threw himself from a window.' Joseph hadn't intended to raise his voice, but there it was. 'He was a boatbuilder. He came into a little money and tried to set up his own business. When he couldn't pay his debts the bailiffs confiscated everything he had and put him in prison. He wasn't a spy or a traitor. He'd tried to enlist but they rejected him because he was too short. He was *innocent*.'

'Yes. That's why we're pursuing this affair.' Ricard held Joseph's gaze. 'But we must do it properly, make sure that what the lawyers call due process is followed. You wouldn't want to arrest the wrong man, would you?'

'Oh no,' he said, 'and I wouldn't want anything to upset next month's elections either.'

After a little while, Ricard said, 'If we can't trust each other ...' His hands opened slowly, as if something was sliding from his grasp.

Which of them hadn't been fingered by panic in those oppressive weeks when all the news of the war was bad? Joseph recalled night after night tangled in sleeplessness, fear ticking down his spine as he tried not to think of the Prussians' manifesto and what it promised to all who hadn't actively opposed the Revolution. He looked at Ricard, slumped in his chair, and longed to say that of course no one held him responsible for the killings.

But there was the whisper that was spreading like infection through the town. He hardened his heart. 'Is it true that two men presented themselves here, at the town hall, demanding the wages they'd been promised for their night's work at the prison?'

'Nonsense!' said Luzac, caressing his empty sleeve.

Chalabre kept his eyes on the stingy flames struggling in the vast fireplace. 'But the kind of men who'd be capable of such a claim . . . Durand comes to mind. And that friend of his from the barges: Lagarde? Lebrun?'

Luzac licked his lips. 'Legrand.'

'Ah, yes.' Chalabre reached into his pocket for a velvet muffler and drew it fussily about his neck. That was the other thing about the lawyer: always impeccably turned out, crisp lace, starched linen. He favoured rich fabrics in deep hues and had an excellent tailor. Joseph could see that it was unfair, as well as unreasonable, to resent a man for the elegance of his dress; nevertheless, he noted that muffler.

'A few years ago Durand and Legrand were both employed in one of my workshops.' The mayor began drumming on his desk. 'Troublemakers! That's how they came to my attention.'

Ricard said, 'And perhaps you were obliged to get rid of them, and now they're seeking revenge by spreading these lies.'

'That's it!' Tapping his blotter. 'Exactly!'

'Well, no doubt a commission would reach the same conclusion.'

Luzac fell back, deflated.

Joseph was sure he knew what had happened. With the elections approaching, the mayor would have been anxious for his office. The news of the revolutionary army's defeats, the widespread fear of a royalist uprising, the prison crowded with political suspects: these things would have come together in Luzac's mind as a heaven-sent opportunity to be rid of the taint of conservatism that had dogged him all summer.

Perhaps a little thing had decided him – a chance meeting, a disreputable face recognised on the other side of the street, a former employee who jostled him as he emerged from the theatre. He had probably intended nothing worse than the exemplary deaths of a few priests; that would have been sure to bring in votes. But it would be just like Luzac to issue instructions so elaborately guarded as to be incomprehensible; like him also to pick men who could be relied on to botch things up.

One thing was certain: he wouldn't stand by and watch while Ricard and Chalabre let the mayor wriggle free. 'This investigation,' he said, 'I insist it's headed by someone impartial. Not some complaisant lackey.'

Chalabre sneezed. Once, twice. He held folds of red-and-gold silk to his nose and glared at them all.

Ricard said quietly, 'I had Saint-Pierre in mind. There can be no suspicion that he is, as you put it, a complaisant lackey.'

Joseph hung his head; he knew he deserved the reproof. Ricard was right, they had to trust each other.

'Well?'

Chalabre looked up from inspecting the contents of his handkerchief and nodded.

'I'm sorry,' said Joseph, 'I didn't mean to imply . . .'

The pork butcher said lightly, 'We've all been unsettled by this terrible affair. It's easy to lose perspective.'

Against the no-colour sky, a scarlet stain was edging over rooftops to the west. Joseph thought of Sophie coming up to him at the wedding, her hand brushing the hair from her eyes. At this very moment she was probably simpering at something the American was saying.

'Wait a minute.' Luzac, licking his lips, was riffling through a stack of files. It took self-control not to intervene, to find whatever he was so awkwardly searching for. They watched, tensely.

At last the mayor drew out a sheet of paper, glanced at it, brandished it at them. 'A letter from Saint-Pierre, demanding that those responsible for the . . . the events be brought to justice.'

'Hardly surprising. One of my men reported him making a disturbance outside the convent when the bodies were being removed.' Chalabre poked once more at the fire. 'Is that settled then? We really should be getting home, these damp autumn evenings are extremely dangerous for the lungs.'

'Don't you see?' cried Luzac. 'Saint-Pierre's biased, compromised.'

'Oh, I don't think so.' Ricard stared at the mayor. 'His opposition to the killings is precisely the advantage you need. It indicates to all concerned that you have nothing to fear, nothing to hide. I would go so far as to say that it practically guarantees your re-election.'

'But . . .' Luzac's rosebud mouth opened and shut, opened and shut. 'But . . .'

'Don't worry. As I've already said, it'll take Saint-Pierre months to sift the evidence. And with time these things have a way of declining in significance.' Chalabre, impatient to be gone, cut to the heart of the matter.

Joseph considered the lawyer's remark tantamount to complicity and said so. 'If the murders were sanctioned by someone in authority, the people have a right to know the facts before rather than after the elections.'

'Don't be a fool,' retorted Chalabre. 'Do you think for a moment that denouncing Lu . . . one of us will achieve anything other than the undoing of everything we've worked for? Do you really want Castelnau to go over to the royalists?'

The room was awash with shadows. But Luzac, making feeble noises behind his desk, made no move to ring for lights.

'Besides,' continued the lawyer smoothly, 'we stand or fall together. In the eyes of our opponents we're all tainted with revolutionary zeal.'

'I haven't done anything that wouldn't stand up to scrutiny. I'm not afraid.'

'You should be. The massacre you're so concerned about should have made it clear that when events gather momentum, the innocent die alongside the guilty.' And Chalabre sneezed again.

Even the way that man blew his nose seemed cynical. 'It

sickens me that everything you say is motivated by political expediency, not remorse over what happened.'

'Politics calls for realism not remorse.' Ricard moved out of the gloom to stand with his back to the fire. 'Chalabre has summed up the situation admirably. Our most pressing goal must be to ensure victory in the elections. Once that's assured, we'll have little to fear. Then whatever Citizen Saint-Pierre finds will be of purely judicial rather than political interest.'

Chalabre, manifestly unnerved by the pork butcher's contagious proximity, said, 'Good, that's settled then,' and began doing up his coat.

'One or two matters.' Ricard glanced at the lawyer, who fell back muttering. 'This business of membership fees: can we agree once and for all to implement a sliding scale, based on income, with the minimum set at thirty *sous*?'

Ricard and Joseph had been campaigning for this all year. They had succeeded in having the annual subscription reduced and made payable monthly, but among the Jacobins' moneyed majority there was widespread nervousness at the idea of a sliding fee: it opened the Club to the raggle-taggle crowds who filled the public sessions on Sundays, and it is one thing to believe in equality and quite another to find yourself fraternising with your footman. Luzac, for one, had been immovable and had rallied the waverers to his way of thinking.

They all looked at the mayor.

The mayor looked dully back.

'Is it wise right now . . .?' Chalabre roused himself from the depths of his muffler. 'They've been frightened enough by these killings.'

'When people are excluded from power they take it into their own hands. By offering our fellow citizens membership of the Club, we'd be able to direct and control their more regrettable tendencies.' Although answering the lawyer, Ricard kept his eyes on Luzac.

The mayor continued to sit very still, contemplating his hand, which lay palm up on his blotter, as if he wasn't sure where this strange pink object came from or what purpose it served. Just as the silence reached breaking point, he said, 'As you please.'

Ricard nodded, as if the concession were a trivial one. 'The other matter we discussed in the council . . . Concerning public health . . .?'

Thus prodded, Luzac began shuffling papers once more. Without looking up, he said, 'The hospital. I'm told you have plans for improving it, modernisation and so on.'

'Doctor?' said Ricard softly, and it was only then that Joseph realised what the mayor was referring to.

'Yes . . . That is, *plans* is perhaps too . . .'

'The municipality believes . . . new post . . . Deputy Director . . . implementing change . . . reporting directly to . . .' Luzac's leaden drone ceased without warning, like a watch whose mechanism winds down in mid-tick.

Joseph said, 'But what about Ducroix?' Dr Ducroix had listened politely enough to his enthusiastic proposals, nodded and smiled, and done nothing.

'Ducroix is set in his ways,' replied Ricard. 'Castelnau needs a young man with energy and vision. The council has every confidence in your abilities and we envisage no difficulty convincing Ducroix and his board of your fitness for the post.' He paused, but Joseph didn't say anything. 'Dr Ducroix might even welcome the opportunity to retire from the directorship, knowing that you would make an able successor.'

Silence.

'Well?' prompted Ricard, smiling. 'What do you say?'

What could he say?

He had courage and ideals and compassion. They knew better than to offer him the world.

So they offered him the opportunity to improve it.

Sophie read the letter to Berthe, who clutched a frying pan to her stomach and stared at a corner of the kitchen table.

My dear Mother,

Sergeant Bernard Pelet is writing this letter for me and I thank him for his service for I know you will be anxious to hear news of me. I would have written sooner but there has been no time as we've been fully occupied with the war. We've seen some fine action and won a great many glorious victories at Valmy and other places. The regiment is stationed in a village outside Worms, a city on the left bank of the Rhine which is a German river. They speak German here. Wine is very dear, upward of sixty sous a bottle, and only our officers can afford it. The quartermaster says beer is no drink for a fighting man and has written to General Custine himself to complain. He's a good fellow. Don't be alarmed, we eat our fill as pork and potatoes are plentiful. On fine days we march along the bank of the river. We have our own band which plays very well. One cannot go far without stumbling across crosses and shrines, for the Germans have not yet been liberated from superstition. We're quartered in a fine clean house with windows. There are two beds between five of us and I'm in the one with only two because of being recently wounded. Don't be alarmed, we outnumbered the Prussian patrol six to three and killed them all. The bullet passed cleanly through my shoulder, the surgeon said it was a miracle. Sometimes I still feel a little weak but the sergeant tells me this is to be expected as I lost a great deal of blood. My old comrade Henri Bonnet who enlisted with me was sadly killed last month when

183

*we attacked a garrison and a great many other good fellows
with him. Don't be alarmed on my account, the wound is
almost healed and I didn't miss any important action. Our
beds are made of straw with a sheet spread over it and a
feather bed on top of the sheet, which is a German custom
and very warm. We play cards of an evening and only yesterday I won a fine leather belt with a brass buckle. Now it's
time for rollcall. Be assured of my warm affection. I kiss you
with all my heart and remember you every night without fail
in my prayers.*

> *Your loving son Matthieu.*

A pot boiled over. Sophie dealt with it, having handed Berthe
the sheet of paper.

'Potatoes,' said Berthe, after a while. She had laid aside the
frying pan and was scanning the letter closely. 'Nasty things.
Why don't they eat bread?'

'Perhaps it's expensive, like wine.'

'Does it say when he wrote this?'

Sophie shook her head. 'There's no date. But Custine
crossed the Rhine about five weeks ago, towards the end of
October. Matthieu must have written before that.'

Berthe put the letter down, but picked it up again immediately. 'Anything could have happened to him by now.'

'He wouldn't want you to worry about him.'

'He's a good boy.' Berthe had folded the letter into a small
square. Now she folded it out again, smoothing the creases
without looking at the paper. 'He never cried when he was a
baby, not even when he was learning to walk and tripped and
cut his head open.' She looked away. 'I thought . . . when you
said there was a letter . . .'

'I know,' said Sophie, very gently.

'That Henri Bonnet! Soldiering was all his idea. He was the
same age as Matthieu but you wouldn't have known it. Thin
and sickly from the start.'

'Eighteen years old. The poor boy.'

'Do you think we could find out where the regiment is and
send him some wine?'

'We could try. It might be difficult.'

'I haven't seen him in over twenty months.'

'I know.'

'Do you think ...' Berthe gripped the back of a chair. 'Would it be a lot of trouble to read the letter again?'

1793

*T*he hospital had been built in the fourteenth century to receive victims of the bubonic plague. It had always catered to the homeless and destitute. Naturally. Why would you go into hospital if you could afford to die at home? No one, neither patient nor physician, had the least expectation of a cure.

A bleak January morning had been set aside for the new deputy director to carry out his tour of inspection. The main building consisted of three long wards constructed around three sides of a rectangle which had once been a garden; ancient brick pathways divided up what was now a sour wasteland of broken glass, rubble and dispirited weeds. A covered walkway ran all around this open space, and on the fourth side lay the dispensary, the outpatients' clinic, the mortuary and so on. Outlying buildings housed kitchens, a refectory, a bakery, a laundry, a woodstore. A chapel (disused) stood to one side of the main courtyard, near the gate.

A second desk had been placed in a rather dark angle of the director's office, which was next to the dispensary. Dr Ducroix trusted that Morel wouldn't object to sharing his quarters? Far from ideal of course, but they were so pressed for space.

'Not at all.' Joseph was eager to please where he could, not wanting resentment at his appointment to interfere with the execution of his plans. Although resentment could not be discerned in Ducroix's manner: his congratulations seemed sincere, his welcome entirely cordial. A pleasant fellow, Ducroix, and competent enough. But energy! enthusiasm! Surely a man needed these qualities to accomplish anything,

189

thought Joseph, polishing his spectacles, while the director held forth about arrangements for a dinner the hospital board would be holding in honour of the new appointment.

At last, they were walking towards the first of the wards.

'Remind me, Morel – when did you last visit us? The wards, I mean.'

'Some nine months ago.'

Ducroix opened the door and stood aside to let him pass.

The ward had been designed to hold twenty-four beds, with two patients to a bed being the usual unsanitary standard. Now it was occupied by eighty or ninety people; they sat propped against walls, or lay on the floor on bundles of rags or sacks stuffed with straw or on the tiles themselves. Here and there, sacking strung from ropes provided makeshift partitions. Five or six dirty children were chasing each other, weaving their way between the patients with laudable agility and being lavishly cursed. A dog with a question-mark tail wandered up to the newcomers and sniffed their boots.

Close at hand a woman was moaning; Joseph lifted a greasy corner of sacking and disclosed a couple in the act of copulation. Leaping back, he kicked over a chamber pot. The dog trotted up, its tail wagging, to investigate the contents.

'As I mentioned, we're pressed for space,' murmured Ducroix.

In the director's office, Joseph accepted a glass of the director's armagnac and mopped his forehead.

'It's not so bad in fine weather.' Ducroix's tone was apologetic. 'Many of them camp out in the garden. Quite a merry scene, sometimes.'

'But the situation is impossible. I had no idea conditions had deteriorated to this extent. And you say the war . . .?'

Ducroix shrugged. 'It's one of the reasons for the over-crowding. You saw the soldiers yourself. Well, it would be more accurate to call them beggars, poor devils, their fighting days are decidedly over. By the way, did you notice Mother Clothilde? In the second ward, taking that man's pulse.'

Joseph recalled the elderly woman dressed in brown, whom he had taken for a relative of the patient. 'That was Mother Clothilde? I didn't recognise her.'

'When the order was dissolved, she returned to her family. They're rather well off, you know, made their money in ship-building. But she was back within weeks; she told me she missed her patients and asked if she might continue working here as a lay volunteer. Three of her nuns have done likewise. Between them, they keep things going.'

'I had envisaged the wards having separate functions: two medical, one surgical.'

'That would be ideal.'

'And new buildings ... pavilion-style, to allow for the free circulation of air.'

'Yes, I believe I still have the plans you drew up.'

'But ...'

'But there's no money, of course. Our municipal funding was never expected to cover costs and donations to the Daughters of Charity have long dried up. Although Mother Clothilde still brings pressure to bear in certain quarters – an altogether remarkable woman, Morel, and no scruples whatsoever about promising eternal salvation in exchange for a legacy – anyway, we receive the occasional gift but it's barely enough for necessities. Twice a week, the sisters go out begging for food.'

Joseph sat at the director's desk with his head in his hands. 'And all those babies!'

'The birth rate always increases when there's a war – the fighting man must be catered to. We're averaging two foundlings a week. They used to be left outside churches; these days, they find them outside the town hall. Progress, I suppose.' Ducroix set his glass down. 'It's fortunate that most of them don't survive.'

Joseph rallied. 'I – we must take action. The first step is obviously to segregate the sick from the indigent.' He drew a sheet of paper to him and began making notes. 'A fund is needed to house the veterans elsewhere and pay for their upkeep. I'll take it up with the authorities immediately.'

'We've been turning the fevers away. Or turning them out

if they develop here. Nothing like fever for spreading from sick men to healthy ones and killing them all.'

'I had thought one of the medical wards could be set aside for fever cases but we can't spare the space.' Joseph scribbled furiously. 'A fever ward. Couldn't we turn the clinic into one?'

'What would become of the outpatients?'

'We'll rig up something for them in the chapel. Don't look at me like that, it's only a building. One or two alterations will be required, that's all – it can't possibly cost much.'

The director raised his eyebrows.

'Ventilation,' continued Joseph. 'If we can't have new buildings, we must have windows – windows that function – in all the wards. I've always said that those fixed panes set high up in the walls are useless. The stench is indescribable. You're acquainted with my views on noxious effluvia?'

'In some detail.'

'Knocking through a few windows – I can't see that ruining the municipal treasury. I'll take it up at once with Ricard.'

'Ah – our new mayor. Well, he could hardly prove less interested in our problems than his predecessor.'

Seized by inspiration, Joseph stopped writing. 'We must set an example.' He tore off his spectacles and waved them in Ducroix's face. 'As you know, my post carries a considerable stipend: I shall ask that the money be diverted to the hospital.'

There was a long pause. The deputy director gazed expectantly at the director. The director gazed dreamily at an engraving that showed a madman running naked through the streets of a plague-stricken city carrying a dish of burning sulphur on his head.

Eventually, Ducroix gave a little start and pulled his watch from his pocket. 'As I thought: almost half-past the hour. Where does the time go? Well, Morel, it's been most instructive and I look forward to hearing more. But I'm afraid I must ask you to excuse me for the present ...' He got to his feet and held out his hand. 'It won't seem so bad,' he said reassuringly, 'when you get used to it.'

Joseph looked in vain for a polite way of saying that that was exactly what he feared.

'The artist,' explained Stephen, artlessly running his fingers through his hair, 'is essentially solitary. In order to depict society with subtlety and penetration he must remain detached from it, as a physician preserves his distance from his patients the better to observe their symptoms.'

His audience looked downcast.

'This inner remoteness must not be mistaken for withdrawal from life itself. On the contrary, the artist must plunge into the world's turbulence, immerse himself in its depths, allow its currents to bear him where they will, if his work is to strike a spark in the soul of his fellow men, to speak to their hearts in the accents of passion.'

His audience brightened.

It was a cold February. Ice encased twigs, gripped railings, captured fountains. They said that in the fields birds were falling out of the yellow-white sky, frozen in flight; they said that if it kept up, the river itself would turn to ice.

For all that, attendance at Stephen's address to the Society for the Appreciation of Art was flatteringly sizeable.

'Look at them,' breathed Claire, 'look at all those triple-chinned old women and their diamond-hung daughters.'

It was evident that the appreciation of art manifested itself chiefly among Castelnau's female population.

'He turns down their invitations, gives lessons to a select few pupils and spends half his time at Montsignac. The remoteness of the artist – it's irresistible,' replied Sophie.

A lady clasping a small dog to her large bosom turned around and shushed them fiercely.

'The inspirational changes sweeping this country have

193

opened the way for entirely new directions in art. Where the development of my own work is concerned, I've abandoned the sterility of classicism for a style that seeks to express emotion in colour, texture and choice of subject. Which do we require: an outmoded aesthetic that counsels duty and the veneration of the past? Or a revolutionary one that urges us to embrace the future with awe and rapture?'

Enthusiastic murmurs indicated that awe and rapture carried the day.

Sophie shut her eyes, the better to observe her symptoms. He kissed me on the 9th of June in the year 1792. I'm eight months older now, if he were to do it tomorrow I'd be sure to part my lips, and I'd take hold of his hand and place it . . .

'Sophie, are you all right? Your breathing sounds most peculiar.'

'Landscape has traditionally been considered an inferior genre. Conservative opinion argues that antiquity is the only fit subject for serious art: we gain in stature, we are enlightened and ennobled by the contemplation of heroes and heroic deeds. According to traditionalists a landscape, however pleasing to the eye, is not an edifying subject.' Here, Stephen sought out the unblinking brown gaze of a ravishingly pretty girl in the front row and fixed his attention on her: 'But when confronted with Nature's sublime harmonies, are we not moved to nobility ourselves? Doesn't the simple, unaffected beauty of the natural world call forth a corresponding desire for goodness and truth in man's breast?'

The girl in the front row blushed, lowered her eyes and relieved her emotions by kicking the lieutenant who had contrived to position himself next to her by dint of stepping ruthlessly on other people's feet. He deemed this a highly auspicious sign and immediately set about composing a declaration to her in his head.

Refreshments were served in the adjoining room, where representative examples of the artist's work hung on the grey-panelled walls. The artist himself, closely attended by his most determined admirers, was making his gradual way from one canvas to the next, speaking of 'pure colour' and 'pictorial symbolism'.

Claire greeted acquaintances and kept an eye on Stephen's progress. Sophie looked at the paintings.

A series of mountain landscapes had storms raging in purple-tinted skies and gloomy foliage swirling in patches of broken colour. A lake whipped into white-capped peaks reared up towards snowy summits; a solitary figure could be discerned on top of the highest mountain. Precipitous rocks loomed above a waterfall and a ruined castle. 'The Sublime is very different from the Beautiful,' warned Stephen. No one disagreed.

A still life contained a pewter jug, a half-glass of wine and candles reflected in a mirror. Another showed a bowl of roses – Sophie frowned and bent closer: those plum-coloured petals bleeding to crimson could only be the Rose des Maures. The shape of the flowers stood up to her inspection; but in her opinion Stephen had quite failed to render the soft, rich pink of the half-open blooms.

Paintings and sketches of the countryside around Montsignac took up an entire wall. Sophie saw a barley field, a road down which a child was driving a flock of geese, the redbrown roofs of the village crowding through a gap in the trees. A clearing in autumn woods. A water-mill, a bridge, the river running greenly. A lane where thick-leaved elms met overhead. Silvery light, bare branches, a boat, a blue-jacketed fisherman with his basket beside him. The crowd stood two and three deep in front of these paintings, people elbowing each other out of the way to make it clear that Art couldn't put anything over them: 'That place with the birch trees, where the stream runs into the river – we drive past it on our way to visit your mother.' 'That strip of meadow, there, with the gate hanging loose, that definitely belongs to my uncle, I'd know it anywhere.'

The lieutenant listened and cracked his knuckles in despair. The pretty girl hadn't so much as glanced in his direction after the lecture and was now to be glimpsed in the thick of the group around that foreigner. He turned his reluctant attention to the nearest canvases. 'Ugly green stuff,' he remarked gloomily to the tall young woman standing beside him.

The president of the Society, an eagle-nosed financier who specialised in still lifes of dead partridge, was not without courage. He had hesitated over accepting the work that was attracting comment at the far end of the room. But Fletcher had been charming and persuasive, and by the time the first decanter was empty and they had made serious inroads on the second, the financier had felt insurrection sizzle in his veins: damn it, they were artists! So the painting had been hung – in the corner where what was left of the afternoon light fell dingiest, it was true. Nevertheless.

It showed an interior: cramped, dirty, inadequate, lit only by firelight. A fiddler stood to one side of the hearth, his face, like most of the room, in shadow. In the foreground, where the light turned her skin to rose and gold, a woman was nursing an infant at her breast. An urchin played at her feet, tussling with a ferociously ugly dog for possession of a bone. There was a predominance of browns and blacks, with here and there a shriek of colour made twice as strident by the surrounding darkness: a yellow neckerchief, an emerald-green blouse.

The lady with the large bosom said that something about the painting made her feel quite ill, and thrust her dog into the lieutenant's startled arms before proceeding with the vapours. The little dog kept up a vicious yapping all the while its mistress was being revived with a fan and lavender water, pausing only to regurgitate its lunch – minced breast of duck and chestnut puree – onto a gold-braided epaulette.

'So provincial!' hissed Claire. 'Everyone has bare breasts in paintings these days, they represent the eternal fecundity of Nature. It's completely respectable.'

The president's wife was saying that what she couldn't understand was why they were all in rags. She knew the Saint-Pierres were hard up but surely it hadn't come to that?

'Really,' said Claire, 'you'd think some people had never heard of the Imagination.'

The artist and his coterie, sensing something amiss, were heading towards the commotion. With commendable presence of mind, the president positioned his wife in front of the canvas – her girth was a stroke of fortune – instructed her on no account to move, seized Stephen by the arm and propelled him in the opposite direction, thanking him for his profoundly illuminating remarks and congratulating him on the tremendous success of the exhibition. But now they should all be thinking of getting home, the weather, you see, and he was sure everyone felt the need of time and ... and solitude, the better to appreciate such originality. Gratified if slightly taken aback, Stephen found himself shaking the presidential hand while a footman stood ready with his coat.

The pretty girl had been whispering to her mother, who stepped forward now with an invitation to them all to repair to her drawing-room. She lived only two streets away and if Mr Fletcher would consent to continue his explanation of Art ...? She was afraid she hadn't followed quite everything he'd said, but her daughter did wonderful things with seed-pods.

Sophie, with her back to the room, watched daylight take cover behind the rooftops.

In some deep-shadowed recess of her mind, she had always known. Why, only the other week she had remarked how fair the child was. And then Stephen's attentiveness, the way he was always there, circling around the baby, turning his head at once if she cried. I put it down to something he'd read in Rousseau, thought Sophie, leaning her forehead against the cold glass, When someone is sincere all the time how can you tell when they mean it?

When she took her hand away, Sophie saw that the handle of the window had left a small red indentation in her palm. All she had felt was a bony cage closing itself around her heart.

And then, unexpectedly, there was a thaw and the worst of the winter melted away in a matter of days. There followed a fortnight of rain, violent downpours at all hours that invariably found Stephen outdoors and unprepared, icy drops dribbling vindictively down his neck, entire streets vanishing in the distance, perspective dissolving in rain.

In the café, jostled by other men crowding in, he caught a glint of light on spectacles. Using his height and elbows to good effect, he made his way to the table where the doctor sat hunched over a glass; the notion that one might prefer to drink alone occurring to Stephen, if at all, only in firm conjunction with people of an entirely different class.

Morel acknowledged him without apparent enthusiasm; but then he was an odd fellow, abrupt and awkward, although good-hearted, he was sure; still, you could see what Claire meant when she said she found him difficult enough going when she was feeling perfectly well. But he roused himself when Stephen ordered a bottle of wine and filled both their glasses: 'Foul weather.'

'Good for business?'

'They die all year round.'

'How do you bear it?'

'It has its moments.'

'Sophie says that now we've lost faith in religion, medicine is the sole repository of our irrational hopes.'

'Does she really.'

Cheerfully: 'It must take a lot out of you.'

'Do you see her often?'

'Who? Oh, Sophie? Well, almost every day. Why do you ask?'

'No reason.' Morel topped up their glasses. 'Ducroix tells me her sister hasn't been well.'

'No.' There was a small puddle of dark wine near his glass. With his forefinger, Stephen began tracing patterns on the table. 'Her confinement wasn't an easy one. She still hasn't recovered her strength.' A five-petalled flower, an isosceles triangle. 'She's far less robust than her sisters.'

'The delicate ones are the hardiest. I've seen it again and again.'

'Really?' He drew an oval, adorned it with ringlets; but left the face blank. 'Caroline – I don't suppose you've seen her – an extraordinarily pretty baby. Advanced for her age, too. She holds up her head unsupported, you know.'

A man paused at their table, greeted the doctor heartily and shook his hand. Morel and he exchanged a few words. The stranger nodded to them both and moved on.

'I adore children,' said Stephen, and sighed. 'Do you have plans to marry, Morel?'

'No, do you?'

Stephen shook his head.

'Why not?'

He looked up to find the spectacles aimed uncompromisingly at him. At that instant, the conviction came to him that Morel knew. Perhaps everyone did – he had no talent for dissimulation. At the idea of someone to whom he could unburden himself without reserve, relief welled up in him: Claire had missed the point, the essential thing was you felt you could rely on Morel. 'I won't ask how you guessed. But isn't it obvious why not?'

'Is it such an obstacle, these days?' Morel had taken off his spectacles and was polishing them. This made him appear much younger – and helpless, as if it would be easy to finish him off, thought Stephen.

He didn't need to ask Claire her opinion of the new divorce laws. 'I can imagine all too well what she'd say. I don't blame her in the least, one reacts to these things from the heart. Sentiments don't always keep pace with revolutionary decrees.'

A man sitting nearby glanced in their direction.

Morel leant forward. 'Keep your voice down and watch what you say. Foreigners can't be too careful. Even Americans.'

'I keep forgetting. Sophie accuses me of looking on your revolution as a minor consequence of ours.'

'You must have a lot to say to each other.'

'Well, you know there's more to Sophie than meets the eye. I didn't appreciate that at first. I was ... well, distracted.'

His smile was foolish, enchanted, utterly disarming. You had only to see it to know the man was in love, thought Joseph. Poor devil. He poured the last of the wine into his own glass. It gave him a grim satisfaction to hear Fletcher admit that Sophie considered herself too good for him. Spitefully, he imagined her living out her days alone, the dusty relic of a world that no longer mattered. He imagined calling on her: he would be gracious, she would stand at the window watching as he left, thinking, If only ...

'I hadn't realised she would actually sacrifice the happiness of two people for the sake of an antiquated principle. Although I suppose there's nothing very surprising about an aristocrat who clings to social distinctions. How people run true to form.'

Slightly taken aback, Stephen realised that Morel was in fact quite drunk. 'It shows a delicacy of feeling,' he protested, 'rather than a concern for distinctions.' What did the man know of Claire, anyway?

But Morel, trying to attract a waiter's attention, seemed to have lost all interest in the subject. 'Another bottle?'

Stephen placed his hand over his half-full glass.

The waiter cleared away the empty bottle and brought Morel his armagnac.

The rain stopped falling.

The man in the red cap who had greeted them on his way in, raised his hand in acknowledgment on his way out.

'A patient?' Stephen would happily have followed the red cap but didn't quite like to leave Morel alone.

'You weren't at the execution this morning then?' At Stephen's look: 'That was the executioner. Quite a personable fellow.'

'Do you often attend executions?'

'I used to when I was young. For a while there was something of a fad for them among medical students. But I was asked to, in this case. My professional opinion of our brand-new guillotine is solicited. I have to write a report.'

'I see, yes. And what did you think of it?'

'Efficient.'

'More humane surely than hanging?'

'Oh yes. Just a swish and a thud.'

'Who was . . .?'

'A miller convicted of hoarding flour. Girard – the executioner – forgot to display the head. He had quite a long talk to me about the whole thing afterwards. He wonders whether the guillotine doesn't take away from his dignity: a professional man like him reduced to pulling on a rope like some village bellringer. I tried to point out that he could take pride in keeping the blade razor-sharp at all times.'

'Large crowd?'

'Not bad, considering the weather. Curiosity about the new machine. And hoarders always pull them in, of course. Although it isn't quite the same spectacle any more, none of that twitching and leaping on the gibbet.'

'They say the King died well.'

'Let me tell you this, Fletcher.' The spectacles glittered. 'There's no such thing as dying well. There's dying. That's all.'

'I see what you mean.'

Joseph swallowed the last of the armagnac: 'Swish.' He banged his glass down on the table: 'Thud.' Stephen watched in some dismay. 'You know what I can't stop thinking, Fletcher?' The spectacles thrust themselves closer. 'It's so quick. They'll be able to kill so many people.'

'ave you seen this week's *Citoyen*?'

'We don't take it. Louis doesn't approve. Why?'

'There's a new club for women. They want both sexes to participate equally in political life and any woman over the age of eighteen can join. There's no membership fee.'

'There is Louis to consider, you see.'

'Stern, pale daughters of the republic sewing garments for soldiers?'

'That would certainly be the angle to emphasise. Do they favour Amazon dress?'

'I believe that kind of thing is confined to Paris.'

'Our local dressmakers are as up-to-the-minute as any. More tea?'

Sophie shook her head. 'I'd like to be ... I don't know, active, useful.' Three of her long strides and she was at the window through which spring was sidling into Isabelle's parlour. In the street below, a man was coming out of the pharmacy. 'There's that lawyer, Chalabre. He must be the only man under the age of forty in Castelnau still wearing a wig. Father says he's a slippery fish.'

'My father says yours is overdoing things.'

'He ought to know, Father sleeps most nights at his house to save himself the journey from Montsignac. When he does come home he closets himself away with files full of depositions. We've barely seen him in weeks.'

'Why is it so complicated?'

'A suspect he was hoping to question turned out to have volunteered and is presently thought to be somewhere in the

Low Countries. Another was found in the river. Two witnesses say he was drunk and lost his footing, but an anonymous letter claims he was set upon and thrown in. There's a bruise on his forehead and the doctors can't be sure whether it happened before or after he drowned.'

'Medical men!' remarked Isabelle, with the air of one who could say more if she chose.

'And the priest who survived the massacre was found dead in prison last month. He appears to have been poisoned. They're still taking statements from the warders and other prisoners.' She wandered back to the sofa, picked up her cup. 'But you know, Father's in his element. He's regained that exalted look we thought only certain puddings could still bring on.'

'Do have another biscuit.'

'How do you manage,' Sophie asked enviously, 'for sugar?' It had been in scarce supply since the slave rebellions in the colonies. 'Half the injustices in the world can be traced to sugar,' her father often remarked. That didn't stop him complaining when there wasn't any.

'Louis's younger son has a contact. We ask no questions.'

Sophie ate biscuits.

After the third, she asked, 'Do you see much of Joseph Morel?'

'No. Why?' Isabelle looked alert.

'I sent him a geranium once. I was wondering what happened to it.'

'Men invariably over-water.' Isabelle continued to eye Sophie. 'Relations have been rather strained since his appointment. He's been badgering Father for years with his schemes for ventilation and goodness knows what else, and now it's difficult to fob him off. Father says it's a great deal of nonsense and you might as well put everyone outside to die in the cold and be done with it. Mind you, he doesn't take to innovation of any kind.'

Sophie fidgeted with her sleeve, where a thread had worked loose.

Isabelle watched, and drank tea. The dark, cramped rooms

above the pharmacy were not what she was used to. But they smelt of resins, balsams, herbs, flowers, fruit, barks, fungi, roots, expressed and distilled oils, spirits, antimony, vinegars, purgatives, opiates, honey, mercury, elixirs, salts, simple and compound syrups. At Christmas Louis had presented her with a bezoar, a concretion found in the alimentary canal of ruminants and believed by ignorant people to be an antidote to poison; he had had it fitted with a gold chain so that she could wear it around her neck. Married life was like the walnut-inlaid drawers that lined one wall of the pharmacy: you slid them open one at a time, hooking your finger into the hollow under the brass handle, and so learnt which ones were best left shut.

Sophie sprang up and walked twice around the sofa. Then she sat down again.

'There are always your roses,' said Isabelle.

'Sometimes,' said the heretic, 'roses aren't enough.'

'It's the change of season. It used to take me that way too.'

'And now? Are you happy?'

Isabelle said, 'Of course everything will be different once we have children.'

'If I took an interest in politics,' said Sophie, 'perhaps I wouldn't spend so much time thinking about ... other things.'

'I'll talk to Louis tonight,' said Isabelle. Thinking, Poor Sophie. First the American and now Joseph. 'But you know, the only effective remedy is plenty of cooling drinks and waiting for it to pass.'

Queueing up to show his papers at the eastern barrier, Joseph saw a familiar froth of light-brown hair and called out to Lisette. She was carrying a basket covered with a cloth and told him she had been to visit her mother, who was ailing. 'There's nothing really wrong with her: she's tired of living, that's all.'

A man wearing a filthy, once-blue jacket, his face half-hidden under a thick beard, was making his way towards them, leaning on crutches. His left leg had been amputated above the knee. He thrust a hat awkwardly at the people waiting in line: 'Alms, for an old soldier.' Joseph shook his head; but Lisette had her purse out and was dropping a coin in the hat. '*Vive la république*,' said the beggar and his eyes, dull brown with red-stained whites, peered into their faces, '*Vive la Révolution*.' He dragged his way on.

A woman in a bonnet trimmed with green ribbons began berating Lisette. 'It only encourages them. My husband says most of the beggars you see around here passing themselves off as veterans have cut off their own legs and arms to sell to butchers.'

'So what?' retorted Lisette. 'They still have to eat.'

'Eat? That's a good one. They spend it on drink and loose women.'

'Beggars are entitled to enjoy themselves, just like everyone else.'

The woman snorted, and turned away to whisper to her companion.

Lisette looked at Joseph, crossed her eyes, stuck out her tongue. Then she was overcome by giggles and at once her hand flew up to cover her mouth.

He took the basket from her, exclaimed at its weight.

'Carrots,' she said, 'and eggs and wine and honey. Between the shop and my sister's garden, we manage. I don't know how other people do. Paul says it's only a matter of time before they control prices, but that won't help with the shortages, will it?'

An indifferent guardsman glanced at their papers and waved them through into Castelnau. They walked side by side through streets from which light was starting to withdraw its attention. The first workers were straggling home, pausing on doorsteps to gather themselves for the moment of return. Children were shouting farewells, pinching each other, pocketing a pebble, a scrap of ribbon, a whistle, running back to make urgent adjustments to arrangements for meeting the next day.

Lisette asked Joseph where he had been, and he told her about the farmer coughing blood while his wife wept and said that their son had been conscripted and what were they to do, what were they to do.

'But the thing is, just having you there is what they need. My mother knows she's dying and she wouldn't mind if she could have Abbé Michel for the last rites. But he disappeared in January. Doctors are like priests: people send for you not because they expect to be saved but because they need to feel they've done their best.'

An alley, a narrow passage smelling of drains, opened off to their left between two wooden houses. A girl stood at the angle of the street, a scrawny girl of sixteen or seventeen with creamy white skin and red-brown hair. Her eyes slid blankly over them, then returned to rest on Joseph before sliding away again.

Lisette looked sideways at him and laughed.

'She's always around here somewhere,' he said, despising himself for blushing.

'There are so many girls these days. It makes Paul angry, he says it's a social disease that has no place in republican France. But it's the same as the beggars, isn't it? They're hungry and they have no other way to eat.'

When they parted, she insisted on presenting him with a jar

of honey, closing his fingers round the pot when he demurred. Then she stood facing him, holding her basket in both hands. A man passing glanced at them, but moved on at once when they looked at him.

'Everyone's afraid, aren't they?' said Lisette. 'Like that man just now. My sister has a friend ... someone denounced her for saying she didn't blame that general for deserting, she hoped her son had the brains to do the same. They came and took her away. I had to ask Paul to intervene.'

'It's been a bad spring.'

'Paul says the Revolution needs men like you. He's been telling me about your plans for cleaning up the streets. That'll be good – all this filth, it's disgusting.'

She had a way of staring, earnest and entreating, that made him shift from foot to foot.

'But you're afraid too, aren't you?' she said. 'That's why you drink.'

'Is that what Ricard ...?' He stopped. The sky was still full of blue light, but around them evening had seeped into the streets. Windows were turning yellow, one by one.

Lisette transferred the basket to her arm and held out her hand. 'You should get married, Joseph.'

ay, and the chestnut trees are heavy with blossom. The man standing at the gate as darkness falls looks up into their branches and remembers a garden, and of all the things he has lost that seems the hardest to bear. It occurs to him that when life wants to punish a man, it requires him to make choices; not that he has a clear recollection of having done so. But here he is, this village, these flowers. He runs his fingers down the trunk of a tree; and at once from the direction of the house comes a furious barking.

Anne's letter identifies the bearer as 'a friend'. Claire and Sophie receive him in their father's study, where he introduces himself only as Pierre and refuses their offer of something to eat; although he accepts a glass of wine readily enough. While Claire is still thanking him, he crosses quickly to the window and closes it, draws the dark-red curtains shut, catches himself observing the frayed silk cord and shabby velvet. One of the ways in which he has changed is this new-found awareness of detail; a pity, he thinks, that it took a Revolution to make him notice things.

When they finish reading and look at him, he doesn't hesitate at all before telling the usual lie: 'A soldier's end. A valiant death.'

Their eyes never leave his face. He looks from one to the other and lies again. 'He didn't regain consciousness. I assure you he didn't suffer.'

Claire says, 'And my husband? Was he with Sébastien when . . .?' Her voice is flat, painfully even. But she's chalk-white and her hands aren't quite steady. Who would have guessed, he thinks, that Monferrant's wife would be so beautiful? Or that she would care so much for her husband?

He nods. 'I returned to England not long afterwards. Your husband was alive and in good spirits when I left.'

'I see.' She turns the letter over in her hands, which are still trembling. 'And that was . . .?'

'In December.'

'Where's the regiment now?'

He shrugs.

'He isn't allowed to say.' Sophie refills his glass and pours one out for Claire. He notices Sophie's hands, how different they are from her sister's smooth, pale fingers. She's the one who takes charge, he thinks, there's someone like that in every household.

Claire says, 'We wondered if my husband . . . with the royalist uprising in the Vendée . . . There are so many stories of émigré officers returning secretly to France to encourage insurrection.'

'You shouldn't believe everything you hear,' he says drily, and drinks his wine. Then he notices the silver bowl of small pink flowers on the edge of the desk: 'Roses de Meaux.' He looks from one woman to the other. 'The first of the season?'

Sophie nods.

'They're early,' he says. 'But then you're so much further south.' He puts out a finger and touches a petal. 'Like little pompoms.'

'Would you like one?'

Immediately he breaks off a half-open bud, which he places carefully in his buttonhole. He picks up his glass and raises it to Sophie. 'Thank you.'

She asks, 'And Anne? She doesn't even say if she and the children are well. We've had no news for months.'

He shakes his head. 'The note was passed on by a mutual acquaintance.'

'We hear such sad stories about émigrés. Entire families begging in the streets.'

'Oh yes,' he says, 'and the terrible food and the unspeakable weather. And the ugly English girls, desperate to be corrupted.'

Claire looks down, into her wine. But Sophie stares back at him and he smiles, because he has a hypothesis, patiently tested over years, that passion runs fiercer in plain women than in pretty ones.

'Why did you come here?' she asks.

He sets down his empty glass. She makes no move to refill it.

'You know,' he says, 'for all the hardship . . . at least our honour is intact.'

'If you find honour compatible with treason.'

'Treason!' He raises an eyebrow. 'And murdering your King – what do you call that?'

'Why did you come here?' asks Sophie again.

'We need money,' he says, 'jewels, gold, whatever you have.'

He's looking at Claire. Her hand, with its rings, flies up to her throat, to the heavy gold chain she always wears these days.

'We don't have any money,' says Sophie, 'and I think you should leave now.'

He ignores her and speaks directly to her sister: 'Your husband risks his life daily in our cause.'

'Your cause,' replies Sophie, 'not ours. We believe in the Revolution.'

'It always amuses me,' he says, 'to hear people use that term as if it signified something new, a departure. If you knew your astronomy you'd realise it describes the fixed course traced by a star as it wheels through the heavens.' He holds up a hand, counts off his fingers: 'French military defeats in Holland, Belgium, the Rhineland. Dumouriez gone over to the Austrians. The Vendée in royalist hands. Riots in Lyon. War with all the major European powers.' He smiles again. 'Never forget, when you speak so confidently of revolutions, that wheels, by their very nature, continue turning.'

There are tears in Claire's eyes. Sophie takes her sister's hand. 'Of course there are setbacks,' she says. 'People make mistakes when they try to put the unimaginable into practice. But at least they're trying.'

210

All he does, very deliberately, is pick up the decanter and pour out more wine. Which he sips lounging back in his chair, his hips thrust forward, watching them realise that wine is not the only thing he could help himself to if he chose.

'We expect . . . our father should be here at any moment.'

'Oh yes,' he says, 'I know all about your father, Mademoiselle de Saint-Pierre.' Then, because he has succeeded in frightening her, he half relents. 'There's no need for alarm. I wouldn't take anything you didn't want to give.'

Something screams, outside in the darkness, and Claire leaps to her feet.

'It's only the owl,' says Sophie.

But her sister is taking off her rings. A white stone, a blue one, blue and white stones together. Then she pauses and holds out her hand to him. 'Here. You do it.' And after a brief tussle the gold band slides over her knuckle and into his palm. 'Here. Take everything.'

He pockets the rings, the bracelet. He looks at her throat.

'No,' she says, 'not this.'

He nods and gets to his feet. 'Thank you, Madame la Marquise. Your husband would be proud of you.'

Claire covers her face with her ringless fingers.

'Please don't trouble your servant,' he says, 'I'll show myself out.' He crosses to the window, slips his hand behind the curtain, undoes the catch.

'Is Hubert really all right?' Sophie, coming up behind him, stands with her hands clasped in front of her. 'If you lied, just to get her jewellery . . .'

He turns and runs his finger lightly down her cheek. 'I'll come back for you, one day.'

The next morning she finds a small pink rose outside the window, where it has fallen unheeded and been trampled into the gravel.

The failure of the spring rains had led to the introduction of the *maximum*, the ceiling on the price of grain. This, in turn, aggravated shortages, occasioned riots, encouraged oratory, filled file after bursting file with triplicate copies of licences, requisition notices, memorandums, letters of denunciation.

How do you reconcile progress and freedom? How do you improve the world if you don't take control of it? It was the conundrum of the age.

Joseph gave it no thought whatsoever, whistling his way through town under the cloudless skies he had come to take for granted that year.

At the site off to one side of the central marketplace, the foundations for the public latrines were being dug. Progress you could measure in bricks and mortar, he thought, that was a great thing.

'Disgusting,' said a woman, standing watching the work.

'Indecent,' agreed her companion. 'But what do you expect these days?'

'Shocking. Next they'll be inviting us to attend the inaugural pissing.'

'Disgraceful. The mayor and councillors have probably gone into training.'

Buoyed up, they began trading cheerful insults with the workmen, who leapt at the opportunity to lay down their picks and engage in verbal battle.

'Good afternoon,' said a voice at his elbow.

'Citizeness Saint-Pierre! What brings you here?'

'Waiting for Berthe,' explained Mathilde. 'But she's probably stuck in a queue somewhere.'

212

He looked at the damp curls straggling out under the limp cotton bonnet. 'Would you do me the honour of having a lemonade with me while you wait?'

They found a table in the shade of an awning and she told him she had come into Castelnau to buy a present for Sophie, whose birthday fell in three days. 'She's fond of flowers so I considered Heliotrope Water, but it's outrageously expensive. And sugar almonds are out of the question this year, they've trebled in price. Don't you think it sad I should be burdened with financial worries at my age? Youth should be a time of carefree mirth.'

'They do very good pastries here. Might I offer you some?'

She made her selection with frowning concentration.

He raised his glass to her. 'Did you solve the problem to your satisfaction?'

She produced a small parcel from her pocket and unwrapped the tissue paper: a pair of hair combs, each carved with a rose. 'They were very reasonably priced at a market stall. I expect they'll fall apart soon. But the alternative was embroidering a piece of cotton and calling it a handkerchief – and neither of us deserves that.'

'I'm sure your thoughtfulness will be appreciated.'

She sipped lemonade, gazing out over the dusty square. 'I worry about Sophie. She's not getting any younger. And if a man can't have beauty or wealth, he requires youthfulness at least.'

A plate of cakes was placed in front of them. Conversation ceased for a while.

At length, Mathilde sat back. 'That was lovely. Thank you.' She licked a fleck of pastry from the corner of her mouth and added, quite unnecessarily, 'My appetite is at odds with my appearance.'

'About your sister,' he began. Then he stopped and fidgeted with his spectacles.

'She's getting over Stephen. At least she no longer makes a point of not looking at him. And I know she thinks well of you. But she has a poor opinion of herself. She needs encouragement.'

213

'I'm not rich,' he said, 'and I was born in Lacapelle. If she thought Fletcher wasn't good enough . . .'

'What a peculiar notion. Sophie isn't like that at all. Even Claire's no longer sure what she thinks about foreigners. Although Americans are a case apart, aren't they, not so much strange as exotic. Like Persian carpets. And it does help that he has money and looks.'

A flock of hopeful sparrows had alighted near their feet. Joseph brushed crumbs in their direction and watched the quarrels break out. He was retracing a conversation in which he had thought Fletcher told him that . . .

Eventually, he said, 'I've probably been very foolish.'

'It wouldn't surprise me. Still, you seem to be competent as well as kind-hearted, which is rare. Everyone's talking about how well you've done with the rubbish. The smell is really quite bearable. Despite this heat, too.'

'The cart goes around twice a week,' he said. He poured the last of the lemonade into her glass and couldn't stop grinning.

'And Dr Ducroix says you've transformed the hospital. He says it quite often, as if he hasn't made up his mind whether to be pleased or not.'

'The council has rented separate housing for the veterans and an orphanage has been set up from funds confiscated by the revolutionary tribunal. That still leaves basic problems like the lack of nursing care.' He offered this information automatically, his mind on quite other things. What was he meant to be doing this evening? How soon could he set about this programme of encouragement? He saw himself riding out to Montsignac, his pockets bulging with sugar almonds.

'You're a credit to the Revolution,' said Mathilde. 'And you have excellent taste in pastries.'

But he wasn't listening. 'About your sister. Do you really think –?'

She nodded. 'In a month or two. Once the roses are over. And one more thing . . .'

'Yes?'

'You stand a much better chance if you take off those spectacles.'

214

onfessing his aversion to the cavernous mayoral office, Ricard ushered them into a small room that opened off it. It was a more intimate space, he explained, it encouraged the exchange of ideas; and it was more democratic too, he had always objected to Luzac's habit of ensconcing himself behind his desk, while the rest of them had to perch about his office. Here there was an oval table, not too large, around which they could take their places 'as equals, to engage in frank discussion'.

The brand-new Central Committee duly admired the ceiling with its painted scenes of *fêtes champêtres* set in gilded panelling, the tall, south-facing windows opening onto a balcony and leaf-filled square. Ricard limped around, drawing attention to the soft blues and reds of the carpet, pointing out the lacquer corner cupboards, running a reverent hand over an exquisite little bronze statue of Hercules. 'The Revolution in Home Furnishings,' muttered Mercier when the mayor's back was turned, and pulled the shutters tight.

When at last they disposed themselves around the table, Joseph wondered if the others were as conscious as he was of the absence of Luzac: their fifth man, whose omission from the Committee was a measure of how far their courses had diverged since the previous autumn. Despite Mercier's precautions, a faint shriek of cicadas penetrated the room. Luzac's owl face loomed in Joseph's mind, pallid and persistent, claws clinging grimly to the rafters.

Accepting only a glass of water, he spotted the printer's knowing smile.

Ricard opened the meeting with a formal statement of the Central Committee's purpose. It was essentially an advisory body, he said, its hand-picked 'experts' would make recommendations to the town council about how best to implement and safeguard revolutionary policy. Chalabre represented security, Mercier the press and public opinion, Joseph the altogether vaguer domain of public welfare.

'What does that mean, exactly?' asked Mercier. With a half-bow to Joseph, sitting across the table: 'No disrespect, of course.'

Ricard said coldly, 'Citizen Morel will advise us about health, sanitation and related practical matters, all vital to public morale. I'd have thought we all knew of his work at the hospital. As well as his achievements with rubbish collection and latrines.'

'Ah yes,' said Mercier, 'garbage and excrement. Behold a revolutionary at work.'

'Can we move on?' Chalabre had produced a little tin of lemon pastilles and was selecting one with care. About to return the sweets to his pocket, he caught the mayor's eye and placed them in the middle of the table.

That summer it was being whispered that the Revolution was coming undone quicker than a whore's petticoats. At meetings of the Convention, the elected representatives of the people screamed insults at each other: Vile bird! Cracked toad! A band of armed Parisians, exercising their Parisian right to set the country straight, put an end to the endless contention by walking into the Convention and walking out with those deputies whose views on matters such as the abolition of private property did not coincide with their own.

In Castelnau, the municipal authorities had received notification of the imminent visit of Citizen Brunel, dispatched from Paris to ensure that the Revolution was progressing to order throughout France. 'Naturally, I don't intend to provide this Brunel fellow with grounds for intervening in our affairs,' said Ricard. 'The very existence of this Committee should be sufficient assurance that in Castelnau we're capable of anticipating problems and dealing with them.'

How many times had they heard Ricard denounce provincial pride? 'I'm a Frenchman,' the mayor was fond of saying, 'that's all that counts.' Yet resentment of Paris twisted away inside Ricard, too. Only in his case it took the form of a determination to outdo – pre-empt, where possible – the revolutionary zeal of the capital. It was like desiring a woman who cared nothing for you but who occasionally used you for her own ends, thought Joseph; she determined the course of your days, no matter whether you opted for pursuit or flight.

'I admit I was wrong.' Mercier, tilting his chair back, smiled at the mayor, looked around the table. 'I told Citizen Ricard that his council would never agree to this Committee.'

'You weren't too wide of the mark,' replied Ricard. 'Our friend Luzac lost no time expressing his objections. Beginning with the fact that neither you nor Morel are elected members of the council.'

'And?'

It was Chalabre who answered. 'Consider the recent events in Paris. Our councillors dread the fervour with which certain options are urged in Castelnau among citizens who are not, shall we say, concerned with social niceties. I myself was moved by the eloquence with which our mayor represented the Committee as a mediating influence between the Club and the council – after all, we know which spoons to use at banquets.'

Ricard waited until the snicker had died down. 'Nevertheless, I've received a formal protest.' Tapping the letter in front of him: 'Signed by Luzac and three other councillors. *Liberty, equality and the sovereignty of the people* ... the usual preamble ...' His eyes moved down the page.

'*An ardent desire to serve the Revolution?*' hazarded Mercier.

'Quite, quite ... Here's the nub of it: *We fear that the existence of the Central Committee will encourage political divisions that strike at the heart of republican unity. We deeply regret that the council, in a moment of misguided if sincere fervour, voted in favour of its establishment.*'

'Let me look at that letter,' said Chalabre.

Ricard handed it over.

'I see that Chauvet is one of the signatories. He abstained

from voting at the council meeting, if I remember correctly. But has since been persuaded to change his mind. Well, I'm almost sure I have a letter in my files accusing one of his farmers of holding back a portion of his harvest.' The lawyer popped one of the small yellow sweets into his mouth and glanced around. 'That should do it, don't you think?'

Mercier shrugged. 'Luzac's behind this – why bother with anyone else?'

'Our friend still enjoys a certain prestige in Castelnau,' said Ricard. 'People remember him as –' he grimaced – 'a hero, the man who defied Caussade. Chauvet is an aristocrat, it's not so long ago his bailiffs were hanging peasants who weren't quick enough with their rents.'

'All the same.' Mercier looked at Chalabre. 'What stage has the investigation of the famous massacre reached?'

The lawyer frowned. 'That's a separate matter altogether.'

'I told you not to put that ponderous old fool Saint-Pierre in charge. You panicked quite unnecessarily in the autumn. Listen to me now: everyone knows Luzac was implicated. Turn up some hard evidence and you have a judicial reason, if you feel you need one, to arrest him.'

Ricard looked at Joseph.

'If Luzac is guilty ...' His spectacles slid down his nose. 'Only you seemed to think there was some doubt about that.'

'We didn't want to jump to conclusions. And we were right not to risk disrupting the elections over the fate of a few priests.'

'There was a boy,' said Joseph, 'and that boat-builder. Among others.'

'Exactly my point,' interrupted Mercier. 'Innocent citizens, small people. What more do you need? Organise the arrest to coincide with Brunel's visit.'

Joseph thought of Luzac, that pathetic sleeve pinned up at the shoulder. 'Saint-Pierre is conducting an investigation. If he hasn't found any evidence ...'

Mercier laughed. 'Isn't that why we have him?' – nodding at Chalabre.

'Save your witticisms for your editorials,' snapped the

lawyer, 'the fools who buy your paper are probably amused by them.'

When the other two left, Joseph hung back. The room felt stale, the air sticky. Ricard folded back the shutters and carried two chairs onto the balcony, where stars had pricked open the dark-blue sky.

'I don't understand why I'm on this Committee,' said Joseph.

'You shouldn't let Mercier needle you.'

'It's not that. But this matter of Luzac . . .' The words blundered softly, like moths. 'The three of you don't need me,' he said.

'I do. I need a man I can trust absolutely.'

Joseph turned his head. Ricard was staring out over the wilderness of dark leaves: 'I need someone who won't betray me.'

'Mercier,' he felt obliged to say, 'Chalabre.' All the while delighted at being singled out.

'Ambitious men. They wouldn't hesitate to sacrifice me – or each other, or anyone else – if it suited them.'

The cicadas, which had fallen into one of their inexplicable silences, shrilled out once more. 'I understand why you shrink from condemning Luzac.' Ricard was taking out his pipe. 'I admire your loyalty. But he can't be allowed to go on, opposing us at every turn. And I'm not squeamish. It's not my business to be.'

'Nor mine. I think I am, all the same.'

'Oh, undoubtedly. But only because you fret over the consequences for others, not because you're afraid for yourself. Self-interest doesn't enter your calculation. That's why I trust you.'

Joseph thought, *Fret*, that isn't right, that's a word that's used about children. But Ricard had changed the subject: 'That American – Fletcher. Chalabre tells me he's given up his lodgings in town and moved out to Montsignac. Do you know what's behind that?'

219

A week earlier the news would have frozen him. Now he smiled. 'He's in love with Saint-Pierre's eldest daughter.'

'Isn't she still married to Monferrant?'

'He's in exile, remember, fighting our armies somewhere.'

'Her husband might be a traitor but he's still her husband,' retorted the mayor. 'Moral squalor is always inexcusable. And typical of that class.'

Joseph had been about to say something about Sophie, wanting to savour her name in his mouth. Wanting also to confide, to explain why the Revolution no longer seemed of overwhelming importance, why he needed time for ordinary things, a woman's smile, life drawing him in like a ripening orchard.

'That American has family in Bordeaux,' continued Ricard. 'Half the deputies who were arrested in Paris came from around there. The Committee should be keeping a close eye on anyone who has connections with the place.'

'Fletcher is an artist,' said Joseph, conscious of magnanimity. 'He's no threat to anyone. To the Revolution, I mean.'

'His association with Saint-Pierre is disturbing. In fact that entire family ... The other girl has taken up with those so-called Republican Women.'

'She's called Sophie.'

'I've no patience at all with their petty carping on equality. As if there weren't ... *ideals*, a Revolution at stake. Do you know, they've written to the council proposing we release funds to establish a lying-in hospital for unmarried mothers. Why not license prostitution while we're about it?'

'Not all unmarried mothers are prostitutes.'

'A literal distinction, not a moral one. Anyway, where do these women find the time? Who's looking after their husbands?'

Joseph smiled into the dark. 'Not all of them have husbands.' And was unable to resist adding, 'She grows roses, you know.'

Clove-scented smoke drifted over the balcony. 'Promise me you'll give me until the next elections?' Ricard's voice grew softer still: 'It'll be settled by then, one way or the other.'

Naturally, there are roses, impossible to escape them in this house, at this season. The bed-curtains are drawn back and Stephen picks out the vase on one of the tables scattered about the room, but in the half-dark he can't tell the colour of the flowers, only that they're not white.

'What are you thinking of?'

The lover's question. 'Roses,' he replies truthfully.

She pinches him. 'It's as bad as talking to Sophie.'

He strokes her cheek. Propping himself up on one elbow, he slides his palm along the dampness of her skin. A copy of *Paul et Virginie*, bound in large-grained, dark-blue morocco, always lies on her night-table; he can see the gold lettering on its spine. It was his first present to her. They speak of it as their book. When they talk of a life together they tell each other of a bamboo house set in a banana grove, of flocks of goats and flights of parakeets. They will have a little dog called Fidèle – 'Nothing like Brutus,' they agree – and plant a coconut tree for each of the children. This evocation of innocence is necessary to them both. But lately he dreams of being held fast in greenery, if only he could reach the other side of the mountains, but pale-green tendrils curl tight around his ribs and the way forward is thick with leaves.

'We'd be safe in Bordeaux,' he says.

'I'm not frightened any longer. Now that you're here all the time. If that man comes back, Sophie and I won't be alone.'

'It's not his side that worries me. It's different in Bordeaux – they've closed down their Jacobin clubs and arrested the leaders.'

'Then go,' she says, moving slightly away, 'go if you're afraid.'

He wants to seize her wrists and oblige her to defend the maddening logic which allows her to be unfaithful to her husband while requiring her to remain at Montsignac until such time as he should come back to claim her. It's as if adultery fastens her to Monferrant far more securely than the vows she set aside with such seeming lightness. A perverse conception of honour that won't allow her to end the marriage, while it shows itself unscrupulous in taking daily – nightly – advantage of her husband's absence. The calculus of desire, inscrutable, operating according to its own rules.

He wants to ask what will happen when Monferrant returns. If he returns. How long is Claire prepared to wait for the husband she never mentions?

And the child. The baby who sucks her ankles, who laughs at sunlight, who opens and shuts both hands at him across a room. My daughter, he thinks fiercely, Claire can't expect me to ... I'll tell Monferrant, if it comes to that.

But surely it won't? Surely she wants him as much as he wants her?

At the same time, even as he knots her hair through his fingers, as he shifts to feel the length of her against his body, he thinks about the time before he knew her and sees a series of arches opening to infinity, he thinks of balloons and the astonishing air.

He has done almost no work since moving to Montsignac.

He stills panic with the resolution that from now on he will rise early and work late. He'll talk to Sophie, speed up arrangements for converting that barn into a studio. There are two portraits due in the autumn, conventional stuff but he needs the discipline; he'll hunt up more commissions, it's only a matter of being agreeable to people. He'll go to Paris soon, spend a fortnight looking at paintings. I'll write to Charles, he thinks, when he gets leave we'll travel south, into the mountains. Or along the coast, as we planned at Christmas.

He kisses her eyelids.

He thinks of seabirds.

She owns one of those pretty little cabinets with elaborately inlaid doors that swing open to reveal a set of drawers; no doubt its marquetry conceals a secret compartment. She has a fondness for objects that invite intimacy and create privacy, dividing up her room around a Chinese screen, a silk hanging, a wallpapered alcove. She sections off her life, as well: her marriage, the future, these subjects are cordoned-off territory where she will not tolerate trespass.

Claire knows that America is not the same as the island where Paul and Virginia love each other chastely, in harmony with Nature. But along the blurred frontier between wakefulness and sleep, all Edens converge. 'Tell me what it's like,' she says, trying to keep things straight, 'there in the New World.' Seeing azure butterflies as large as her palm, lace-edged waves beside a ribbon of shore.

'Wider,' he replies without hesitation.

Her eyes fly open.

He speaks urgently into the scented darkness: 'We must be sincere. We must talk about ... *everything.*'

She slides her hand under his shirt.

As was to be expected, the assassination of Marat by a girl called Charlotte Corday was all anyone could talk about.

'They say she's beautiful,' said the woman sitting on the other side of Isabelle, 'no man who lays eyes on her can help falling in love with her.'

'I suspect the tribunal will be immune.'

'They say,' lowering her voice, 'that she had his child. Strangled it at birth.'

Another woman turned around. 'Nonsense. She's a virgin brought up by nuns. They probably put her up to it.'

'Wouldn't a respectable girl have waited until he was out of his bath and dressed? It proves she's immoral.'

'They say she's fond of cats.'

'It was an ordinary kitchen knife, you know, one with a five-inch blade.'

A handbell called the fourteen Republican Women to order. They met once a fortnight in a low-beamed room above a bakery. Until recently, the room had been used for storing flour, and sacks were still heaped in one corner. Fine white dust settled in the folds of the women's skirts and escaped in ghostly puffs when they shook out their hair at night.

Their president, a brisk woman called Suzanne Lambert, wasted no time on inessentials; she was married to an actor and had developed a ruthlessness in getting to the point. 'Dear friends: Yesterday I received a letter from the Central Committee informing me that we have until the end of the month to disband our association. After that date, the Republican Women will be formally proscribed. Should we continue to meet in defiance of the order, we'll be arrested and prosecuted.'

She paused. Theatrical conversation, for all its disadvantages, was instructive about delivery.

When the uproar had subsided, she went on. 'I think it reasonable to deduce that we've all been judged guilty of Charlotte Corday's crime. However, the reason the Committee advances for its decision is that associations such as ours *foster disunity and dissension at the expense of the national interest*.'

A woman sitting in the front row enquired if the Committee had the authority to disband them. Mme Lambert shrugged.

'It's all that girl's fault,' hissed Isabelle's neighbour. 'They keep asking her for the names of her accomplices and she keeps insisting women are capable of independent action.'

'The letter concludes by reminding us that the Jacobins recently voted to admit women to their meetings – as observers, not as members, of course. We are urged to avail ourselves of the opportunity to *swell with pride at the oratory talent and political astuteness* of our husbands.' Mme Lambert smiled grimly. 'I'm sure you all recognise that editorial flair. The wistful note can perhaps be attributed to an incident you won't see reported in *Le Citoyen*: Anne Mercier has left her husband and is seeking a divorce.'

'I'm not surprised,' whispered Isabelle to Sophie, 'he must have swelled once too often for her to go on pretending she didn't notice.'

The baker's wife had a poor opinion of men. Apprised of the fate of the Republican Women, she sent up her condolences and a tray of freshly baked cinnamon meringues. She had no patience with politics herself; but what harm were those girls doing?

The baker, to whom the question was addressed, cut himself another wedge of cheese. For his part, he was tired of meeting strange women on the stairs; and what if one of them took it into her head to murder him in his bath? He could see it now: there he was, all wrinkled and soapy, at a terrible disadvantage, while a harridan in scarlet bore down on him with an axe. He chewed steadily, his eyes on his plate, congratulating himself on his narrow escape.

It was in December, thinks Saint-Pierre, two or three days before Christmas. He remembers opening a window and the way a line of snow collapsed inwards, onto the ledge; but that might have been on another occasion. He had stood on one foot beside his grandmother, leaning against this very table, and she showed him how to make cruchade. Half a century later, he still finds himself craving its warm, sweet blandness.

His older daughters wrinkle their noses at it, but his grandson loves cruchade and Mathilde is not altogether immune. A dish for children and old men. A winter dish, unsuited to high summer. But Berthe would of course have served it at dinner, if he'd asked. He didn't, for three reasons: he takes pleasure in preparing it himself; he believes his version superior to Berthe's; he doesn't want to have to share.

The mixture of maize flour, milk and a little butter has cooked slowly, thickening to the right consistency. He turns it out onto a linen cloth and blows on it, willing it to cool faster.

The night house sighs and shifts. Then settles itself, groaning. Through the kitchen window he can see a lopsided white moon.

Having forsaken Mathilde for the smells from the kitchen, Brutus yawns – the roof of his mouth is black-mottled pink, an unpleasant sight – and positions himself where Saint-Pierre is bound to trip over him. When this happens, he bears the reproaches unblinkingly, even finding it in his heart to lick Saint-Pierre's avenging hand, and hunkers down to fix his yellow gaze on the table. A little puddle of hopeful drool forms gradually on the tiles.

There is no armagnac to be found, so Saint-Pierre pours out a glass of Berthe's plum brandy. He can't resist breaking off a corncr of the solidifying cruchade. His eyebrows twitch in anticipation.

A witness has come forward. He says he was paid by Luzac to silence a man called Durand. At the time, this Durand was going around the taverns boasting that he was on the mayor's payroll and had played an instrumental role in the prison killings, so the witness wasn't surprised that Luzac wanted him out of the way. He lay in wait as Durand reeled down the quays one misty November night, intending to break his head open with an iron bar. With a drunk's astonishing luck, Durand staggered at the crucial moment and the blow glanced off his head; but then he lost his footing, slipped on the wct stones and toppled backwards into the river.

Asked why he had decided to break his silence, the witness, an out-of-work carder called Mazel, replied virtuously that his conscience had given him no rest since Durand's body had been fished from the river. Besides, he added, peering up through stubby, fluttering lashes at Saint-Pierre, Luzac had told him plainly that he suspected Durand of anti-revolutionary activity. Since he himself was the sworn enemy of all such traitors, he had felt no qualms about Durand's fate. At the time, he had believed like the rest of Castelnau, that Luzac was a good republican and revolutionary. 'So who was I, a poor, ignorant man, to doubt what he said?'

It was not an implausible story. Yet it troubled Saint-Pierre at several points and he went over his objections with Chalabre. There was the character of the witness, for a start: Mazel had been in and out of jail for various petty crimes ever since he was a boy, was known to the police as a thief and a liar. Could the fellow's word be worth anything at all? What was more, Mazel was a skinny weasel of a man; why would Luzac choose him to do away with Durand, who had been tall and hefty? And if by some outlandish chance Mazel was telling the truth, where was the money? The carder was unable to produce a single *sou* of the small fortune he had allegedly been paid, claiming he had lost most of it at cards and squandered the rest on alcohol and women. Yet the man Saint-Pierre sent to make enquiries at certain establishments reported that Mazel's acquaintances all denied the carder giving any sign of having recently come into money.

Chalabre heard him out courteously, nodding his appreciation of Saint-Pierre's misgivings. 'Yes, yes, indeed, Citizen Saint-Pierre, I congratulate you as always on the perspicacity of your observations. Undoubtedly a more rigorous investigation will find that Mazel has distorted events through malice or stupidity, a creature like that is incapable of telling a straight story. Perhaps he had an accomplice; perhaps he has hidden the money to avoid handing it over. But these are questions that can wait for the trial, yes?'

'And the most peculiar aspect of this whole thing: Why is Mazel confessing to a crime as serious as this? That nonsense about his conscience troubling him is transparently false.'

'I agree it's surprising. But it's common knowledge that our former mayor and his circle have expressed support for the deputies arrested in Paris last month, which is to say, traitors. And they've made no secret of wanting to close down our Club, now that it's no longer their gentlemen's association. Granted, Mazel is a profoundly unattractive character in almost every respect, but it doesn't necessarily follow that he's not a good patriot. He might well feel betrayed by men like Luzac.'

Saint-Pierre didn't bother to hide his scepticism.

'You shouldn't underestimate the contempt in which ordinary citizens hold enemies of the State,' said the lawyer primly. 'If we don't act on this evidence, could we ourselves be considered guilty of betraying the Revolution?'

Not even a fool could have missed that.

'Besides,' went on Chalabre in a gentler tone, as if he had seen the spurt of fear in the magistrate's eyes, 'you once told me you yourself suspected official involvement in the prison killings. Who else could have been responsible?'

So Saint-Pierre had approved the warrant for Luzac's arrest.

He can't lay his hands on any sugar either – really, where does Berthe squirrel these things away? – but a pot of her apricot jam from the previous summer will do just as well. In fact, he prefers jam. With the point of a knife, he draws a diamond grid on the surface of the cruchade; then he cuts along the lines.

What he hasn't told Chalabre is that his informant reported talking to a prostitute who said she was certain Mazel had turned police spy. Only the previous week she had surprised Mazel deep in conversation with two men everyone knew worked for the public prosecutor; so she couldn't understand why he'd been arrested, but that was the police for you, what were they there for if not to make life difficult for honest citizens?

He begins frying. The butter sizzles, and Saint-Pierre is growing a little deaf; so he doesn't hear the door open and is startled into dropping his spoon when a voice behind him says, 'I didn't think it could be an intruder. Then again, you take food so seriously in this country, I couldn't be sure. For all I know, it might be customary to break into houses just to cook –'

Stephen grabs wildly at a chair to save himself, and hits his elbow on a corner of the table as he crashes to the floor. Head on one side, Brutus contemplates him for a long moment, rehearsing possibilities; then he rearranges himself with his back to the newcomer.

'Spit,' says Stephen bitterly, clutching his elbow, heaving himself onto a chair. 'Cold spit. Disgusting. Three times in a fortnight. Hound of hell.'

Saint-Pierre is wielding a slotted spoon, lifting the golden-yellow diamonds onto a plate. 'He's getting older. Drooling more, biting less.'

'I'll try to think of it that way.'

'You know,' says Saint-Pierre reflectively, 'it was that same Christmas that I first noticed – when someone comes in out of the cold, it's not until after the door shuts that you feel the draught.'

Rubbing his bruises, Stephen contemplates this remark, eventually concluding that its surface is free of crevices where he might reasonably be expected to find a toehold. He watches as a thick layer of apricot jam is spread on the cruchade. 'The sky tonight, just above the horizon at sunset,' he remarks. 'Exactly that shade of orange.'

'It's an old regional dish.' Saint-Pierre holds out the plate. 'Not to everyone's taste,' he says hopefully. 'Try a small piece.'

'Delicious.'

Saint-Pierre sighs.

*I*n Paris they had decided to backdate the future, which was deemed to have begun with the founding of the Republic, one and indivisible, in the autumn of 1792. So twelve months later, the first of the brand-new calendars proclaimed that it was already Year II. It was as if they had drawn a line under the past, added up the sum of its achievements and found the total unimpressive, thought Joseph. As if they had wasted enough time, and now had no more to lose.

Saint-Pierre's eyes followed Joseph's. Vendémiaire, the month of the *vendange* or wine harvest. The picture on the calendar showed a statuesque young woman, her arms full of grapes, and vine leaves twined around her brow. Her bare, round breasts hinted at a voluptuousness in piquant contrast to her accusatory gaze.

'It makes a change from Saint Mark.'

'I beg your pardon?'

'Patron saint of vineyards.'

'Ah.' Joseph's spectacles twisted in his hands. 'Yes, it's certainly different.'

'You're poets, you men of the Revolution. The names you've conjured – Brumaire, the misty month, Prairial, the month of meadows.'

'It's the cult of Nature. Liberated from the Christian superstitions that burdened the old calendar, republicans will live in harmony with the rhythms of the natural world.'

'Which apparently accords them a single day of rest every ten days. Are you quite sure they wanted to be liberated from Sundays?'

'Units of ten are more logical.'

'Only because of an arbitrary quirk of arithmetic. What if we counted in nines or twelves?'

Joseph felt, with something not unlike desperation, that the conversation was getting away from him.

The clerk who sat in the cubby hole outside Saint-Pierre's room came diffidently in after knocking and presented the magistrate with one, two, four documents that urgently required his signature.

With an effort, Joseph succeeded in not looking at the woman on the calendar. Every surface in the cramped office – desk, cupboards, chairs, floor – overflowed with deed boxes, and bundle upon bundle of documents bound with scarlet tape. There was a narrow window, cobweb-laced, facing east. He noticed the smell of sealing wax, and a line of purposeful ants striking out obliquely from behind a bookcase.

Before the door had quite shut on the clerk, he blurted out why he had come.

After a long silence, during which Joseph stared at the ants, the magistrate said, 'And Sophie? Does she . . . ?'

'I thought it right to speak to you first.' Immediately that struck him as both presumptuous and clumsy; although it had seemed the honourable course of action, when night after night he had walked about the shuttered streets and miserably watched scruple beat down desire. 'The Committee . . . you might not approve . . .'

'Very punctilious of you,' said Saint-Pierre. Rather drily, thought Joseph; but he lacked the nerve to raise his eyes to the magistrate's face.

'She once gave me a geranium,' he mumbled.

'Luzac is to be tried by the revolutionary tribunal rather than in my court. Chalabre informed me yesterday that the charge has been changed to one of sedition – the prison murders representing an attempt to turn popular opinion against the Revolution.'

'I know.'

'I know you do. By order of the Central Committee. Tell me, Morel, when the Committee decided to have Luzac's case handed on to the tribunal, were you aware that he had counter-accused our mayor of complicity in the massacre?'

Certain of his ground, Joseph looked up at once. 'Luzac will say anything to save himself, won't he? Ricard is an orator and a priest-hater, his speeches to the Club were colourful. Beyond that . . .' He shrugged.

'Luzac alleges that the killings were entirely Ricard's idea. He claims that Durand, the fellow they fished from the river, met them both for instructions. Later, when there was an uproar over the massacre, Ricard arranged to have Durand murdered – who by, Luzac doesn't know. He says that Durand had an accomplice, believed to have volunteered and since reported missing in action, who was in fact silenced before my investigation could question him. He denies ever meeting Mazel, and insists that the man's evidence is a web of lies spun by Ricard or Chalabre or both.'

'Well, the trial will prove the truth or falsehood of his allegations.'

'My dear Morel, the revolutionary tribunal proves exactly what it sets out to prove. As you well know.'

Joseph stared at his hands, lying pinkly on his knees.

'But you probably haven't heard the news with which my clerk greeted me today: Mazel was found hanging in his cell this morning. Overcome by remorse in the night, according to the governor of the prison.' Saint-Pierre paused. 'Odd that it should have happened the night after he was moved, most unaccountably, to a solitary cell.'

There was no mistaking the dryness that time.

Joseph said, 'I promised Ricard until the end of next summer.' He said, and it sounded like a plea, 'They outvote me three to one.'

'You're widely perceived as a good man, an honourable man. You were the reason the council agreed to the Committee. Did you know that?'

Miserably, he shook his head.

'As I was the reason the outrage over the killings was brought under control. Society likes its conscience personified. Its scapegoats too. The law was invented to circumvent that, to make right and wrong an expression of a collective will that

233

resonates beyond individual responsibility. You and I should have remembered that.' Saint-Pierre leant forward. 'They've made it clear they don't need me any longer, Morel. How much longer do you think they'll need you?'

'You're wrong about Ricard,' he insisted. 'He's a good man too, utterly dedicated. He wants a better life for his children, for everyone. He can be ...' what was the word? – 'rigorous, but I assure you he always acts in the best interests of the Revolution.'

'How terrifying.'

After a while Joseph said, 'I owe him so much, you see.'

'When you came in I was composing my letter of resignation. And since, for my daughters' sake, I have no wish to be provocative, the reason I cite is my failing health.' The magistrate smiled. 'How many men have resigned from public office in the last twelve months on the grounds of ill health? As a physician, you must have remarked the epidemic.'

Joseph opened his mouth.

Saint-Pierre forestalled him. 'As to Sophie: my daughters have long done as they pleased. Sophie is of age, and quite capable of making up her own mind about marriage, as I'm sure you realise. But as a scrupulous man you came to me first, a courtesy I appreciate. And so I'd ask you to consider this before you go any further: Sophie is an aristocrat, her sister is married to an émigré, her father has fallen short of the Revolution's requirements. If you were to marry her, wouldn't that be the excuse they needed?'

'Five minutes ago you implied they didn't need an excuse – that it would only be a matter of time before they ... turn against me.'

'Quite so.' The voice was very gentle. 'But you see, just now it was Sophie's safety I had in mind.'

'I'd make certain she came to no harm ... I'd protect her,' he protested.

The magistrate said nothing.

Footsteps hurried past in the passage and the line of ants had started to double back on itself.

'What should I do?' asked Joseph.

*H*er father thinks how characteristic it is of Sophie to tackle difficulties without flinching, not because she welcomes them but in order to get them out of the way as soon as possible. On upward stretches she's always a good few lengths ahead of him, climbing with resolute strides, whereas he picks his way leisurely over the rising ground, looking around him, taking in the view, noticing a patch of purple bellflowers, stepping aside to avoid a caramel-brown beetle. There is his heart to be considered; and then he cannot get out of the habit of always thinking he has plenty of time, wide bends in a slow green river looping into the distance.

He wonders if all only children share the illusion that it is other people who grow old.

But he knows he'll catch up and perhaps overtake Sophie on the downhill slope, where he makes steady progress and she takes sideways steps and is nervous of falling. And what might be concluded from that, he asks himself; perhaps simply that he has a regrettable tendency to sift the evidence in search of alternative explanations that fit the facts.

He tries to explain a version of this to Sophie, who is waiting for him at the top of the crest in the lee of a hawthorn hedge.

'I don't trust people who don't consider alternatives,' she says, as he lowers himself carefully onto the grass. 'They pride themselves on being practical when all they really are is unimaginative.'

'Well, there's such a thing as too much imagination.'

'Don't let Stephen hear you say that.'

He watches her twist free from the bag she has insisted on carrying, slung across one shoulder. At one time he had believed that she and Fletcher ... and immediately his mind springs away like a frightened hare, because he can't bring himself to contemplate what he knows is happening, and what will become of Claire – what can she be storing up but sadness?

Sophie hands him a bunch of small, golden grapes, thinking she knows why he looks so unhappy. 'You'll have time to finish your book,' she says, 'and we'll go walking every day. And if we sell those two fields there'll be enough money, even if Matty keeps growing at this rate.'

'In my grandfather's day,' he says, looking out over the valley, 'we owned it all – as far you can see.' An observation prompted not by regret but by mild astonishment at time's erosion of certainties.

Sophie spits a pip – thoop! – into the heart of a clump of yellowing nettles.

Before he can help himself, the question comes: 'What do you think of Joseph Morel?'

She frowns at a grape and tosses it down the hillside, where invisible rooks are calling. 'It's such a long time since I've seen him. I don't suppose his official duties have encouraged him to modify his opinion of people like us.'

'Perhaps his presence on the Committee spares everyone the worst of its zeal.'

It was what Morel had argued, maintaining that Ricard, at least, sought his opinions and could often be brought around to his way of thinking: 'We're friends, you see.' He had cited a municipal fund for poor relief, the housing of destitute war veterans and improvements in public sanitation; had spoken optimistically about a lying-in hospital that would provide working women with much-needed bed rest. Under Saint-Pierre's sceptical gaze he had admitted that when it came to 'political situations' and the measures taken to deal with them, his influence was minimal. 'But I promised him until the end of next summer.'

Sophie uncoils herself, rising to her feet in a single smooth movement. Saint-Pierre thinks, I'll never climb a tree again, never go running down a hill, never leap onto a horse or take the stairs two at a time.

October has been one clear, pale day after another. Sophie's rolled-back sleeves show forearms that are still tanned light gold. She brushes a strand of hair from her eyes and reaches for the fat blackberries prickling through the hedge, whose architecture is emerging once more from the clutter of summer. Saint-Pierre watches, aware that she hasn't answered his question. And he's no longer sure he was right to urge caution, to advise waiting, counsel prudence until ... Until what? What can be the end of it?

Morel had promised not to speak to Sophie until seeing out his term on the Committee. He had promised reluctantly, staring at his feet, quite obviously wishing he'd gone straight to her instead. Nevertheless, he had given his word.

Morel doesn't have long to live, of that Saint-Pierre is sure. The doctor is riddled with doubt, a terminal disease in times of revolution. They won't tolerate his symptomatic scruples much longer. What could such a marriage bring Sophie but grief? And worse, perhaps.

But the warm breath of suspicion whispers in his ear, hinting that hand in hand with his instinct to keep her safe goes a desire to keep her close, at his side, easing his days. Another selfish old fool, he thinks, is that all I've become?

When Sophie's bag is full she returns to sit beside him. Saint-Pierre, wishing to go on eating grapes in the autumn sunshine for as long as possible, begins talking about restaurants. He disapproves – of course – of this Parisian fad. Not that he blames the proprietors, cooks formerly employed in aristocratic kitchens, who found themselves out of work and set up these establishments where the provincial deputies are flocking to eat. 'Those poor devils haven't had a home-cooked meal in years,' says Saint-Pierre feelingly. 'No good ever comes of hanging about Paris.'

But for once, Sophie isn't paying attention. 'Father,' she says, 'there's something I want to do.'

237

At the barrier, the first guard had called a second over to examine Sophie's papers and she had been required to turn out her bag and her pockets. They lingered over the figures she had scribbled on the back of a draper's bill:

One bushel of flour	158
One bushel of barley	22
One bushel of oats	22
One pound of salt	96
Two litres of oil	110
12 lamp wicks	24
One pound of Marseilles soap	23
One ell of cloth	86
Two pairs of stockings	64
A passable hat	<u>220</u>
	827

'That's a large quantity of dried foodstuffs.' The second guard, the older of the two, thrust his face close to hers: 'Are you hoarding provisions?'

'Certainly not. There are eight people in the house, not counting two young children, a dog and two horses.'

Behind her, a woman trailing a sullen child clucked sympathy: 'Just like a man. No idea what it takes to feed a family.'

'What is the purpose of your visit to Castelnau?'

'I have an appointment with Dr Joseph Morel,' said Sophie, hoping she wouldn't be asked to prove it.

The first guard was running his finger down the list, his lips moving. 'You've added this up wrong: it comes to 825 not

827.' He held out the paper for her to check.

The second guard tapped the side of his head and rolled his eyes: 'Women. No head for figures.'

'Anyone can make a mistake.' Sophie's champion raised her voice and crossed her arms over her chest. 'With the cost of everything, it's impossible to keep track.' She waited a minute to see if the challenge would be taken up. When it wasn't, she craned her neck in shameless scrutiny of the list. 'My dear,' turning to Sophie, 'they're charging you far too much for wicks. If you go to my sister, she won't ask more than eighteen *livres* a dozen. The shop's on the rue de la Convention, you can't miss it. Be sure to tell her I sent you.'

'Thank you very much.'

'Is that the hat you paid all that money for? It's wicked –' glaring at the guards – 'what some people think they can get away with during a revolution.'

The porter at the hospital pointed her towards the director's office. She had timed her visit for midday, knowing that Dr Ducroix would be arriving at Isabelle's for lunch at that hour.

She had kept her overshoes on until reaching the gate, but the courtyard must have been muddy from the recent rain. About to knock, she glanced down and saw that her new red shoes were streaked with dirt. Instantly her nerve deserted her; but it was too late, she had rapped on the panelling and there was his voice.

Joseph rose to greet her, blinking rapidly, offering her a chair, apologising for Ducroix's absence – he assumed it was his colleague she wanted to see – asking whether he should ring for refreshments, telling her that if she hurried she might be able to catch Ducroix, he had been gone scarcely five minutes.

'My enquiry could just as well be directed to you,' she said, accepting the chair and removing a saucer that had once contained milk from the seat.

He relieved her of the saucer and apologised again, muttering something about kittens and waving a vague hand towards the wards. Then he said, looking not at her but at the litter of papers on his desk, 'How might I assist you?'

Sophie quailed. She began to apologise for disturbing him, for having no appointment, she knew how very busy he must be, she shouldn't presume to take up his time . . .

He interrupted quietly: 'I'm entirely at your disposal.'

'My sister – that is, my younger sister – told me you might be looking for someone to help with nursing. I would have to be shown what to do. But I have a little experience, I attended to my mother throughout her illness . . .' In desperation, she summoned Professor Kölreuter to her aid: he skipped about a landscape ordered with geometric precision, and curious flowers bloomed at his touch.

Suddenly, Joseph pulled off his spectacles.

'I could spare one or two days a week,' she said. 'But I quite see that might not be convenient . . .'

'How soon can you start?'

'Next week?'

'Excellent.' Then his face clouded over. 'But you should see the wards first, before you engage yourself. And I should warn you, the conditions are less than hygienic. People who work here often look pale and frequently fall ill.'

'You yourself look very well,' she said.

He twirled his spectacles with such force that they clattered to the floor. He dived to retrieve them, his voice floating up to her: 'But I have a strong constitution and one that's accustomed to contact with disease.'

'Two days a week – it doesn't seem an inordinate risk to me.'

Scrabbling about on his knees, he banged his elbow on the desk and didn't even notice the pain.

1794

'Once upon a time there was a hunchback and every-one made fun of him. One day when he was walking in the woods and weeping at his fate, he came across three witches dancing in a circle. *Monday, Tuesday, Wednesday*, sang each witch in turn, *Monday, Tuesday, Wednesday*. The hunchback watched for a while and then joined in their dance. *Monday, Tuesday, Wednesday*, sang out each of the witches and the hunchback added: *Thursday. Monday, Tuesday, Wednesday*, and he chimed in again: *Thursday*. The witches thought this a fine thing and laughed a great deal. They had been dancing and singing since the beginning of time and were longing for novelty. So they struck the hunchback on his hump, which immediately rolled away into the bushes. For the first time in his life he could stand up straight; and shouting with joy he ran away and back to his village, where he married the pretti-est girl and lived a long and merry and prosperous life. But once a month, on the night of the full moon, he had to return to the clearing in the forest and dance and sing with the witches, for so he had promised them and he was a man of his word.

'By and by a second hunchback, an outcast and a wanderer, came to the village and heard the story of how the first hunch-back had been miraculously cured. And the second hunchback begged the first, who was now a woodsman, to tell him how he had got rid of his hump. But the woodsman would only smile and shake his head. He had promised the witches never to reveal what had happened in the clearing that night, and he was a man of his word, stopping his pretty wife's mouth with kisses if ever she asked too many questions.

'But the hunchback was a persistent fellow, and he bided his time and watched closely, and in this way, on the night of the full moon, he saw the woodsman tiptoe out of his house and shut the door softly and set off along the path that led to the forest. The hunchback followed at a safe distance, keeping to the shadows and taking care not to step on any twigs. By and by he heard voices and they guided him to the moonlit clearing. Peeping out from behind an oak tree, he watched the dancers: *Monday, Tuesday, Wednesday*, sang each witch in turn and the woodsman joined in, singing *Thursday* in his clear, strong voice. *Monday, Tuesday, Wednesday* and *Thursday, Monday, Tuesday, Wednesday* and *Thursday*. And so they held hands and danced and sang by the light of the moon.

'Now the hunchback was no fool. He bided his time and watched closely, and Oh-ho, he said to himself, a man doesn't need moonlight to see what's going on here. So when they sang *Monday, Tuesday, Wednesday* and *Thursday*, he ran out into the clearing and chimed in: *Friday. Monday, Tuesday, Wednesday, Thursday*, went the song, and the hunchback joined in the dance, holding hands and singing *Friday*.

'Then the witches flew into a terrible rage and struck the hunchback between his shoulders. And the woodsman's hump flew out of the bushes and fastened itself to the hunchback's spine. So now he had not one hump but two, and he ran away howling and was never seen again.'

'Is that all?'

'Yes.'

'But that's terrible,' he protested. 'The second fellow's only trying to take control of his destiny. If you're going to tell that story to children, surely his initiative should be rewarded. Otherwise, where's the moral in it?'

'You could think of it as an allegory about what happens to artists who lack originality.'

'It would never be allowed in America.'

Olivier wound his arms around Sophie's neck, a tactic that usually proved successful. 'Tell me that story again?'

Since November, she had spent the fourth and ninth days of every ten-day *décadi* at the hospital. Her midday meal was provided free of charge; also two blue aprons, freshly laundered. Unlike the nursing sisters she was not entitled to the use of wood, coal, salt, candles or household linen; but a handcloth and soap were set aside for her personal use by Mother Clothilde, who enjoined her to scour her hands every hour, and immediately if they came into contact with a patient of dubious moral character.

She was assigned to one of the wards, where she was required to serve the patients soup, bread and wine in accordance with the doctors' prescriptions, to shave them and to ensure they were provided with clean linen, clean bandages and other necessities. She supervised the ward's paid servant, and was responsible for the hospital's woodstore and for recording admissions to her ward. Mother Clothilde – even Dr Morel couldn't bring himself to address her as Citizen – instructed Sophie in how to take a pulse in order to assess its strength, firmness and rhythm (regular or erratic, languid or racing?). She was expected to grind powders and mix syrups in the dispensary under the eye of the visiting apothecary. They were always running short of tincture of laudanum: two ounces of opium to a pint of wine mixed with an ounce of saffron and a pinch of ground cinnamon. Sophie was to simmer the liquid over a vapour bath, strain and bottle it. She helped with the dressing of wounds, which meant doing what she was told. She prepared linseed poultices and applied them to abscesses to drain the noxious matter. Although not required to administer bleedings, a service provided by the apprentice surgeon, she was expected to show proficiency and calm in the handling of leeches.

Blistering was the subject of controversy. It had long been accepted that artificially provoked pain was beneficial to patients because it provided distraction from their original symptoms and dislodged sickness. The traditional irritant was a plaster made from cantharides, Burgundian pitch, euphorbia powder, yeast, wax and mustard seeds. The blisters were pierced and kept open to let the poison escape. But Dr Morel was sceptical about the therapeutic value of the treatment. If it had to be resorted to, he advocated heating small cups and upending them on the patient's scalp or back to produce the desired effect. Everyone took sides and had an opinion on the matter.

The director and deputy director made their ward rounds in the morning and afternoon respectively. Each round was supposed to last no more than an hour, an average of thirty seconds per invalid. But Joseph would linger at bedsides, taking notes. Sophie observed that while he paid courteous attention to his patients' descriptions of their ailments, he never relied solely on their accounts, as Ducroix did, for diagnosis. Joseph's examinations always took longer because he would tap chests, sniff wounds, look at tongues, pull down eyelids, listen to breathing. A patient's urine, stools, expectorations and vomit had to be preserved until the deputy director had scrutinised them.

When his round was over and he came to sit with her, as he unfailingly did, at her desk placed in a recess at one end of the ward, she asked him why he paid such close attention to the patients' physical symptoms. 'Because medicine is a science,' he replied, 'and scientific knowledge is based on observable phenomena. For instance: the presence of a clear oily matter in a viscous expectoration is a sure sign of purulence. Such cases are usually mortal.'

'But what if the patient's account contradicts what you observe?'

'Then the patient is mistaken. People often exaggerate or become confused about their symptoms.'

He had put on his spectacles to examine her admission notes. *A man was brought in at half-past nine*, she had written. *He was insensible and could not tell us his name. He died at ten minutes past ten. He appeared to be about twenty-five years old.*

He resisted despair.

She was frowning, picking over what he had said. 'But who is to say that there are no errors of interpretation in the conclusions you draw from your observations?'

He considered this novel point of view. 'That might well be true,' he said at last, 'but I couldn't go on doing this work if I thought it was.'

'You see? Reason will do as long as science confines itself to explaining the world. But acting in it, changing things, human endeavour: that requires faith.'

Sophie had already remarked Dr Morel's gentleness. She had watched as he sat listening to an old woman's ramblings, his coarse-fingered hands smoothing the bed-cover. She had seen for herself that when he flung up his chin and laughed, you couldn't help smiling. Now she turned to look at him as she spoke. And something in his face –

The clockwork universe fell apart in cogs and springs. Then reassembled itself differently.

Her day began at eight o'clock and ended at half-past six. Its progression was strictly ordered: distributing the wood, sponging the invalids' faces and hands, bringing the register up to date, the servant sluicing down the ward, the physicians' and surgeons' visits, Mother Clothilde's lips moving silently before the meal they took around a table that the years had scrubbed thin. Yet, walking to Isabelle's, where she spent the night, Sophie was conscious of time only as patches of shadow and light, fatigue blunting the day's well-defined edges.

Hardest to bear was the smell. The promised windows were yet to materialise; in the meantime, Joseph had given orders for the doors at either end of each ward to be left open at all times. He had also enforced the long-standing but never adhered-to regulation that limited a single patient to a bed. Need was such, however, that straw pallets were also brought in. The patients lying on these complained bitterly of the draughts at floor level, and the able-bodied among them persisted in climbing onto the nearest beds, unleashing a fresh clamour of laments and curses from the original occupants. In the end, the doors were left barely ajar. The reek of sweat, urine, vomit, diarrhoea, dirty bandages, vinegar and the concoctions prescribed by the physicians began at crescendo and mounted until, by the end of the day, she would have to leave the ward every quarter of an hour to snatch gulping breaths in the walkway.

One blustery morning in early spring when she wasn't expected, she presented herself at Dr Ducroix's office requesting permission to clear the waste ground enclosed by the main building. She had brought plants from Montsignac, she explained, they were in a cart waiting at the gate. It would be a dreadful waste not to make use of them, now they were here. And with the fine weather approaching, convalescent patients could be encouraged to spend time out of doors, breathing in fresh air, which would surely benefit their health and please Dr Morel. Perhaps a little weeding wouldn't be out of the question?

Behind the kitchens ran a wide strip of land where carrots, turnips, cabbages, beans, peas and medicinal herbs were grown for the hospital's use. This was the domain of an arthritic individual named Taine, half-blind, more than half-deaf, stooped like a willow, who savagely repelled all trespassers. No one, not even Mother Clothilde, could remember when he had attached himself to the hospital or knew anything of his antecedents. When addressed he made a noise like barking and laid about the air with a blackthorn stick.

The winter past had brought Taine a cough that stopped him in his shuffling tracks, whole days when pain kept him nailed to his pallet in the damp outbuilding he called home. In this weakened state, he had lowered his guard. A boy who hung around the hospital and did the things no one else wanted to do in return for his board was summoned to the kitchen garden, where he displayed a preternatural aptitude for interpreting Taine's utterances. What passed for Luc's childhood had begun on a farm; he understood work, weather, the quickening earth. Taine did not beat him much more than was necessary.

This same jug-eared boy was detailed to assist Sophie. Under Joseph's regime, all the rubbish and the worst of the rubble had already been removed from the old garden between the wards. Working together, Sophie and Luc now uprooted weeds, cleared away stones, turned the soil, broke up clods, raked the earth, discovered a mildewy red leather purse (empty except for a three-cornered button made of bone). She crumbled a handful of soil, showing the boy how dark and loamy it was where they had turned it. 'Earthworms,' he said, eager to impress, holding up a translucent pink wriggle.

Roses, lavender, rosemary waited, their roots wrapped in damp rags. An uninviting sack that Sophie kept protectively close was opened a fraction to reveal a quantity of well-rotted dung. This was to be used exclusively as top dressing for the roses, she instructed, it was not to be squandered on mere herbs. And on no account was Taine to learn of its existence or he would be after it for his vegetables. Thrilling to his role, Luc swore elaborate secrecy.

They edged a path with herbs. They planted two beds with triangular arrangements of roses, spreading the roots out, covering them with soil, then holding each bush in position and pressing the earth into place around it with their feet. When the plant had been trodden in, the rest of the earth was shovelled close around it. 'Damasks,' said Sophie, 'pinky-red double flowers with sixty petals each. Unrivalled for scent.'

The morning wore itself out. They stretched their arms and told each other how hard they'd worked. She had to leave with more than half the planting yet to be completed, but promised to return the following day. Luc, enslaved, stood waving at the gate.

Joseph, arriving shortly afterwards, was informed of what they had done and went out to see for himself. The afternoon had grown dark, the wind colder. He broke off a sprig of rosemary, walked about filling his lungs with the smell of earth. The first drops of rain were falling as he began tearing at the scented leathery spikes in his hand, stripping them from their stalk like so many unwanted promises.

The cottage stood at the far end of the street. It had a lean-to pigsty at the side and a garden with a dungheap and vegetable patch at the back. One of a pair, the only houses in the village still owned by the Saint-Pierres, it had stood vacant over the winter since the death of the previous tenant, rain coming in through the roof that there had been no money to repair. Stephen had quietly come to the rescue; it was a small return for all that hot water, he said.

'Look, Jacques, an apple tree.'

'Apples are all very well for young folk with strong teeth. Sweet, juicy pears, that's what I like. I don't see any pear trees. Nor plums.'

'You know you can come up to the orchard whenever you like and pick all the fruit you want.'

'It's a fair step and rising ground. If I take another nasty fall it'll be the end of me. I don't suppose I'll last beyond Christmas in any case. I daresay no one will be sorry to see me go.'

'I'll bring you pears every day they're in season,' pleaded Mathilde.

'How long do you suppose those new tiles will last? Drip, drip, drip with the first summer storm and I'll be bound to catch one of those coughs you never recover from.' With a ridged ochre fingernail he prised loose a strip of bark, then another. More than ever he resembled an ancient, leafless twig.

'Stephen's fetching you a piglet from the Costes' farm. It's meant to be a surprise.'

'What use do I have for a pig? I'll be fattening worms long before it's fit to kill.'

251

Mathilde ran around to the back where a pile of weeds lay beside the vegetable bed and Sophie was resting on her spade with her hair coming down. 'I want Jacques to stay with us, why can't he stay?'

'You know why. You wouldn't want him to fall down the stairs again, would you?'

'It's a horrible little house. There are no windows and it smells.'

'It's better than the almshouse in Castelnau.' Sophie dug grimly, trying not to think about Jacques, alone for the first time in seventy-six years. He had insisted on sending for a notary to draw up his will. He wanted his entire estate – two shirts, a pair of breeches, two pairs of drawers, a waistcoat, two handkerchiefs, three pairs of stockings, two bonnets (one wool, one cotton), a pair of slippers and a framed print of Saint Agatha's martyrdom – to be sold at auction. The proceeds, along with the nine *livres* that represented his savings, were to be sent 'to the blacks in Africa'. Asked if he had any particular blacks in mind, he replied, 'The blackest.'

'He'll be sad all the time,' wept Mathilde, 'you know he will.'

'Everyone in the village knows him.'

'He doesn't like most of them.'

'Berthe'll bring his dinner every day, and we'll all visit him. It won't be so bad,' said Sophie, willing herself to believe it.

'Do you think he'd like to have my portrait of Brutus?'

A mud-splattered piglet with a rope around its neck came trotting down the street, splashing through puddles. Stephen, struggling to balance Caroline in the crook of his other arm, was brought up short by the sight of an old man embracing a tree: a flourish of white blossom against a blue sky, two paper-thin petals stuck to a crumpling face.

252

*T*hey were waiting for Joseph in the director's office, as he knew they would be. There was no need for them to ask; his failure was apparent before he entered the room, in the way his footsteps dragged to the door.

Mother Clothilde crossed herself, and he hadn't the heart to reprove her.

He had arrived earlier that day to find the hospital in an uproar. One of the servants, a slow-witted woman called Bette Roussel who worked in the laundry, had attended the previous day's executions. Among those destined for the guillotine had been a priest; when his head fell, drops of blood spurted onto the ground. Later, when the spectacle was over, Bette had been observed furtively gathering up the blood-stained gravel. She had been arrested on the spot on a charge of conspiracy.

As soon as he had heard the story, Joseph had gone to see Ricard.

There were three red-blotched pink roses in a glass on Ducroix's desk. Joseph leant against the wall near the door.

'I did your round for you,' said Ducroix. 'The old man with the goitre has died.'

'Bette is barely capable of distinguishing a pillowslip from a tablecloth. Abbé Maury was her confessor, he attended her father on his deathbed. How could she even begin to understand why the Revolution thought fit to execute him? Has it reached the point where you people can't tell simple-mindedness from sedition?' Thin-lipped, Mother Clothilde swept from the room, holding her skirt clear as if Joseph were a pool of something unpleasant on the floor.

253

'I explained all that,' he said to Ducroix, 'and more. Ricard referred me to Chalabre. Chalabre said he couldn't possibly make an exception on my behalf. What would people think if the Central Committee were to set itself above the law?'

He stayed on after Ducroix had left, sitting at his desk while light shifted on the walls. Late afternoon, a time he found intolerable no matter what the day had brought, closed in on him like incipient illness.

In the garden, birds were calling. He thought of Bette's water-logged red hands, so like his mother's. He thought of Luzac, protesting his innocence to the last, telling an appreciative crowd he had willingly sacrificed his arm for the Revolution, he hadn't realised it wouldn't be satisfied with anything less than his head.

For something to do, he opened the central register and began to read. Skin disorders were, as always, well represented: tinea (7 cases), scabies (4), malignant abscesses (11), ulcerated sores (22), scurvy (9), erysipelas (34). Three cases of paralysis, forty-four sore throats, one inflammation of the testicles. Several catarrhs. The usual pulmonary disorders, including nine instances of phthisis. Vomiting with and without stomach pains. Discomfort when urinating. Dysentery. Rheumatisms (28 cases). Fevers: continuous, intermittent, spotted, low. Hernia, dropsy, sunstroke.

At the end of the month, he would transfer the information to a graph that charted the incidence of individual diseases against the calendar. He knew in advance that fevers tended to increase sharply over the summer, supporting his theory that they were a by-product of the noxious emanations which were at their most virulent in warm weather. Conversely death rates, recorded on a different chart, could be seen to fall at that time of year; the largest number of fatalities occurred as a result of chest complaints, and it was in the cold months that these raged.

You kept meticulous records, wrestling information from chaos. Nothing made sense if viewed in isolation. You had to discern the patterns.

Earlier that year, Paris had decreed that henceforth all political suspects were to be transferred to the capital for trial. Castelnau protested vigorously. Mercier's pen had outdone itself: *Between the people and their enemies there can be nothing but the sword. Only when it is seen to fall swiftly by the very citizens who have identified the treachery in their neighbours' hearts can we be certain of keeping revolutionary ardour at the white-hot pitch with which it burns in Castelnau.* Whether stunned by Mercier's eloquence or suffocated by its own bureaucratic tangles, the Convention relented: Castelnau kept its tribunal. The victory was marked with bonfires and the distribution of a poem composed by a minor municipal official. It began: 'O *Castelnau! All who have suckled at your bounteous breasts . . .*'

Executions now took place every four days, crimes against the Revolution accounting for an average of five deaths each time.

Errors of interpretation. He was no longer sure he had the faith to disregard them.

Outside, a vague commotion – scraping, tapping, creaking, the rustle of voices – signalled that the patients who had been placed around the garden to profit from sunshine and fresh air were being shifted back to their wards. He drew a sheet of paper towards him and began to write.

By the time he had finished, the room had been claimed by shadows. He heard the dull clang of something metallic – a knife, a pan, a tin tray? – dropped in the passage. About to light a lamp, he thought, Why bother? The grey half-dark filtering in through the window would easily last as long as he needed.

He was groping for the bottle in the cupboard next to Ducroix's desk when someone knocked at the door. He had heard no footfall. They came silently, after dark, that was when they knocked, and produced their warrants and searched the house and took you away. Locked in with fear, his heart scrabbled madly.

She stood there on one foot, wearing her outdoor clothes. 'I didn't like to leave without making sure you were all right.'

He put out his hand, drew her into the room, shut the door. 'Sophie,' he said, keeping hold of her wrist, 'I intend to resign from the Committee. I've drafted a letter to Ricard.'

'I'm sure you've made the right decision. And certainly a courageous one.'

'Does that mean you think it's foolish?'

'Oh no,' she said seriously, 'in that case I'd have said you were being brave.'

And so he began to kiss her.

Having woken early, Joseph walked through streets where shadows still struck cold, until he emerged onto the quays and warmth fell across his shoulders like a friendly arm. A small boy and two old codgers were fishing in the sun-dazzled river. There were white birds like clumsy stitching on blue cloth, filling the air with querulous cries.

Ça ira, he roared, striding past the bridge, *ça ira*! So that the sentry picking his teeth gazed after him sourly, wondering what that fellow had to sing about.

They were setting up the market on the square at the end of his street. A woman who couldn't stop yawning sold him an enormous bunch of white lilac, which he placed in the jug on his washstand. The scent poured into his room, someone went clattering down the stairs, there was a button missing from his shirt.

All over Castelnau, the padlocking of churches at the Committee's decree met with outraged resistance. Textile workers threatened strike action; stevedores and bargemen carried it out. Petitions from all quarters protested the infringement of a citizen's right to choose his place and manner of worship. Injustice, coinciding with fine spring weather, brought the streets out in a rash of demonstrations: carters, pawnbrokers, vintners, cobblers, fishwives, journeymen, barbers, knife-grinders, smith-farriers, stonemasons, tailors, ratcatchers, bookbinders, fortune-tellers, flautists, singers of ballads, sellers of violets, smugglers of armagnac. Neighbours who hadn't spoken to each other for years seethed in huddles on landings.

At question time in the Club itself, a cabinetmaker asked point-blank whether Paris had decreed the closure of the churches; the mayor had to admit that the decision had been taken on his own initiative. The padlocks were removed the following morning by the same locksmiths who had clamped them in place.

At the emergency meeting of the Committee, Mercier tried to shrug off the fiasco: 'A priest-ridden people cling to their rituals. They'll come round in time.'

'And until they do,' said Joseph, 'we can guillotine them.'

No one pounced on him. Not that he cared, any longer.

'If the conservatives form an alliance with the workers ...' There was no need for Chalabre to finish his sentence.

It was Ricard, of course, who came up with the counter-strategy: since direct attacks on the Church simply played into enemy hands, why not supply an alternative to Christianity instead? He had in mind a series of celebrations based on the new calendar that would gradually, imperceptibly, replace the old liturgical feasts and saints' days while providing working people with the same opportunities for rest and self-indulgence. A Festival of Youth in spring, a Festival of Marriage in summer, an Agricultural Festival in autumn.

Joseph had intended to talk to Ricard before formally tendering his resignation. But the mayor hurried from the Committee while their deliberations were still winding down, late for a meeting with the leaders of the striking river-workers. And four days had already gone past.

Telling himself that Ricard would understand, he placed the envelope on the mayor's desk and followed Mercier down the stairs.

By a stroke of good fortune, the town hall had just taken delivery of a statue of Rousseau commissioned the previous year. The Festival of Liberty, the first of the new feasts, was hastily organised around it.

Floréal was the month of flowers. On the square in front of the Temple of Reason – once known as the Cathédrale de Saint-Denis – there were banks of red and white roses. Leafy branches and marigold garlands adorned the surrounding buildings, and the rue de la Liberté was lined with people wearing white: the men standing on the right with their sons, the women and girls on the left, everyone carrying bouquets of flowers or baskets of fruit.

Tiers of benches had been reserved for dignitaries along one side of the square. Taking his place, Joseph was obliged to pass directly behind the mayor. He hesitated – and Ricard, turning around, greeted him as amiably as ever.

Relief and gratitude manifested themselves as a stream of platitudes: a perfect day, the town looked splendid, everyone was to be congratulated, he hoped the mayor was well? And where was Lisette, it had been such a long time since he had seen her. She had woken with a bad headache, said Ricard: 'She's never been one for the warm weather.'

People were threading their way along the row behind him. Ricard extended his hand; he grasped it, moved on.

A battalion of boys came marching up under a banner: *He gave us Émile as our model*. He would have to remember that for Matty. In the massed choir on the adjacent side of the square, he picked out two small girls resplendent in white silk and blue sashes, holding hands, their red hair glinting in the sun.

Sunlight, music, a flag-hung morning.

The stainless voices of children.

He thought how easy it was to dismiss it all as cheap sentiment, orchestrated emotion. But he saw it as the human drift towards brotherhood, a stumbling impulse to achieve goodness, and found himself intensely moved.

Overnight, a young oak tree had been planted in the centre of the square. In its shade, the veiled statue waited on its plinth. As the songs died down Ricard and a cluster of councillors left their seats for the dais that had been erected alongside the statue. The mayor had on a plumed hat, and his green coat was the same shade as the oak leaves. Joseph saw one of the little girls nudge her sister, nodding towards their father, who towered over the other men as he limped up the steps to the platform.

He thought, I should have gone to see him, I should have explained. But regret slipped past him like a fish and was gone without a ripple. These days, although he brimmed over with a vague, smiling benevolence, other people seemed neither interesting nor relevant. 'Sophie', he often said aloud, startling people around him, 'Sophie'. Time spent away from her passed in alert dreaminess.

Ricard's voice was rolling out over the hushed square. The oak represented the resurrection of freedom in France, said the mayor, it was the genealogical tree of the great family of the free who would one day inherit the world. The oak tree would grow, and endure for generations. The children who gathered beneath its branches today would return years hence with their own children and grandchildren and tell them with pride of the heroic days when men tore off their chains and liberty was born.

There was a stirring on Joseph's left. He glanced sideways to see a woman dabbing at red-rimmed eyes with a lavender-scented handkerchief. Evidently, he wasn't the only one leaning in to the day's pull.

Then she sneezed violently, three times. Hay fever, he realised, and smiled.

A moment later he heard the shot. The pattern of the crowd shifted instantly, as if an invisible hand had shuffled a board.

He saw Ricard lying on the platform, his plumed hat spiralling away to fetch up against the foot of the oak tree.

Stephen was thought to be out painting in the woods and her father – she peered into his study, checked with Berthe – hadn't been seen since breakfast. But Claire was discovered reading a novel on the sofa, and Mathilde was winkled out of an attic when a muffled sneeze betrayed her.

'Do you have to play up here? There's a cobweb in your hair.' But Sophie appeared distracted.

'We weren't playing.' Mathilde clambered out of the basket after Brutus and squeezed past strategically positioned odds and ends. 'We were seeing if we still fitted.'

Claire was collected on their way out: 'Really, Sophie, just when Adolfo is about to discover the casket with Sir Percy's letters to Emiglia.'

It was late spring: the garden was an extravagance of roses. Even Claire seemed disposed to linger. But Sophie strode along until they reached a bed on the other side of the hedge, where she stopped and pointed.

'An Apothecary's Rose,' said Mathilde, at the sight of the two crimson buds. Then, coming closer, 'Isn't it?'

'Look at that red. And the leaves, with that faint sheen.'

'Really, Sophie – have you dragged us out here for guessing games with roses? That doctor won't tolerate your preoccupation with the finer points of botany once you're married. A husband expects to be the focus of his wife's attention.'

'*I* know – it's one of those China roses. They've got leaves like that.'

'Smell it.' And when Mathilde obeyed: 'You see? Nothing like a China rose. And the buds are larger as well as darker.'

'Stop making a mystery of things, Sophie, you know I can't

abide that. Tell us what you mean or I'm going back inside.'

Sophie had begun smiling and now she couldn't stop. She tickled Brutus's ears and laughed. 'I've been crossing Autumn Damasks with China roses for years now. Nothing like this has ever happened before.'

'But these flowers are crimson. Darker than a China rose,' objected Mathilde, 'and nothing like those pink damasks.'

'Last year there were seedlings with white flowers. And I've had every shade of pink. But the reds have predominated, always. Only I never thought I'd get such a dark one, along with that scent.' Irregularity, thought Sophie, scratching Brutus's stomach, stooping to kiss Professor Kölreuter's hand.

'Will you be able to sell it? Like the China roses?'

'If it survives. If I succeed in propagating it.'

'Will there be enough for presents? Or just things like winter stockings?'

Claire was examining the phenomenon. 'It's a remarkable colour, I must say. What a pity you're not getting married until September – you could have included one in your bouquet.'

That started Sophie smiling again.

'If it's descended from those two . . .' Mathilde was working it out – 'Will it flower again in autumn?'

'I'm not counting on it,' lied Sophie shamelessly.

'Oh Sophie – you'll be famous.'

'If it's new, don't you have to give it a name?' asked Claire. 'What are you going to call it?'

Hopefully: 'Brutus?'

'Mmm . . . Probably not.'

'Promise it won't be something awful like Innocence?'

'What about Carbuncle?'

Her sisters giggled.

Brutus lay on a dead snail, with his paws in the air, and wriggled joyfully.

Claire began recounting Emiglia's vicissitudes but kept forgetting details that later turned out to be crucial. Mathilde sprawled beside her, concentrating: 'But why didn't her old nurse say who her father really was?' 'What colour was the cat?'

Sophie thought how random life was, a thing of accident and casual opportunity. She closed her eyes and there were crammed red petals, she rolled their crimson weight on her tongue.

ide by side, they strolled in companionable silence through the late-afternoon streets. People made way for them and whispered. Now and then a man would step forward to shake Ricard's hand or clap him on the shoulder.

Joseph thought, This is like before.

In the grain market, lanterns had been strung from the rafters and a fiddler was tuning up. Two men were assembling trestle tables. A band of children swirled past, eating nougat.

'In the end it was as good as anything they might have put on in Paris, don't you think?' Ricard had stopped and was filling his pipe in his unhurried way. 'Despite the interruption.'

The bullet had chipped Rousseau's left hand, glanced off and lodged itself in the trunk of the oak tree. The would-be assassin, an out-of-work pastrycook, had been overpowered within seconds. Most people, apart from those in the immediate vicinity of the incident, hadn't grasped what had happened, assuming the gunshot to be part of the festivities. A few had even flung themselves to the ground, believing their mayor to be giving the signal for the family of the free to prostrate themselves before the philosopher's statue.

Joseph said, 'I know I promised you until the elections.' The words running together, an unintelligible rush. 'I'm sorry,' he persisted.

Ricard, drawing on his pipe, waved away apology.

A bear shambled past on all fours, led by a chain attached to the iron collar around its neck. 'I hate that,' said Joseph. 'Do you know how they teach them to dance? They stand a cub on a bucket of red-hot coals and play music while it shifts from foot to foot in agony.'

They heard cheering from the park, where the pig races were being held. A small girl, urged on by admiring parents, trotted up to offer the mayor a red carnation. Ricard patted the child's head and tucked the flower into his buttonhole.

There was a wine shop on the corner of a street and a knot of drinkers among the barrels outside. Revolution or no, gentlemen favoured delicate wines imported from other provinces, while your working man swilled the local *gros rouge*, gargling as he went for added efficacy. Fresh sawdust stretched the statutory distance from the mouth of the shop; that had been Joseph's initiative, it absorbed the worst of the smell and made things easier for the street-cleaners. He wondered, with shy pride, whether Ricard had noticed.

In front of the town hall, the mayor paused. 'Why don't you come up, later on? There'll be an excellent view of the fireworks. Mercier might be there – if he can tear himself away from whichever whorehouse he's patronising.'

That was blatant slander. Mercier, incandescent with the drama of the day's events, would certainly be at his desk denouncing treachery, hinting at conspiracy, demanding retribution. There would be a pamphlet out before dawn. Joseph knew all this; but how could he resist the invitation to complicity?

All the same: 'I'm riding out to Montsignac,' he explained, 'dinner with the Saint-Pierres.'

Ricard said easily, 'Taken up with them again?' And continued, before Joseph could answer: 'Chalabre sent me a note. That pastrycook has admitted that his brother-in-law used to be Luzac's valet.'

'You think there's a connection?'

'I'm certain of it. They won't rest until they've destroyed the Revolution and consolidated the interests of their class. I know you think we take excessive measures. But you make the classic mistake of believing everyone's like you. We're not dealing with men of goodwill.'

Joseph shifted bear-like from one large boot to the other.

'*Diagnosis is only the first step – it's curing the ailment that matters*. It was you who taught mc that, doctor.'

Men and women came laughing along the street. The mayor waited until they had gone past. 'A surgeon must wield his knife ruthlessly.'

'That's why people flinch from surgery.'

Ricard said, 'This is what I've missed, being able to talk freely. We mustn't let our differences stand in the way of friendship.'

'Of course not.' He seized gratefully on the proof at hand: 'I've been meaning to tell you: I'm going to be married in the autumn.'

air head to dark, they lay on their backs in the long grass by the river. Leaf shadows patterned their faces; their chests rose and fell.

He jerked awake. 'How musically you snore, Matty.'

'I've been lying here enduring your racket for hours. Too polite to say anything.'

'Remind me to drown you when I get up.'

Insects clamoured in the grass. Brutus flexed his paws and made high yelping noises.

'I wonder if he knows what dreaming is.'

'Do you?'

Stephen turned his eyes sideways and there were clumps of loosestrife by the water. He ran his hand down a bright purple spire: spear-shaped leaves clasping the stem, whorled arrangements of petals. It left a slight stickiness on his fingers.

'Did you eat the last slice of tart?'

'Of course.'

'Of course.'

There were birch leaves and alder, and restless interstices of blue. 'Charles's letter said he took his general up in his balloon for a view of the battlefield at Fleurus. He's convinced it made all the difference to the outcome.'

'You never took me ballooning like you said you would. And I'll be thirteen next month and childhood but a distant dream.'

'When Charles comes home. I promise.'

A water-rat was a streak of bubbles on the surface of the river.

But his eyes were closing.

Unmoored, he drifted with the afternoon.

'I'll come with you,' said Mathilde in answer to Joseph's question. Whereupon Stephen kicked her under the table; and Saint-Pierre roused himself to say, 'Why, Matty – afraid of another drubbing at chess?'

So there he was, alone with Sophie. Leaves, grass, the darkening sky, these things lent an illusion of coolness to the sluggish air in the garden.

She was slapping at her arms. 'Why do they bite me and not you?'

'Perhaps your skin's finer. Or your blood sweeter. Perhaps even mosquitoes fall in love with you.'

Sophie said nothing for a while. Then she took his hand. 'You were so quiet at dinner. Is anything the matter?'

Frogs sang mockingly from the river.

The question had been poisoning him for weeks. That evening it was a thick phlegm that hurt his lungs, a black bile mounting in his throat. 'Fletcher,' he managed to say, 'was he . . . Do you . . .?' Dreading her contempt, despising himself, afraid to look at her.

'Once,' said Sophie, 'but not any more.' She stopped walking.

Afterwards, he pointed: 'Look – a falling star.'

'That's what we need,' she said, pinching his arm, 'a telescope and a tower. We'd sit up there, night after night, in all seasons. Our lunar tables would run to seven hundred pages of very small print when published to universal acclaim.'

'A common interest?'

'Exactly. It will save having to talk to each other.'

He brought his face up close to hers, contorting his features: 'But will we be rigorous?'

'We'll be taken for Germans.'

'*Gott in Himmel*. What about children?'

'We'll need several. With names like Hypatia and Alde-baran. They'll check our calculations and take you to task over your mistakes.'

She had led him by circuitous paths into the orchard. There was a sweet stench of fermentation; something small and frightened rustling overhead. He leant against a cherry tree and looked up at the rounded weight of its fruit.

'About Fletcher . . .' He drew her closer. 'I'm sorry.'

'That's quite all right,' said Sophie. And a little later, 'In fact . . . there's something I want to ask you.'

'Yes?'

'Why is it that the first thing you do when you see me is whip off your spectacles?'

'Do you think I look better with them on?'

Head on one side, she gave it consideration: 'Well, no.'

'Sophie,' he said, 'will you always astonish me?'

eople were saying there had never been such a summer, a bone sky, the furious air. Joseph walked along an avenue of plane trees and the shade wrapped itself around him closer than an overcoat. There was no longer any difference between breathing and gasping. Like a swimmer, you made your way forward effortfully, breasting clammy resistance.

He thought of champagne, each drop an icy explosion in his throat. He wondered what Sophie was doing and calculated that in less than eight hours he would see her again.

The gravelled streets had a hard white stare you couldn't meet. The carts went rattling through the town every other day now, and every house displayed a neat list of residents' names, posted next to the front door. Everywhere you looked you saw the slogan *Égalité ou la mort*: it bloomed on walls, was carved into tree-trunks. Denunciations proliferated like flies. Terror was one of those diseases no one spoke of; it tapped its victims on the shoulder, erupted in a knot of rosy pustules.

All this reached him in undertones, the rumour of a distant conflict. The summer gathered itself around Sophie. He had never dared imagine such happiness.

As he passed under an archway, pinpricks of light shimmered before his eyes and he almost trod on a cat. Its mouth opened noiselessly, a clean pink flower blossoming in the shadows.

At the hospital, the courtyard was a quivering expanse. The porter's skin was waxy and there were stains under his eyes.

Nevertheless, something that could have been animation flickered in a face dulled by lack of sleep: he glanced furtively at Joseph, passed a furry tongue over cracked lips as if about to say something; but lowered his gaze, his features blunting over once again.

All these impressions held an instant, and then took off. It was far too hot for pursuit.

He stepped into the welcome dimness of his office and a man with flame-coloured hair rose to greet him.

They hadn't seen each other since the day of the festival, and the change in Ricard was immediately apparent. The mayor would never be anything but colossal; nevertheless, he seemed diminished, thinner, stooped, the flesh sagging on his face. His hair had grown longer, straying over his collar, darker where sweat glued it to his skull. Only his eyes were the same, that pale, cloudless blue like the sky rinsed clean by rain.

They shook hands; and Joseph was conscious of his damp palm in Ricard's cool, dry fingers.

'You'll forgive me for dispensing with preambles.' The mayor paused – and Joseph was sure he knew what he was about to hear, he had been expecting it ever since he had tendered his resignation.

'You – that is, the Committee wishes to relieve me of my duties here.'

Ricard looked at him as a parent might look at a child whose prattle indicates a freedom from adult cares which is at once diverting and irritating. 'No, listen –' He stopped again. 'I'm sorry if I appear abrupt. I don't have much time.' Gripping the arms of his chair. 'If it were the usual scum I wouldn't trouble you. But it involves ... other elements. Well, there's no point in talking in riddles: Chalabre has been stirring things up against me, trotting between what remains of the Luzac faction and every other fool who hates me because the Revolution hasn't lined his pockets or fulfilled whatever petty ambition torments him.'

'Chalabre?'

'I know, I couldn't bring myself to believe it at first either. But lawyers – they're born crooked, and Chalabre has plenty of ambition of his own. And then he's of their class, of course. He's perfectly placed to mastermind a coup, with his spider-web of informers and the tribunal to back up his arguments.'

Slices of lemon floated in a carafe of water on Joseph's desk. Ricard helped himself to a tumbler, downed the contents, refilled his glass. 'Listen: you remember that pastrycook, Gillet, who tried to kill me? Chalabre was quick to point out that he had connections with Luzac. But he didn't tell me that his own wife used to hire Gillet to help in the kitchens when she was entertaining. The man used to frequent Chalabre's house.' Jabbing the desk with his finger to emphasise each word.

'Chalabre probably hadn't the faintest idea who made the pastries his wife produced at their parties.'

Ricard was shaking his head. 'I've always felt he could betray us.'

'There's no shortage of people who'd cheer Chalabre on his way to the guillotine. Is your information reliable?'

'It was Mercier who told me.'

'Well, Mercier! Every time a flea bites him he suspects a conspiracy.' The edges of the conversation were growing hazy, threatening to warp into a headache. Here I am, Joseph thought, talking about pastries and betrayal in the middle of a heatwave.

Ricard's blue eyes raked over him. 'Has Chalabre been talking to you?'

'The day after I resigned from the Committee he sent a note informing me he was changing his physician. I haven't seen him in months.'

The mayor slumped back in his chair and passed his hand over his face. 'I'm sorry. I ...'

'It's all right,' he said.

'Here's why I came: I know the president of the Jacobins in Cahors, I've written requesting as many men as they can spare. Chalabre won't dare make a move if the numbers are against him. Will you take the letter for me?'

A bluebottle swayed in through the window, described a drunken arc above their heads and thudded onto the desk. It buzzed twice and lay still.

'There's no one else I can trust, Joseph.'

It was the first time Ricard had called him by his name. 'Of course.' He held out his hand for the envelope. 'I'll leave tomorrow morning.'

'No, as soon as possible, now. It's urgent, there's no time to lose.'

Joseph was turning the envelope over in his hands: 'I'm expected at Montsignac tonight.'

Ricard said quietly, 'There's another thing.'

Something in that uninflected voice. At once, Joseph's hands grew still.

'Monferrant has been arrested near Paris in the company of an English spy. They've probably already been executed. A warrant is being prepared for the arrest of his wife.'

'His wife?' he echoed stupidly.

'Get word to her – I'll see to it that nothing happens today. Is there someone you can send?'

The boy from the kitchens. Joseph nodded, swallowed, managed to ask, 'The rest of the family . . .?'

Ricard was already on his feet. 'It's Monferrant's wife they want. As soon as she's out of the way, they'll seize the property he transferred to her.'

'I can't thank you enough.'

'The least return. I'll save a more fitting expression of my gratitude for another occasion.'

Suddenly, Joseph put his head back and sniffed. An unexpected breeze had risen, and with it a stench . . . 'In this heat,' he said, 'those open carts . . .'

'That's the dead cow they hauled from the river this morning.' Ricard's tone was incisive. But he lingered at the door, looked incuriously, indifferently around the room, looked down. Looked at last into Joseph's face and said, 'Everything's gone badly since you resigned.'

They shook hands. Then the door closed.

Pinching his nostrils shut, Joseph scribbled frantically. His mouth was dry but Ricard had emptied the carafe. What if I hadn't agreed to take the letter, he thought, what would have happened then?

Sophie read: *Your brother-in-law has been arrested in Paris and condemned as a traitor. Tomorrow they arrest your sister. Tell her to leave at once, without delay. Don't be afraid, there's no danger for anyone else.*

Early afternoon. They had all been asleep. Their tongues were still thick, their eyes gummy with dreams.

In the terrible silence, Saint-Pierre asked, 'Why didn't Morel come himself?'

'He says he's obliged to leave Castelnau on urgent business for a few days – not more than three, he hopes.' He must have been pressed for time – the scrawled lines bore neither salutation nor signature.

'Where can I go?' whispered Claire. 'The children ...'

'We'll go to Bordeaux. By river.' Stephen spoke calmly, without hesitation. The sequence of swift images had always been there, waiting to claim him. 'We'll make our way across the fields until we're downstream of Castelnau and find a boat to take us. We'll be safe – it's the roads they check.'

They stared at him. His disordered hair drew what light there was in the shuttered room. There was a splatter of indigo on one of his cuffs.

He thought, This afternoon contains the rest of my life. The past receded like a green promontory; he pulled away, over the waves, trusting to the horizon.

'There's no time to lose,' he reminded them. 'We should heed Morel's advice to go at once.'

'The children ...'

'They're upstairs, asleep.' Sophie took her sister's hand,

drawing Claire to her feet. 'Come with me – they'll need you. I'll pack your things.'

'Only essentials,' said Stephen.

Claire spoke to him as if they were alone in the room: 'You don't have to do this. If they find you with me, helping us . . .'

'They won't find anyone. I'll see to the horses.' And he was gone.

Stuffing the improbably small garments of children into a bag embroidered with dark birds, Sophie thought at last of Hubert and shivered.

But Joseph, insisted her selfish heart, where was Joseph?

The way he looked down when entering a room full of people, his hands.

I know you'll be eager to hear all the details of my journey. And so, although I hope to see you before sunset tomorrow and satisfy your curiosity in full, I've decided to set down some impressions of my travels – so that you might know that you are present in my thoughts this evening, as indeed you are at every moment of every day.

The beauty of this country north of the Garonne is so striking and so various that I'll attempt only a general description. As you leave Cahors, the mountain of rock rises so steeply that you fear it must at any moment tumble down into the town. But the high land affords an excellent and immense prospect of ridges, vales and gentle slopes. By late morning I was riding through a green yet precipitous landscape, all hill and valley. There were hanging woods of chestnuts, deep vales where the sparkling river ran swiftly, pretty little water towns clinging to the cliffs above. Walnuts are much cultivated here; also rye and wheat and of course vines. Around noon, I found myself riding past an avenue of mulberry trees; the fruit red-purple and delicious, the sweetest I've ever tasted.

The houses add to the beauty of the landscape – white, square-built, with rather flat roofs but only a few windows. I'm told that many of the peasants own their own land. All the same, the air of general well-being notwithstanding, I saw barefoot, stunted women by the side of the road, stooping to fill their aprons with weeds for their cows, the sun beating fiercely down on them. And so must conclude that even in the richest country, there are those who are excluded by the circumstances of their birth from sharing in the prosperity around them. We have had five years of Revolution – five hundred might see some improvement in the wretchedness of these lives.

In the afternoon, a rolling, calcareous country, very white and glaring under the sun. I would have feared for my mare's hooves; but the road was excellent, of pounded granite, firm and level, blessedly free of stones. The Pyrenees remain invisible, of course. I imagine the stupefaction of a stranger who has journeyed south day after day in a season such as this, never suspecting the existence of the mountains – until he wakes one morning to find the haze dispelled, rain on its way and immense snowy peaks rearing under his nose!

Now I know you'll ask what I have been eating in these foreign places – at least your father is sure to! – so let me assure you that I've just dined very satisfactorily on sorrel soup, a pigeon, green peas, veal sweetbreads, biscuits, nectarines, a bottle of good red wine and a glass of walnut liqueur, all for ninety-four *sous*. This is the supper served at the Soleil d'Or, not far from Moissac, where I've taken a room for the night. The inn is uncommonly clean, and my room whitewashed, not hung with the usual filthy tapestries where spiders and moths multiply undisturbed. The serving-girl who attended me was likewise clean and neat; the landlord, on the other hand, is a filthy old fellow with villainous moustaches, a frightful wig (where I swear the spiders and moths took refuge when the tapestries were burnt midway through the last century) and a wall-eye. The girl is his niece and as quick and pretty as her uncle is slovenly and slow-witted. Over supper she told me a most entertaining

Here he paused and, after reflection, scratched out the last sentence and a half.

But I see that I've forgotten to say anything about Cahors. Well, that's not to be wondered at for in fact I found it an ill-favoured place, the streets neither wide nor straight – close, ill-built, dirty, stinking. The very opposite of Castelnau, with its fine houses and handsome promenades. The inn at which I lodged was the Poisson Rouge – a squalid establishment with four beds to a room and at least twice as many papers of clashing design on the wall. (A parenthesis to remind us both that when we are married – that phrase is so much to my liking that I shall write it a second time – when we are married, we must not fail to visit Montpellier, a city you are certain to find delightful in every respect.)

But to return to Cahors (which I fervently hope never to do): I was obliged to spend rather longer there than I'd envisaged, as the person I had to see was unable to receive me immediately. However, once he was free from his duties, my business was speedily discharged; to my relief, as I wouldn't wish to spend more than a single night at the Poisson Rouge, even if I didn't have you as an incentive to speed me home. But here I should note, in case you should find me only disagreeable and carping, that the wine on which the town's reputation is founded is truly excellent. The true *vin de Grève*, as it's called, comes from the vineyards on the rocky hills due south of Cahors, and acquires its name from the gravelly soil of the region. I drank a bottle that was six years old and cost only eighteen *sous*, a very fair price for such a splendid, full-bodied wine. But you will judge of its quality yourself, for I have two more bottles in my bag and we'll drink them together tomorrow night.

Sophie, so many things I've seen and would like to describe for you: such as the *bories*, conical huts built of flat grey stones, very common in these parts; or a grassy field full of small golden flowers, bright as coins, and spiky purple ones, which you would recognise at once. But reading over what I've written I see that it parades its little store of the strange, quaint and absurd, offering up a smoke-screen of exoticism when, like all accounts of journeys, whatever interest it might possess can only lie in what it reveals of the traveller's heart. Which in the present case, dearest, has room for little other than love and longing for you. I hardly dare imagine how sad and fearful these days must have been for your family, and would have done anything in my power to be at your side through those trials. But it could not be so; as you will understand tomorrow, when I can disclose the reason for my journey. So that by the time you read these words, you will have forgiven me, I hope, for what must seem like the most base desertion; and I trust that the first separation we have had to endure will also be our last.

The judge, who is wearing a white cravat and black robe, once sat next to Saint-Pierre at an official dinner and finished the evening slumped face-first in a chocolate soufflé. A decade later, Saint-Pierre can still recall the keen disappointment he felt at having to make do with apple charlotte.

He notices that someone has forgotten to dust the bust of Marat which stands on a pedestal near the door: a silvery thread runs from the martyr's nose to his ear and the spider itself, small and brown, crouches like a beauty spot at the corner of his mouth. This evidence of human fallibility soothes Saint-Pierre, this tiny imperfection in the system's smooth functioning. Efficiency is the order of the day. Until now he hasn't appreciated how this works against the prisoners: if things happen fast enough they seem inevitable. You are arrested; twenty-four hours later you are tried. After that ... But Saint-Pierre closes his eyes. The courtroom is crowded and airless, which must be why he's finding it difficult to breathe.

Morel sent them a letter, he remembers that clearly: striped sunlight slicing a shuttered room. Afternoons aren't designed for farewells, he thinks, something about the hard yellow angle of the light renders gestures stiff and over-rehearsed. The children, woken abruptly and subjected to kissing, were heavy-eyed and inclined to complain. He knows he was clumsy, folding Claire so fiercely to his chest that in the end she struggled to free herself.

All that night he had kept walking: in the clammy orchard, by the interminable river. He imagined sentries strung out across the road to halt her; lanterns raised along the riverbank, a shouted challenge to the boat slipping over dark water.

Why isn't he there with her? How could he have entrusted her to Fletcher?

The courtroom sways.

Lombard, the pear-faced prosecutor, is reading out the first charge, running a finger around the collar of his robe. A violinist has been denounced by one of his pupils for *Unpatriotic slander*: he has described the music composed for the Festival of Marriage as 'sentimental caterwauling' and has confessed to spending all national feast days in bed with his ears stopped up and the curtains drawn.

In the interests of expediting justice the tribunal is forbidden to call witnesses. Defence counsels are likewise deemed unnecessary: jurymen are good citizens, quite capable of looking into their hearts and reaching the correct verdict when not muddled and misdirected by legal cunning. To further pare down the complexity of the tribunal's task, all prisoners are either acquitted or condemned to death.

The violinist is among the unfortunate majority. 'The executioner will be doing me a favour, Citizens – no more caterwauling.' This sally brings applause from the public gallery, which is full to bursting as usual; spirited defiance which poses no threat to anyone's comfort always meets with approval. Besides, the violinist has chocolate-brown eyes and a torrent of dark curls. One or two women are already feeling for their handkerchiefs.

They had anticipated the house being searched, but with Claire safely gone that had seemed no more than a disagreeable intrusion. Joseph's note had been folded away in Sophie's desk, it not having occurred to the Saint-Pierres that their private papers might be of interest to the police. Until the agent came downstairs brandishing the sheet of paper.

Pain shoots up his arm but is gone in an instant. It leaves him breathless and lucid. He judges himself guilty of inattention, selfishness, complacency. Even Monferrant, he thinks, even a fool like that could see what was coming. A moment later he remembers what has happened to Hubert.

The heat gathers him up and holds him close. For whole

voluptuous moments, he considers yielding to its embrace.

By the door of his cell two guards had been playing chess with a set in which the heads of the kings and queens were missing. At dinner – beans in suet, bread, a few greyish lumps that might have been meat – a prisoner held a tin plate to his cheek and produced, with perfect tonalities, the sound of a hunting horn; he was hoping to deflect the hounds, he said, and even the guards had laughed.

A prostitute who has boasted that she charges Jacobins twice as much as other clients is accused of *Depraving morals and impairing the purity and energy of the Revolution*. Guilty.

A farm labourer has been denounced for refusing to work on Sundays and claiming that the day is sacred, thereby *Corrupting the public conscience*. Guilty.

A seamstress has *Undermined national interests* by expressing pessimism about the outcome of the battle of Fleurus; that the revolutionary army carried the day is cited by Lombard as proof that her intentions were entirely malicious. But the seamstress has a trump card: no sooner has her charge been read than she announces she is pregnant. This occasions a long digression, while the prosecutor explains that the suspect was away from home attending a sick relative when her treachery was brought to the attention of the authorities – hence the delay in arresting her. On her return she learnt what had happened, and it is Lombard's sincere belief that she thereupon hastily got herself with child. He begs the jury to pay no heed to this vexing circumstance, beyond noting it as further evidence of the prisoner's perfidy. But the seamstress's luck holds. In any event, her life would have to be spared until after the birth; the jurors, looking in their hearts, find magnanimity indistinguishable from sentimentality and acquit her. The judge admonishes the police for wasting the tribunal's time and resources.

Lombard grows redder and fans himself with a file.

Everyone knows that the tribunal has never acquitted an aristocrat.

Sophie speaks rapidly and without hesitation: 'My sister is guilty only of having made an unfortunate marriage. When I heard that her husband had been arrested, I urged her to flee of course, she's my sister. My father had nothing to do with the arrangements I made.'

'That's nonsense,' says Saint-Pierre at once, 'I alone am entirely responsible.'

'The prisoner will not speak unless he is addressed,' says Lombard smartly. He adjusts his robe, consults his papers, takes his time; it's not every day a magistrate falls into his hands. 'The boy who delivered the note was instructed to give it to no one but your daughter. In any case, she has already admitted her guilt.'

Sophie is asked her sister's whereabouts: 'She intended to go south, towards the mountains. Perhaps to Spain.'

Who wrote the letter that warned them?

She looks down at the balustrade.

'The jury will note the prisoner's refusal to co-operate with the tribunal. In any case, the boy has provided the necessary information.'

Saint-Pierre ignores Lombard and speaks to the judge, who is making a show of taking notes, thus avoiding having to look at the prisoner. 'The charge is *Aiding counter-revolution*. But where is the sister, the father, who would have acted otherwise?' His tormentors hold him down on the marble floor, waiting for him to speak. The right words will redeem him, of that he is certain; but they have their hands around his throat, a cold blade pressed against his flesh.

'We fail our children often enough,' he hears himself say, 'but nothing, not even a revolution, stops us loving them.'

Sophie, standing beside him, has grown very still.

'Would you find love a treasonable offence?'

The violinist cheers.

One of the jurors hawks and spits.

Lombard says irritably, 'A citizen's supreme allegiance is to his country. A patriot would have alerted the authorities to his daughter's flight – incontrovertible proof, I might remind the jury, of her guilt. In any case, this isn't the first time the prisoner has sought to pervert the course of justice. When investigating the activities of Étienne Luzac, condemned for crimes against the Revolution and subsequently executed on 22 Vendémiaire in the Year II, the prisoner dragged his feet to the point where the public prosecutor was obliged to close the investigation and refer the case to this tribunal, where Luzac's guilt was swiftly established.'

'I was never appointed to investigate Luzac,' he cries, stung by the twist that is being given to the evidence. 'My task was to determine who initiated the killings at the former convent – a question which remains unanswered, since the evidence produced at Luzac's trial was a mass of contradictions.'

Lombard mops his forehead, glowing with self-satisfaction. The judge coughs, draws out his watch and stares at it.

Then the walls start closing in. Saint-Pierre tries to ward them off, but his hands are tied in front of him and –

the red air

ut as it turned out, after Joseph had been ferried across the river, the excellence of the road declined; and when he was still half a day's ride from Castelnau, his mare went lame. The delay this necessitated was longer than might have been anticipated. The blacksmith at the nearest village having been conscripted into the army, the forge had reverted to his father – a chronically combative ancient, who, having grasped that Joseph was anxious to press on with his journey, announced that it was already past the usual time for his midday meal. On no account could he delay it further, or forgo the siesta that followed, these things being his democratic right and common sense besides, no matter what foreigners – eyeing Joseph distastefully – might be accustomed to, it being well known that they were numbskulls and fornicators to a man. He waited a moment, thrusting out his chin on which a few wiry grey hairs still sprouted truculently; shuffling off with bad grace when the stranger failed to take the bait. And Joseph was left to cool his heels for well over three hours, passing the time as best he could at the adjoining inn, toying with a plate of unappetising eggs and failing to make conversation with the partially deaf landlord.

It was like those dreams in which everything takes place in maddening detail and wrongly.

So that the moon – pallid and slow, as if it had slept badly – had already laboured its way above the horizon and twilight was well advanced by the time he reached Castelnau and detoured round the town to take the road to Montsignac. He found the house in darkness, shuttered and still; he hesitated a while at the gate, for it was barely half-past ten and he couldn't believe that the household had retired so early on a warm summer night. But his mare, with oats and straw on her mind, pawed the gravel and whinnied in protest; and it occurred to him that the Saint-Pierres might well have craved their beds after the upheavals of the past few days. And so, with a last piercing look at her window – but he couldn't persuade himself, however hard he stared, that there was a glimmer of yellow on the other side of the shutters – he turned his horse around.

Anxiety plucked at his sleeve, all along the pitchy lanes. He put it down to finding himself in the countryside after dark, hedges breathing on either side of him. Branches met overhead, obscuring the sky; and where leaves let the moon slip past their guard, shadows pooled inkier still.

Then he remembered that he had been away three nights, which meant that Sophie would be at the hospital the following day. He would go there straight after breakfast and surprise her. Leaning low over the mare's neck, he grasped a fistful of her coarse black mane. 'Faster,' he whispered into her flickering ear, 'go faster.'

Once the mare was stabled he discovered he was tremendously hungry, not having eaten since noon – if pushing a glutinous mess around a plate with a piece of rye bread can be described as eating.

The streets were full of people: fanning themselves in doorways, strolling, laughing outside taverns. In the middle of a square, a woman was singing in Italian, something lilting and high, from an opera no doubt. It trailed him down the street that led to the river, where there would be a café and, with any luck, a breeze from the water; he hummed a few bars under his breath.

Ahead of him on the corner the Victoire was laying amber oblongs of light over the cobblestones. A man hurrying away glanced at him in passing; and they recognised each other at the same moment.

'Morel!' Chalabre's fingers hooked over his arm, there was

gherkin breath in his face, he was being pushed against a wall, into the shadows. 'Why did you come back?'

The clatter of the café was only yards away; Joseph's blood beat louder still. If his absence had been noted it could only mean that his movements were being tracked. 'A family matter,' he managed to say. 'I was called away for a few days.'

The fingers tightened on his flesh. People were dying of heatstroke, so naturally Chalabre was muffled up in a jacket – impeccably cut, irreproachably styled. The silver grey cloth looked soft and expensive. 'I tried to find you. As soon as the boy was picked up. Your note was found, of course, when they were arrested. We have to talk, Morel, he'll murder us all if we don't stop him. He's been spreading rumours about me –'

He had never liked gherkins, his empty stomach heaved. 'What do you mean by *they*? Who was arrested with the marquise?'

'Monferrant's wife? But she and the American ... haven't you been helping them escape?'

'Who?' he shouted, and clutched at a silvery lapel, slimy as fish-skin.

Chalabre's voice went on and on.

The sentries on duty outside the charcuterie were standing about with their jackets unbuttoned and their hats pushed back on their heads. Recognising Joseph, the older of the two launched into a grievance about the heat, his bad knee, the long hours, the inadequate pay.

When the door opened, stale air and the smell of cooking engulfed him.

Someone was exclaiming, drawing him into the dim passageway, where the tiles were cool against his cheek. In the dining room there was a shiny red cloth on the table, the window stood open and the smell was far worse.

His hands closed on the back of a chair.

Ricard in shirt-sleeves, reaching for the decanter, clicked his tongue in disapproval: 'I gave that fellow instructions to say nothing, to send you directly here. I've had him waiting at your house ever since ... A dreadful business.'

The glass rattled against Joseph's teeth.

'Chalabre must have had me followed to the hospital, got wind of our conversation, I told you he has spies everywhere.'

He shut his eyes.

'And ... your journey?' Ricard's voice was tentative.

He kept drinking.

'A dreadful business. Tragic.'

He fumbled in his shirt, drew out the note he had been handed in Cahors, pushed it across the table. Ricard broke the seal and unfolded the paper. His eyes slid rapidly from side to side.

Joseph looked at his glass. Why was it empty?

The mayor pulled out a chair – a grating shriek against the floorboards – and sat down. 'I'll take care of all the arrangements, of course. You'll have to lie low for a few days. But only until the reinforcements arrive.'

The oilcloth wasn't red at all, but brown. On it stood a loaf, a breadboard, a knife, half a creamy yellow cheese oozing onto a flowered plate. Two candles. A bowl of greengages. A pipe. That morning's *Citoyen* lying open, upside down. He noticed the date: 8 Thermidor.

He said, 'I spoke to Chalabre.'

Ricard's eyes had returned to the letter. Now they were clear, unblinking blue. He took his tobacco from his pocket and his eyes never left Joseph's face.

'I know you arranged the arrests.'

'Joseph – '

His name, again. He couldn't help laughing.

'You mustn't believe anything that man –' Ricard's fingers were hovering around his mouth.

'If Chalabre was behind it he wouldn't have waited for her sister to escape, he'd have sent agents to the house that very day. You wanted Claire to get away so you'd have something to charge Sophie with.'

'Joseph, I –'

'*Why did you do it?*'

The voice behind his shoulder was as unexpected as rain: 'People who see things differently from my husband are always punished,' said Lisette. Under her silky green wrap she was wearing an ivory chemise; her feet were small and bare. 'Did you really think he wouldn't punish you?'

Ricard said, 'Don't be a fool.' And, 'It's the hot weather, you see, Morel.'

But Joseph was staring at Lisette.

She stepped into the room, out of the shadows.

The mayor pushed back his chair – that sound! – and got to his feet with his usual deliberateness.

She was turning her arms this way and that for Joseph to see. 'When I was a girl I slept with men for money. But I didn't tell Paul until after we were married.' The wrap slid off, and onto the floor. And reaching past Joseph, she picked up the breadknife.

'She inflicts those injuries on herself, doctor, I've tried reason, entreaty.' Ricard was coming around from the other side of the table, his hand out, those pretty, tapering fingers.

But Joseph reached her first.

Her constant effort to scour her life clean: why had he seen pride, where he should have recognised fear?

She offered no resistance when he took the knife away from her.

There was a student bending over a pinky-grey cadaver, each varnished detail of the memory sealed and bright. Then he was turning his wrist, and the knife slid sweetly in between the bones.

At eight o'clock the sun in the courtyard is like a blade.

The previous night they chalked a number on her door, so she knew that the footsteps would stop there this morning.

The prisoners' correspondence is read by the governor, so she hasn't written to Joseph. But she has given the guard a letter for her father, who has not regained consciousness, and another for Mathilde. She has written that she will always love them. She asks them to remember her.

One of the inconveniences of publicly appointed death is its predisposition to banality.

The men are already waiting in the cart. She sees the violinist, his curls cropped short. And beyond him, a wizened brown face, bright monkey eyes . . .

'Rinaldi!'

His usual shy smile.

It's then she begins to cry.

The pedlar would like to take her hand but his own are tied behind his back, so the best he can do, as their journey begins, is to stand as close to her as possible, he leans his face against her shoulder, they sway around a corner and it's shady under the plane trees, and then the cart creaks out into the sun again, and they have arrived.

1799

September, a day of skies that dissolve between blue and grey, the wind not cold exactly but honed along its edge. He draws the air deep into his lungs, savouring its clean saltiness.

They've taken off their shoes and stockings and are walking on the curving beach to the south of the port where the houses cluster like mussels. The sea is streaked purple and brown where slate-black rocks run down into the water. His son's toes curl over the sand as he staggers along, holding up his hands and laughing at a liver-and-white setter who is making foolish, barking dashes at unruffled gulls.

Over the years he has grown attached to the little girls. How could it be otherwise? They are children, they fall over and hurt themselves, one of them is frightened of moths, the other confides that what she loves best in the world is the moon in water. They cry and laugh easily; they slip small hands into his and ask earnest questions, gazing up at him with unguarded blue eyes.

But he didn't have to learn to love his son, tenderness, involuntary as the tide, flooding him from the moment he first held the tiny body in his arms. Already he discerns intelligence in the child's reasoning, in the bright hazel eyes and quick movements he has inherited from his mother; and something too of his own tenacity, a dogged concentration that steadies the boy and fills his gestures with purpose.

Windblown seabirds wheel and call.

He respects the bone-bare contours of this coast, all excess trimmed by wind and water.

Straight-kneed, his son plumps down on the pale sand, where a trail of emerald-green seaweed has caught his attention among the ochre and olive bladderwrack. He wraps it around his fat wrists, murmuring to himself like the ocean. The dog shakes itself, sending cold spray flying, then flops by the child and starts chewing a stick.

Something makes Joseph turn around and look back down the beach.

A woman dressed in black is standing at the place where the road runs down to the grass-tufted dunes. After a moment, she raises her hand. He hesitates, glancing at the child and the dog; then begins walking slowly towards her.

There is salt-spray on his spectacles; he wipes them on his shirt.

Black ringlets escape from her black bonnet, whipping across her face. She pushes them away, holding her head on one side at an angle he knows, and he calls: 'Claire?' And begins running, scuffing up sand.

She smiles.

He stumbles into her embrace.

'Joseph, dear Joseph,' says Mathilde, and pats his sleeve over and over.

She says, 'Your wife told me I'd find you here. She said there's no keeping you away from the sea, she's always coming across sand in your pockets.'

She says, 'Father died eleven weeks ago.'

She says, 'I must say those new spectacles are a great improvement.'

So once again the waves pull back, and the past is a litter of bright stones on a beach, sea-smoothed glass, sea-drowned feathers, not a day goes past when he doesn't pick over its familiar array.

'We tried to find you,' says Mathilde at last. 'Dr Ducroix went looking for you, but your landlady said you'd gone away.'

'We left as soon as they let me go. When they heard what had happened in Paris, when everything changed. We couldn't have stayed in Castelnau. For Lisette, for the girls – it was intolerable.'

'They still talk about you there, you know. How you killed

296

our monster, our Robespierre. They'd have erected a statue of you if you'd stayed.'

He says, 'It was intolerable for me too.'

He says, 'I often wanted to write. But what was there to say?'

He says, 'Matty, how thin you are. Too thin.'

It's true, her wrists are prominent, there are bluish stains under her eyes, her face is still luminous but paper-white, and her cheeks are already losing their roundness. At certain angles he can see the urgency of bones pressing up under her flesh.

She looks beautiful.

She looks ill.

'I intend to grow buxom in the New World,' she says. 'According to Claire, it's a statutory requirement of plantation life.'

She is to sail from Bordeaux, sixty miles to the north, at the end of the week: 'Everyone says the crossing is hideous so I expect I'll enjoy it.'

She tells him that Dr Ducroix refuses to retire, that Isabelle has a son, that Chalabre has been mayor of Castelnau for the past three years.

Montsignac has been sold, she tells him, as they stand there, poised on the rim of the world, on the brink of a new century whose petals lie folded close around unimaginable secrets. 'Pierre Coste bought it, do you remember Pierre? The house, what was left of the land, the furniture, even that clock. I told him it didn't keep good time, but he said that was why God gave us the sun and the stars and anyway there was no arguing with his wife when she took a fancy into her head.'

Over her shoulder he sees a carriage, waiting at the bend in the road. Beyond it, the heath reaches far into the hinterland, vast sandy tracts covered with pine trees that are grown for their resin; in winter, his house smells of the cones the children like to throw on the fire. But most of the region's sparse population is wretchedly poor: the sale of resin brings handsome profits to those who own the land, so there is no incentive to improve the soil for general cultivation.

People starve here.

When he kisses his wife, he tastes salt.

Ocean, sky, heathland: a country bleached as driftwood. He clung to its wreckage and it brought him salt-laden winds, the scent of pine, fine white sand that finds its way into every-thing, fingernails, puddings, he takes down a book and there are the grains, lodged between its pages.

'It's beautiful here,' she says, looking out to sea. 'Do you know, until this morning I'd never seen the ocean?'

The setter has been leaping in and out of the shallows, chasing retreating waves and pouncing on foam. Now, having taken belated note of the intruder, it gallops down the beach, skids to a halt, pretends to growl, ignores Joseph's remon-strances, flings itself joyfully on Mathilde's skirts.

She bends, strokes its silky head, and, 'Brutus,' he says. 'What happened to Brutus?'

'He was the first one they killed. He was shut up in the kitchen but he escaped, of course, and bit the arresting officer. So they shot him.' Straightening up, she looks at him. 'It's funny, I always thought they'd come at night. But it was morning, we'd just finished breakfast.'

The marram grass on the dunes is knotted with pink bindweed.

In the rockpools, wind shakes the water.

She tells Joseph she has a present for him in the carriage. 'Wait here,' she says, 'and keep your eyes shut.'

When she allows him to look, there's a rosebush at his feet.

'Pierre spotted it half choked by weeds when he was going around the garden.'

It's misshapen, overgrown, burdened with flowers.

He can't see very clearly.

'Look,' she's saying, 'look.'

There's a wooden label, tied to the lowest branch. And on it, in paint so faded that it's barely legible: *L'Avenir*.

The Future.

He takes off his spectacles.

He hides his face in dark-red roses.

'Papa!'

With the dog running in wild circles around him, the child has stumped his way over the beach and is standing at the foot of the dunes, looking up at them, uncertain what to do next.

'Papa!' he calls again, and holds up his arms.

Acknowledgments

Many thanks to: everyone at Random House Australia and Chatto & Windus, especially Jane Palfreyman and Alison Samuel; my agent, Sarah Lutyens; Judith Lukin-Amundsen and Sara White for editorial advice, and Judith for copy-editing as well; Vicki Beale for the photograph; and Chris Andrews, my first and best reader.

Sources

I'm particularly indebted to Simon Schama's monumental *Citizens: A Chronicle of the French Revolution*, which I've plundered for information and anecdote. For further discussion of the Revolution, see: Alfred Cobban, *A History of Modern France, Volume I: The Old Regime and the Revolution 1715–1799* (Penguin 1963); Jean-Paul Bertaud, *La vie quotidienne en France au temps de la Révolution (1789–1795)* (Hachette 1983); Robert Laurent and Geneviève Gavignaud, *La Révolution française dans le Langeudoc méditerranéen* (Bibliothèque historique Privat 1987); Jean Robiquet, *La vie quotidienne au temps de la Révolution* (Hachette 1938).

For the social and cultural background to eighteenth-century French life, I drew on: Philippe Ariès and Georges Duby (general editors), *A History of Private Life, Volume III: Passions of the Renaissance* (Roger Chartier, editor; Arthur Goldhammer, translator; Harvard University Press 1989); Robert Darnton, *The Great Cat Massacre and Other Episodes in French Cultural History* (Penguin 1991); Margaret H Darrow, *Family, Class, and Inheritance in Southern France, 1775–1825* (Princeton University Press 1989); Franklin L Ford, *Robe and Sword: The Regrouping of the French Aristocracy after Louis XIV* (Harvard University Press 1953); Louis-Sébastien Mercier, *The Waiting City* (J P Lipincott 1933); Daniel Roche, *La France des Lumières* (Fayard 1993); Arthur Young, *Travels in France* (edited by Constantia Maxwell; Cambridge University Press 1929).

Graham Stuart Thomas's *The Old Shrub Roses* (Dent 1979), the standard reference work on pre-nineteenth-century

302

roses, was indispensable to the writing of this book. For further reading about roses and their history, see: Allen Paterson, *The History of the Rose* (Collins 1983); Roger Phillips and Martin Ryx, *The Quest for the Rose* (Random House 1993); Nancy Steen, *The Charm of Old Roses* (Reed 1966). S Andrew Schulman's *Yesterday's Rose* (www.Country-Lane.com/yr/) is an informative web site on the subject.

For the history of gardening and plant science, see: Ralph Dutton, *The English Garden* (Batsford 1945); Richard Gorer, *The Development of Garden Flowers* (Eyre & Spottiswoode 1975); H F Roberts, *Plant Hybridization before Mendel* (Hafner 1965).

James C Riley's *The Eighteenth-Century Campaign to Avoid Disease* (Macmillan 1987) was essential to my understanding of scientific and medical thought in the Enlightenment. For more about the history of medicine, see: Colin Jones, *The Charitable Imperative: Hospitals and Nursing in Ancien Régime and Revolutionary France* (Routledge 1989); Roy Porter (editor), *The Cambridge Illustrated History of Medicine* (Cambridge University Press 1996); Roselyne Rey, *The History of Pain* (translated by Louise Elliott Wallace, J A Cadden and S W Cadden; Harvard University Press 1995).

For the history of food, see: Giles MacDonogh, *A Palate in Revolution: Grimod de la Reynière and the Almanach des Gourmands* (Robin Clark 1987); Raymond Oliver, *The French at Table* (The Wine & Food Society 1967); Maguelonne Toussaint-Samat, *A History of Food* (translated by Anthea Bell; Blackwell 1993); Barbara Ketcham Wheaton, *Savouring the Past: The French Kitchen and Table from 1300 to 1789* (Chatto & Windus 1983).